OPENING GAMBIT

TILLY WALLACE

v10022022

ISBN: 978-0-473-62037-0

Published by Ribbonwood Press

To be the first to hear about Tilly's new releases, sign up at:

https://www.tillywallace.com/newsletter

ONE

L ondon, July 1788

THE ROOM off the cellar admitted no light or warmth. Likewise, no cries of despair escaped its thick stone walls. Sera balled up her fists until her nails dug into her palms and held in the scream. While no one outside the room might hear, *she* would, and she refused to release the pent-up rage.

She stood before a long, narrow workbench. On its surface waited a row of bottles in various pretty hues. Her guardian and master, Lord Branvale, had left her with a simple spell to cast over a range of potions to preserve them and stop the oils from going rancid. Yet her mind struggled to grasp the threads needed to weave the magic together.

Bah. She hated preservative spells—they grated over

her skin in an unpleasant fashion. How she longed to craft magic that worked with Mother Nature. To encourage trees to soar to unusual heights, or orchids to bloom in the middle of winter. Her fingers itched to dig in the soil and to have dirt under her nails.

Instead, she was making things that glowed prettily in a bottle as they sat on a lady's dressing table. Every day, Branvale berated her and bemoaned the fact that the council had decided she should be allowed to live. All her failures simply proved the inferiority of women mages, and would justify the council's policy of smothering baby girls so that their power might transfer to more deserving males.

Sera let out a gasp as a fingernail punctured her skin and a droplet of blood welled up. With an effort, she let out a deep breath and shook her hands free of tension. Her anger must be directed not at herself, but at the ignorant men who controlled her life.

At the age of five, every mage was taken from their parents and given to a mentor to be trained in the use of magic, and to learn the history of mages in England. Plucked from the arms of a mother who must have loved her, the council thrust Sera at a man who peered down his nose at her, scoffed at her feeble attempts, and constantly reminded her of the inferiority of her sex.

She wanted to scream. Stupid, small-minded, ignorant men. A certainty dwelt in her bones that she possessed more ability than any of them, but she needed to find her unique way of casting. Every day, she vowed to prove them all wrong and to light up the sky with her gift. Except she struggled to light the tinder in the grate.

A long sigh escaped her, and her shoulders sagged. With hands flat on the bench, she bowed her head and, for a single, lonely second, despair flashed through her. Then she shook it away. Again. She must try again. Only if she finished the task could she escape the stuffy room.

Branvale had a reputation for his potions and lotions that removed wrinkles, brightened the skin, and returned the sparkle to ageing eyes. He thought his method proprietary and that no one could ever replicate it. Except Sera spent long hours refining his work once he had done the mixing and casting. She knew the contents off by heart, including the fact that his secret spells were little more than pleasant-smelling illusions.

Closing her eyes, she considered the required spell anew. This time, she ignored the method her master had drummed into her and considered her own way of achieving the same end. Instead of infusing a preservative into the potions that were sought after by noble ladies, Sera worked with the oils and herbs to extend their lifespan.

Her way took longer, each ingredient individually examined and coaxed into altering its form. Rather than forcing them to comply, she enhanced them from the inside. By the time she finished, the entire row of bottles vibrated with a faint song and a sparkle added to their glow. Work done, she placed stoppers in the bottles.

Arching her back, she relieved muscles cramped

from a day bent over the table. Then Sera removed her apron and hung it on a hook by the door, before scrubbing her hands in a bowl of water. She tossed the dirty water down a drain in the corner, where it gurgled and swirled before racing off to join the rest of the wastewater on its course to the river.

She hurried from what had once been a storeroom and along the servants' hallway. A quick glance at the clock in the servants' hall as she passed confirmed she had perhaps an hour before Lord Branvale returned and demanded to see her work. She hurried on to the bright kitchen.

In the most warm and welcoming room of the entire house, Sera pulled out a chair and sat at the long oak table. The skylight above cast watery sunlight over her as she poured a mug of light ale from the jug and took several long gulps of the refreshing drink. Her throat was parched from a long day in the former cellar, and her stomach complained about the lack of sustenance.

'Here, that stomach's so loud you'd wake sleeping babes." Rosie Privatt, the cook, used a towel to pick up a plate from the stove and carry it over. Under the cast iron lid, she had kept warm a few slices of beef, potatoes, and long beans. Short in stature, Rosie had a generous smile and a kind nature. When Sera had joined the household, Rosie had been the cook's assistant and, from their first day together, she had treated the young mage like a sibling.

"You are a gem, Rosie. I would starve without you."

Sera picked up a fork and silenced her grumbling stomach.

Her statement was literally true, as their master often worked Sera for long hours with no respite. He didn't care if she ate or not, but he certainly ensured that he never skipped a meal. Not that she received any special lack of attention; Branvale treated all the servants under his roof poorly. His status as one of England's twelve mages confirmed, in his mind, his superiority over everyone else.

In many ways, Sera preferred the way he treated her, as she found kindred spirits below stairs. They existed in their own world in the twilight rooms beneath the town house. Staff became her family and ensured she was fed. In return, she did what she could to protect them and crafted small enchantments and wards that made their lives easier.

Sera lived on a knife's edge, never knowing when the experiment of letting her live would be declared a failure. Twice a year, she was trotted out to the Mage Council to be assessed and to attempt to grow a blade of grass in the barren soil around the tower. After her lacklustre performance, the older mages would cluster together like a pack of vultures. Some shook their heads and murmured how her power was wasted inside a female vessel.

"Thank you, Rosie," Sera said after finishing her meal.

She washed the plate and cutlery in the hot water left in the sink and put the dishes away. Then she snatched an apple from a bowl and pushed through the

5

back door into the courtyard that opened to the mews beyond. High walls surrounded the yard, to shield from noble view the servants, tradespeople, and the laundry hanging to dry. A thick wooden door allowed access to the garden on the other side of their enclosing wall.

Sera's first step onto the grass brought a wash of contentment over her body. Through the small kitchen garden, she emerged into the contemplation walk, the only part of the garden ever used by Lord Branvale, with its neat pattern of pathways laid out from a central pond and its tidy geometric beds. Through a gap cut in the yew hedge, the rest of the garden stretched wild and unattended.

Several feet into the wild flowers, a shimmer arose from the ground and stretched upward. A visible reminder of another way her body and mind were controlled. The mage in charge of her education had tethered her to the house and grounds. While she couldn't walk all the way to the back of the garden or slip into the mews beyond, she could sit under a spreading elm.

The light faded to a soft yellow as the afternoon lengthened. As she bit into the apple, a sparrow flew down and perched on her outstretched finger. It tilted its head and chirped.

"What have you seen today, my friend?" she asked the small bird.

The bird looked up and flapped its wings. Sera let her mind touch the bird's, and in an instant, she soared high with it and skimmed over the rooftops. She circled with its friends and they flew as a mob toward an area of damp lawn where insects and worms prowled.

"Thank you," she whispered as she released the bird's mind. They might imprison her form in the house, but her mind could escape thanks to her feathered friends.

"Sera?" a voice called from the other side of the high stone wall. A scrabbling noise gave way to a huff as a girl's face appeared.

Sera's best friend in the entire world, Katherine Napier, hauled herself up and sat on the wide lintel. With sharp features, hair in myriad brown tones like feathers, and a pointed nose, the young woman resembled a bird herself. She also possessed a keen mind and a fierce loyalty to her imprisoned neighbour.

"Hello, Kitty. What news from the outside world?" Sera walked to the bottom of the wall to peer up at her friend. How she longed to climb the tree and drop to the other side!

"Father has asked discreet questions of his noble associates about what will happen when you turn eighteen. Apparently Branvale intends to petition the king that you remain in his custody. The council has agreed with him that they should extend your apprenticeship until you are at least twenty-five." Kitty delivered the words softly, but the spark in her eyes revealed the depth of her indignation on Sera's behalf.

The world turned white in a sudden snowstorm of rage. Her fingers pressed into the apple's flesh. Then, with great effort and a deep breath, Sera swallowed her retort. She needed to reserve her anger for the man responsible, not the friend who had merely delivered the message. The sweet apple turned tart in her mouth, and she tossed the remains under a shrub, where the nocturnal creatures of the garden could dine on it after dark.

"They cannot stop me from taking up my position." On reaching the age of eighteen, mages entered the service of England and took their seat on the Mage Council. They were given a rank equivalent to that of a duke and, in return for their service to their country, were granted a house and a stipend from the Crown.

"Not if we act quickly, they cannot. Apparently there is some hurriedly drafted proposal before Parliament to change the gender neutral Mage Act into one that refers throughout to *male*, *man*, and *masculine*. They think to exclude troublesome women from claiming the full rights due to mages." Kitty huffed. "Father is slowing it down as best he can. Thankfully, he has several enlightened friends who are rather keen to see what happens when you are set loose on the council."

Kitty's father, the Honourable Samuel Napier, was the third son of a viscount. Grasping the chance to make his own way in the world, he had distinguished himself in the law and established a well-respected practice of solicitors. He had then made some canny investments and derived a yearly income from his enterprises greater than that of his older brother or even their father's heir.

Sera leaned on the wall, the rough stone pressing through her shabby gown at her back. "They judge me and declare I cannot fly, before I ever have the chance to leave the nest and test my wings."

Kitty dangled her legs over the wall and hung on to a branch of the elm for balance. "We have two days to figure out an escape plan and to get you to court. Once you claim what is rightfully yours, their efforts to change the legislation will be for nothing. They cannot put you back into a box."

A sad smile touched Sera's lips. She had tried to push through the barrier or to walk out the front door, but no spell or incantation allowed her past. Branvale had to create a door for her through his creation, as he did when she took lessons with Kitty or he needed to parade her before the council. The wide bracelet on her left wrist itched, and idly, she scratched under the metal. "We'll keep trying. There has to be a way. I simply haven't found it yet."

A grin spread across Kitty's face, and her eyes sparkled. "I believe in you, Sera, as does Father. You will find a way and you will show them all."

"I couldn't do it without you." People's belief in her might be the exact magic she needed to break free. She fully intended to walk out of the house the day she turned eighteen, which meant coming up with a way to shatter Branvale's barrier.

"I don't intend to miss a minute of what is coming! I want to see the looks on their faces." Kitty laughed, spread her arms wide, and nearly toppled from her perch.

Sera shot out a blast of air to rebalance her friend.

"Well, I need to think. I only have two days to figure out how to pass through the barrier."

"I'll be waiting for you on this side of the wall," Kitty called.

Sera pushed through the oak door to the courtyard to return to the kitchen. Over the previous years, the servants had grown accustomed to a mage sitting with them below stairs. Or perhaps they were sympathetic to the lonely child who had joined the household. Among them, Sera found a measure of companionship, and in the cosy kitchen, the social divide fell away. Now, she sipped a cup of tea while their chatter washed over her.

Jake Hogan, Branvale's valet, sat across from her, polishing a pair of boots for their master. "Blasted tea is cold," he muttered. Nothing put a shine to the leather like a bit of spit, which needed a hot cup of tea to keep the mouth moist. Of a tall, thin build, he had light brown hair and an intense pale stare that often unnerved the younger maids.

"Let me." Sera put down her cup and picked up his, cradling it in her palms. A few whispered words, and soon a waft of steam curled from the surface.

"Thanks, Sera—you have your uses after all." He toasted her with the cup, then slurped a mouthful of piping-hot liquid. He swallowed, then spat a clean globule at the boot into which his left hand had been thrust.

"Yes, a bright future awaits me as a tea lady at the theatre. It will always be piping hot for the toffs." The comment elicited chuckles from the others, but the words fell cold through her middle.

She stared at her hands and wondered what was wrong with her. Part of her refused to believe that her inability to cast resided solely with her gender. Her mind imagined spells and enchantments far beyond the level of skill her hands displayed. Why would her brain play such a trick on her, if it weren't possible? No. She believed the deficit was either in Branvale's training methods or in something else. Most likely the fog that descended over her thoughts when she grasped for the words of power.

Branvale kept her working in the windowless old storage room, when her hands itched for soil under her nails and her ears strained for birdsong. What if her magic needed to be close to nature to work to its full potential?

Goosebumps raced up her arms, and she rubbed at them before rising from her seat and taking her cup to the sink. "He's back. I had better go wait for him."

Her body reacted when the other mage approached the house, a helpful warning signal that allowed her a few moments to scurry back into the dark.

"I'll make sure his supper is hot." Rosie swung her legs over the bench seat.

While mages could summon food from thin air, it lacked any nourishment. You could eat an entire banquet of magical food and still be hungry, with nothing of any substance inside you.

Sera hurried to the workroom and donned her apron. When the heavy tread sent a shiver through the stairs by the door, she hunched over a book, reading about the feats performed by mages in the Tudor period.

The door swung open and banged on the wall behind it. 'Did you manage that pathetic little spell today?" Branvale crossed his arms over his chest. Of average height and build, he projected an imposing air that made people around him look up and take notice.

Sera suspected he cast an enchantment over himself to ensure he *was* noticed. Certainly his luminous blue eyes weren't a natural colour. It amused her that he could alter his eyes, but hadn't figured out how to make himself taller.

Schooling her features into a neutral expression, she closed the book and turned to her gaoler.

Two

Sera gestured to the array of bottles, their contents glowing in the low light. "Yes, Lord Branvale. All the potions have the preservative activated, and I added a luminosity to the liquid."

He held one hand over the row, judging her work by sending a touch of his magic to assess hers. One vial at the end of the bench refused to glow, its contents remaining a thick, dark red. When his palm stopped over that one, he plucked it from the row and placed it in his pocket. "For my special client," he murmured.

The contents of that particular bottle sent a shiver through Sera. The substance possessed a heavy viscosity like treacle. Try as she might, she couldn't discern the purpose of the potion, almost as though Branvale had cloaked those ingredients.

"You were supposed to use the spell I entrusted you with, not do something else." His lips pulled upward at the corners. In other people, that might have made a smile. But not in him.

'I sought only to ensure the satisfaction of your customers, Lord Branvale. The bottles will emit a magical sparkle as they sit on a dressing table that will look fetching by candlelight." If you were wealthy enough to buy beauty potions from a mage, you wanted something that looked expensive and ensorcelled.

The spell to cast the glow gave her an idea. It would make a far safer light for the servants than carrying a candle up and down the steep stairs. All she needed was a shape to contain the spell. A mushroom popped into her mind, with a cap that could be tapped to turn the light off and on. Or glass jars could become lanterns that never failed or succumbed to the wind. That would be her next project for the staff.

A grunt came from across the room as Branvale picked up a bottle, uncorked it, and sniffed the contents. 'Why did you not use the spell I gave you?"

'I—" She got no further.

'Useless girl. Let me guess—you couldn't get it to work?" He shook his head and Sera could practically see him numbering her faults in his mind.

'Instead of adding a preservative, I increased the lifespan of the ingredients. I believe that will also make the effects of the potion last longer," she murmured. Her way made a better lotion for the women to rub into their faces—one that would actually work.

'Next time, do as you are told. No one wants a girl who thinks for herself. Pack them up ready for dispatch in the morning." He turned on his heel.

"Yes, Lord Branvale." She bowed her head, but only to hide the defiance in her eyes. Only a few more days, and she would be mistress of her future.

When he stormed out the door, she turned to her last task for the day. She wrapped each bottle in tissue paper, then placed it with care in a wooden crate. Straw made padding between each bottle, to ensure they didn't bump against each other and crack while being delivered.

Finally done, she left the cellar. Her body followed the path from memory as her mind tackled how to break through Branvale's barrier. For years she had tried, and at most only succeeded in poking her fingers through. She refused to believe that Branvale could outwit her. Every day she fixed potions crafted by his magic and Sera *knew*, deep inside herself, that she was the better mage.

As she climbed the servants' stairs hidden within the walls of the house to her attic bedroom, loud voices in the entranceway caught her attention. She paused on the landing that opened to the entrance hall. Curiosity made her crack the door open as her master swept into the hall, summoned by Elliot Bryn, one of the footmen.

A man prowled the tiles, his hat wedged tight on his head and a dark overcoat around his body as though he were the embodiment of a storm. The stranger waved a tight roll of paper as soon as Branvale appeared. "It didn't work! I demand my money back."

Branvale waved Elliot away, but declined to escort the intruder to his study or the drawing room.

Whoever it was, he was not welcome in this house. Only when he thought they were alone did her master turn on the interloper. "If it didn't work, then you failed to read the incantation properly."

The short, squat man peered up at the marginally taller mage. "I read it exactly as you wrote it. No man, mage or not, crosses me. Give me my money back, or there will be trouble."

Branvale laughed. "I am not responsible for the incompetence of others. Begone." The mage flung out his hands, and the man slid backward as though a sudden gust of wind pushed against him.

"You'll be sorry we ever crossed paths!" the man yelled as he tumbled out the now-open front door, which slammed shut on him.

Branvale turned and narrowed his bright blue gaze as he surveyed the hall. Sera held the door shut and slowed her breathing. While she sensed his presence, he seemed unaware of hers. Only when his footsteps had retreated to his study did she let out a breath and carry on up the stairs.

IN HER ALMOST THIRTEEN years under Branvale's control, Sera had acquired exactly two friends. She didn't count the staff, because they were family. And like family, sometimes they didn't get on, rubbed up against one another, or had their petty squabbles. But at the end of the day, they were fiercely loyal to one another.

A friend was someone different—another person who liked her and wanted to spend time in her company.

Kitty was her best and closest friend, although with only two, there wasn't much competition for the title. The other was Lady Abigail Crawley. She was older than Sera by a handful of years, and Branvale had brought the noblewoman into the house to educate Sera in the more delicate ways of society.

When Sera turned thirteen, the gleam in the eyes of those on the Mage Council changed into something more speculative. There were muttered questions about Sera's lack of manners and grace, and how on earth could she ever be presented at court when she acted like a wild animal?

As it transpired, leaving her to the care of the servants didn't create a woman capable of gliding through the palace and being paraded before the king and queen—something that Branvale would one day have to do with Seraphina. Her master faced a barrage of well-deserved criticism for the fact that Sera didn't lift her pinkie when she drank her tea, had been known to bite, and walked with the long strides of a man while hiking up her skirts. Lady Abigail was engaged and had begun regular visits to school Sera in how a proper lady behaved.

Sera hated the composed and elegant young woman

on sight. Branvale had chosen her, which made her character suspect, and Sera didn't want to learn how to behave properly. Lady Abigail reciprocated Sera's animosity. Over a succession of tense teas, Sera learned Abigail hadn't wanted the task. Her grandfather, Lord Rowan, the oldest mage on the council, had suggested his granddaughter as the most appropriate person to impart some natural grace to the awkward girl mage.

As they spent more time in each other's company and realised they had a common foe, a friendship grew. Abigail disliked the way her mage grandfather dictated her life. Sera disliked the way *all* mages sought to control her every move. Rosie often muttered that too many cooks ruined a fine meal. Perhaps too many mages pulling her strings exhausted Sera's natural magical abilities?

Today, Sera fetched the good tea service from the butler's pantry and wiped the cups before setting the tray. She carried it into the small parlour, the only room she was permitted to use when Lady Abigail visited. She perched on the edge of a chair, back straight, feet together, as the clock chimed the hour, and waited for Elliot to admit her visitor.

Sera rose as the door opened and curtseyed deeply to her friend. Abigail's mother had married an earl, elevating her friend far above her own common birth. At the age of eighteen, Sera herself would receive an honorary title and the status of a duchess. That title attached to the mage only and did not elevate their descendants, who had to fend for themselves.

Abigail clapped her hands. "Good. That one would satisfy Queen Charlotte herself."

"I fear your fine work has deprived the court of a spectacle. I wonder if they expect a wild and half-naked mage, snarling at the end of a leash." Sera waited for Abigail to sit before taking the adjoining chair.

"I fear you are right. Many whisper about you at court. Some refer to you as *the witch*. Perhaps before you are presented, you could elongate your nose, place a large wart on the end, and sprout hairs from your chin?" Abigail clasped her elegant hands in her lap. Her light brown hair had been expertly coiffed and pinned under a hat perched at a jaunty angle. She possessed the ample proportions and pale complexion much favoured by painters. Humour gleamed in her brown eyes.

"I could blacken my teeth and affect a hump as well, to give them the witch they long to see?" Unlike her friend, Sera resembled a starving waif, begging in the street. Taller than most women, her irregular meals failed to put meat on her bones. While she attempted to pin up her dark locks, they seemed to possess their own magic and at least one strand always defied her attempts to secure it.

Sera poured tea, then added a dash of milk and a teaspoon of sugar before passing the cup and saucer to Abigail.

"They have not seen the likes of you before—that sparks both their curiosity and their concerns." Her friend sipped her tea and regarded her over the rim of her cup.

As the granddaughter of a mage, a trace of magic

flowed through Abigail's veins. The descendants of mages were referred to as *aftermages*. While nowhere near as powerful as mages, they were touched with a variety of gifts. Abigail had a talent acceptable to society—her gift was music. Her exceptional singing voice was sought after to grace soirées and parties.

Mages were rare anomalies. At any one time, only twelve lived on British soil. When a mage died, his power flowed to a babe born in the same instant somewhere in England. Oddly, when a mage fathered children, they were powerless, but the next generation and those that followed all possessed a diminishing trace of magic. Once the seventh generation was born, the magic disappeared from that line and never reappeared. Mother Nature herself imposed a limit on how many people had magic in their blood.

"If there had been more women mages throughout history, people would have stories to draw upon to allay their concerns." Sera's fingers tightened on the cup and it rattled on the saucer. She was the first female mage to reach adulthood in hundreds of years.

"Well, you will soon be presented at court and society will see that you are a refined young woman. I expect you will make a marvellous match by the end of the year." Abigail sipped her tea with her pinkie finger perfectly extended.

Sera ruined her composure by spluttering a mouthful of tea back into the cup, and a small amount went up her nose. With a push of magic, she managed to get the cup and saucer on the table before they fell, and dabbed at her face with a handkerchief. Taking a breath to calm herself, she narrowed her gaze at her friend. "What match?"

Abigail winked as she took another sip. "Come now, do not play coy with me. Your forthcoming status as a mage makes you rather eligible on the marriage market. I expect the council will receive several offers for your hand."

Anger rolled from Sera and her hands curled into fists. The teacup and pot rattled on the table. Her sole focus had been escape. It had never occurred to her that the council would auction her off like a prize brood-mare. Her breath came short in her chest as panic set in. Only by digging her nails into her palms and focusing on the stab of pain could she bring herself under control.

She had endured until now by telling herself that once she turned eighteen, she would be free. Anyone who thought to manoeuvre her like a pawn would discover the depths of her resolve. Ideas spun in her head, but first, she had to escape. With an effort, she drew a deep breath and placed a smile on her face. "Then let us hope I make a good impression when presented to King George, and all your hard work pays off."

"Lord Branvale has yet to set a date for when that will be, so we still have plenty of time to ensure everything goes perfectly." Abigail reached for a tiny biscuit.

How could her master not have set a date yet? She turned eighteen in a matter of hours. All the more reason to break free. She would die waiting for Branvale and the council to open her cage and let her out.

At the end of Abigail's visit, she kissed Sera's cheek and murmured early good wishes for her birthday as they parted company. "I will visit on the day of your presentation and bring my maid to help you dress," her friend promised.

Sera nodded and swallowed the lump in her throat. "You know I value your help," she murmured. A shiver alerted her to Branvale's presence in the house, and she would say no more with his spells listening to her every word.

The remainder of the day passed without incident. Sera returned the tea tray to the kitchen and washed up before continuing with the spellwork waiting for her in the cellar room. That evening, Branvale went out, while Sera ate in the kitchen with the other staff.

"I know him upstairs won't request anything, but I shall find time to bake you a cake tomorrow, to celebrate." Rosie rested a hand on Sera's shoulder as she rose from her chair.

"I don't need a cake, Rosie. I'll not have you getting into trouble if you take the time to make one." From long experience over the years, she predicted Branvale would find some other task to keep the staff busy and conveniently forget his ward's milestone birthday. Usually he entertained at home and made the day all about himself, and ensured no one had time to draw breath enough to so much as wish her well.

Would eighteen be any different? No. If anything, he would grip her all the tighter.

Rosie waved away her concerns. "We all know what he's like. One of these days he'll get what he deserves."

"Imagine if he knew I spat on more than just his boots," Jake muttered, and the other staff laughed.

Sera shook her head. Branvale was not well liked. The only good thing they could say about him was that he paid them on time every quarter day. Nobles didn't seem to grasp the fact that it was foolish to ill-treat those who prepared your meals.

"I'll see you all in the morning." Sera said her good-nights and walked up the dark, narrow stairs to her room. As she undressed and folded her gown, part of her hoped everything would change tomorrow. But the realistic bit of her brain pointed out it would be another day, like all the others before it.

She climbed into bed and pulled the blanket over her shoulders, curling up under its warmth. "No, something will change. I feel it," she whispered as she let herself drift off to sleep.

A few hours later, a *clank* awoke her with a start. The sound vibrated through her limbs, and she shook as it rushed over her. Sera sat up and stared around at her dark room. Clouds obscured most of the moon, and only thin strips of silvery light reached through the small window. Below, a clock chimed twelve.

That must have been what woke her. The clock seemed awfully loud tonight. Each chime echoed through her body.

"Happy birthday to me." Her eighteenth birthday and the day, supposedly, she came into her own as one of England's twelve mages. If she were ever allowed to step into that role. The Mage Council prevaricated about her fate and could potentially delay any decision for years.

A sigh heaved through her, and she pushed her pillow up so she might lean against the wall. A single tear welled up in her eye, and Sera wiped it away. Part of her had always imagined a glorious future awaiting her as soon as she turned eighteen. That dream crashed to earth and smashed into a thousand pieces as an imaginary Branvale laughed in her face. He wouldn't release her—Abigail's slip that he had yet to organise a date for her presentation at court proved it.

The bracelet on her wrist developed a maddening itch, and she rubbed the surrounding skin. Tree branches spread in one direction over the beaten copper, and pretty filigree roots swirled in another. The size of the piece made it hard to get her nails under it to scratch. As her fingers passed over the metal, an image flashed through her mind—thin roots spread from the tree, through the bracelet, and into her veins. As it went, it poisoned her blood and sapped her magic.

A memory surfaced. On her first day with Lord Branvale, he had snapped the bracelet around her young wrist, and pain had flared up her arm. He had scowled and berated her for her ingratitude that a pretty piece of jewellery to make her feel welcome had made her cry.

That was the last time she had ever shed a tear in front of him.

Frustration built within Sera. Men controlled her life. They made decisions about her, as though she were only a decoration to be placed on a table. Or worse. She was a broken vase no one wanted, that would soon be tossed on a refuse heap.

"No more," she rasped. She would grow old and wither waiting for Branvale to free her, or for the Mage Council to allow her to take her seat.

If the things due to her were not given, they would be taken. And that required her freedom.

THREE

S era stared at the bracelet. The itching increased until it seemed to burn. "What *are* you?"

She passed a fingertip over its surface and a silver tendril rose and snagged on her nail. She tugged, and with a stab of pain, a short thread came loose from her arm and slithered through the filigree work. With a shake, Sera tossed the gossamer thread to the floor.

She did it again, pinching a thread attached to the metal. Then, taking a deep breath, she yanked it from her arm. Her hand trembled, but her mind grew certain about what she had to do. Narrowing her gaze, she whispered frosty words at the spiderweb-thin roots, until they froze. Pain raced through her body, and Sera gasped as ice burned in her veins. Gritting her teeth, she bent over her wrist. With her finger and thumb, she grasped a silver tendril and tugged it free of her arm. As it popped out of the bracelet, she flung it away and seized the next one.

At times, the pain almost made her faint, and she

leaned back against the wall. Her vision swam in darkness and chills wracked her body, while her heart beat with a frantic drumming. Sweat dribbled down the side of her face, and she wiped it on her arm. Some tendrils were short, others raced up her arm and across her torso. One snaked around her throat.

While the agony seared her, with the removal of each root, a soothing balm rushed to fill the void left behind. She grew stronger, even as the tendrils fought to remain inside her body. They erupted in barbs to shred her veins as she tugged them free. A surge of new magic healed the damage and prevented her from bleeding out.

By the time the clock struck one, a pile of silver threads writhed on the floor. The last one stubbornly refused to be evicted from her body. She ground her jaw to stop from crying out as she wound it around her finger. Inch by inch, it emerged from her wrist. Tears rolled down her cheeks, and she shook with the effort, but still she reeled in the strand. With a *pop*, the last one burst free, and Sera tossed it on the heap with the others. The bracelet cracked open at a previously unseen hinge, and she threw it into the far corner of the room.

Sera dropped back on the bed, sweat coating her skin. With each breath, the pain evaporated and in its wake...she was reborn. Power flowed through her limbs, like a river where children pile up rocks to dam the water flow, but a heavy rain washes them all away. Finally, the obstruction cleared.

With a flick of her wrist, she set fire to the strands

and then dispersed the ash before the planks of the floor caught fire, too.

"I'm free." But now was not the time to fall into an exhausted sleep. She needed to escape while the house slumbered. Quickly, she dressed in a plain gown, shrugged on a casaquin and shawl, and laced boots on her feet. Then she swept up the bracelet in a handkerchief and tied the ends in a knot before tucking it into her belt. "I don't know what you are, but I intend to find out."

Down the servants' stairs she crept, for once grateful to have been made to use them. It made her escape easier. In the kitchen, she cast one last look around before slipping through the back door.

"I'm sorry, Rosie," she whispered to the cook, who had promised her a birthday cake. "But I will be back for you."

Outside, the moon guided her. Through the heavy door and out into the garden, now washed in silver. The boundary barrier shimmered in the moonlight, the faint line she could never cross. Until now.

Sera placed both her hands on it and whispered, "Begone." The wall shook, then without a sound, it shattered into thousands of pieces that dropped and disappeared into the earth.

At last, she could do whatever she wanted—and first on her list was climbing the tree. Sera scrambled up the spreading elm and along a limb to where it reached into the neighbouring garden. She dangled for a moment, her feet swinging in the night air, before she let go and dropped to the ground.

"Free," she whispered, staring at Branvale's wall from the Napier family side. Sera stretched her arms up over her head and spun in a circle. The exhaustion disappeared, replaced by excitement at the possibilities now before her.

Scooping up a handful of pebbles, Sera used her magic to direct them at Kitty's window until it opened and her friend stared out at her. "About time you escaped. I'll be right down."

Within a few minutes, a light drifted through the house and the terrace door opened.

"Happy birthday." Kitty threw her arms around Sera and hugged her tight. "Come back to my room and we'll figure out how you will storm the palace."

"How do you know that is what I plan to do?" Sera frowned.

Kitty snorted and linked her arm with Sera's. "Please. You have been my friend forever. Of course I know exactly what you intend to do."

Kitty picked up the candle in its silver holder and carried it in one hand as the two young women trod on silent feet through the house and up the stairs to Kitty's bedroom. She clicked the door shut and placed the candle beside the bed.

Sera unlaced her boots and climbed on the bed next to her friend. Kitty spread a coverlet over the two of them to keep warm. They talked for most of the night, thinking up and discarding various ways to sneak Seraphina into the palace. In the quietest moments, they whispered of their hopes for the future.

Sleep claimed them at some point, and Sera woke as

dawn blushed across the sky. A cart rattled along the street outside, most likely a tradesman making early deliveries. She slipped from bed and walked to the window, watching the people below.

"I'm famished," a sleepy voice said from behind her.

"Plotting does make one hungry." Sera rubbed at her wrist. The pain had vanished, but a dull ache remained. An angry red scar in the shape of the tree carved on the bracelet now marked her skin. Without a doubt, Branvale had shackled her with magic and weakened her. But to what end?

She would find out what he had done to her, but there was a more important task first. She had to present herself to the king before the Mage Council moved against her.

"Let's get you dressed." Sera waved her hands, and the blanket peeled itself off her friend.

Kitty grumbled as she rose and crossed to the armoire. She threw it open and selected a gown to wear while Sera tugged her boots on.

They descended to the dining room, and despite the early hour, Mr Napier was already up and having his breakfast.

"Happy birthday, Sera." He toasted her with his coffee cup and then gestured to a large box on the table, in front of a vacant chair.

Sera reached out and touched the dark red ribbon. "For me?"

Mr Napier smiled. "Of course. Kitty's birthday was two months ago."

Kitty pulled out the chair next to the box and sat.

The footman moved forward to pour her hot chocolate.

Sera untied the ribbon and took her time lifting the lid. Peeling back the tissue paper revealed a silken gown in bold green and white stripes. 'Oh!" she breathed. With careful hands, she lifted the dress from the box. The open front would reveal a decorated stomacher. The gown possessed the fashionable sack-back, where the fabric was arranged in box pleats that fell loose from the shoulder to the floor, forming a slight train.

"There are...other things to wear underneath that I frankly don't understand. I had them delivered to Kitty's room." He offered a bashful smile.

Sera raced around the table and flung her arms around her friend's father. "Thank you, sir. It is the most marvellous gown I have ever owned."

"You cannot go to court without a fashionable gown. I would have *both* my girls well attired." He kissed the top of her head and let her go, pride burning in his eyes.

She returned to her place to stare at the gown, her vision blurred from unshed tears. Ever since she was young, Kitty's father had welcomed Sera into their home and had always treated her like a daughter. At least here, she had found the small measure of paternal affection that her life lacked. She blinked away the tears.

"Any news of my parents?" she asked as one footman moved the box and gown to the end of the table while another held out her chair.

Mr Napier shook his head. "No. The Mage Council has refused every request for their details I have made on your behalf. But now that you are eighteen, you will be able to access those records for yourself in the mage tower."

The footman used silver tongs to place toast on her plate and then selected an egg from a silver-domed warmer.

"There is another matter I wish to discuss with you, sir." Sera buttered her toast and took a bite from a corner.

"Anything for you, Duchess." He winked over his coffee.

She nearly choked on her toast at the use of her new title, and Kitty reached out and smacked her on the back. A gulp of rich chocolate soothed the rough spot raised by the coughing. *Duchess. I am Lady Seraphina Winyard.* Having survived to the age of eighteen, she was now elevated to that rank. For the rest of her life, she would be treated as one of the highest-ranking nobles in the land.

Such a title presented new opportunities, and she had much to do.

"With my new position comes a stipend from the Crown, and the opportunity to earn an income through the fruits of my labours. I intend to be most industrious to ensure my freedom, and wish you might manage my finances." Sera ran a finger along the handle of the delicate cup. Magic poured through her limbs like water along a river after a heavy snow melt.

Branvale had blocked her gift—but why? Had the Mage Council conspired with him to limit her ability, or had Branvale acted alone?

Kitty's father leaned back in his chair and folded the newspaper with care. A small smile crinkled his eyes. Grey touched his temples. Despite his age, he remained a handsome man. Such was his enduring love for his wife that, once widowed, he had never remarried. 'I ensured both of you were taught numbers and accounts so that you would not be reliant on anyone else to maintain your finances. Knowledge is power, remember that.'

Sera nodded. She had received a most excellent education thanks to Mr Napier. When she appeared next door, Kitty's father had approached Lord Branvale with an offer. He had employed a tutor for his daughter and suggested that Sera could attend lessons at no charge to Lord Branvale. The mage leapt at the opportunity. Sera long suspected it was because it removed the sulky child from his house for a few hours each day. Whatever his reasons, the girls became fast friends, and vowed nothing would ever separate them.

Lessons had become the high point of her day, for they meant a few hours in Kitty's company. Only when the girls grew into young women did Branvale stop the tutoring and substitute Lady Abigail to teach her social graces. Not that Branvale could come between the two friends. They talked often over the wall, and Kitty dropped books into Sera's open arms, which she studied up in her room.

Sera chewed another end of toast. 'I fully intend to be involved in financial decisions, but I would prefer that you handle the business side on my behalf, and ensure that the Mage Council does not touch so much as a ha'penny of my earnings."

Mr Napier inclined his head. "I would be honoured to be your man of business."

The first step on a new road was taken.

"How exactly will we gain entrance to the palace?" Kitty asked as she tackled her breakfast.

"We? You do not have to do this, Kitty." Seraphina rested a hand on her friend's arm. She had already placed her in danger by seeking her aid. What would the Mage Council do against one with no magic for helping her defy their rules?

Kitty rolled her eyes, which increased her friend's resemblance to an all-seeing bird. "Of course I'm going. I'm not letting you confront them on your own. Besides, why should I miss all the fun and have to read secondhand accounts in the scandal sheets? I so want to see the looks on their faces when you stand before them!"

Seraphina heaved a resigned sigh. "None of this would be possible without you, but I don't like the idea of placing you in danger."

Kitty cast around the room and then leaned toward Sera as though she shared a great confidence. "I have no fear for my safety. I will let you in on a secret—I happen to be friends with the greatest mage England has ever known."

Sera laughed. Once, she had doubted Kitty's words, but since removing the bracelet, magic filled every part of her and it had become possible to believe in herself. "Since you insist on accompanying me, the answer to your question as to how we enter the palace is a simple matter. I am a mage. I will walk through the front door as though I am expected."

Mr Napier waved the footman over with his platter of sausage and sliced potatoes. "You must move with haste, Sera. The Mage Council is rather regretting the ambiguous and neutral language used in the Mage Act. As it currently stands, the legislation applies to a mage of any gender or species even. Some mutter it might even allow for an Unnatural mage, if there were such a thing. I am sure Kitty told you of their rush to designate different treatment and entitlements for male and female mages."

"Kitty told me, and I cannot thank you enough for stalling the amendments to the act." Her fingers curled around the handle of her cup. How frightened those men must be to force Parliament to act in haste, all because a girl would attain the age of eighteen years.

He picked up his cutlery and sliced sausage into bite-sized pieces. "It's no great hardship. I rather delight in crafting the awkward questions for our friends to ask, that the Mage Council's representatives do not wish to answer. How they squirm on the House floor."

Sera needed to act while she had surprise on her side. Branvale would think her still asleep under his roof and the Mage Council didn't yet know she had escaped. "We will waste no time. I intend to appear at court today. It is my birthday, after all."

"I shall have the carriage made ready. What time do you intend to depart?" Mr Napier asked.

'One o'clock. Let's catch the king early, as soon as the court has roused for the day," Kitty said.

'I shall send a note to Abigail. She has offered to help me prepare." How Sera wanted both her friends present! Although she had noticed that outspoken Kitty became much quieter in Abigail's presence. Most likely because Kitty was merely an Honourable's daughter. It didn't matter that her father had created his fortune through his business dealings—he would always be the third son of a noble and without a title of his own.

The maids were called upon to help the young women prepare for battle. Or that was how Sera imagined it in her mind. What if they were barred entry at the first gate? What if soldiers seized her on command of the Mage Council? She ran through the small number of spells Branvale had taught her—but had no defensive spells to use. With eyes half-closed, she let the maids remove her clothes, scrub her clean, and start afresh with the new underthings and gown.

If Sera imagined a problem, the magic whispered through her veins and suggested a solution. In the hours since she had removed the bracelet from her wrist, that ability had grown stronger. Her fingers itched to cast spells to immobilise guards, smash open gates, or blow aside nattering courtiers.

Can I really do all that? she asked the magic spinning through her.

Yes, came the answer. Although until she tested her new wings by jumping, she wouldn't know whether she could fly or not.

Abigail sent a message by return as they prepared. While she could not join them—she had been summoned to wait upon the queen—she would be present at court to support Sera.

At long last, they were ready. Sera's hair was piled high on her head, and feathers were pinned to one side that matched the green stripe of her gown. Kitty wore a dark grey gown with autumnal leaves in red and gold embroidered over it.

They descended the stairs to where Kitty's father stood by the front door. 'I will come with you, but will not be admitted. I will wait along the road with the horses ready, if for some reason you both coming running out of the palace."

Kitty laughed, but Sera bit the inside of her cheek. As amusing as the picture was in her mind, they might yet flee down the stairs like Cinderella when the clock struck twelve. She clasped her hands to stop their trembling as they walked out the front door to the waiting carriage.

They journeyed through London to St James's Palace, used by King George III when not at his preferred home of Windsor Castle. Thankfully, they didn't need to undertake the journey to Berkshire today.

'Soon court will relocate again. The king refurbishes Buckingham House for Queen Charlotte and turns it into a palace," Mr Napier mused on the journey.

'What of the rumours that he is going mad?" Kitty asked her father.

"There is some truth to them, sadly. He is being treated by the best aftermage gifted physicians in our land, but they struggle to discover what plagues his mind. Let us pray their efforts will be rewarded." Silence fell, each lost in their own thoughts about how events might unfold.

The carriage stopped outside the imposing stone facade of the palace. "I think this is your battle, Sera. I am here for you, but my work is best done behind the scenes."

She nodded and would be forever grateful for his support. Now, she needed to show the Mage Council and society that she was a force to be reckoned with. She could not do that by using Mr Napier as a mouthpiece in this matter. The time had come to stand front and centre and demand the king's attention.

A footman opened the carriage door and handed down first Sera and then Kitty. Kitty looped her arm through Sera's. "Let us storm the castle," she said with a sparkle in her brown eyes.

FOUR

Somewhat to her disappointment, Sera didn't need to call upon her magic to ease their progress. Their clothing and bearing alone opened many doors to them. None of the footmen questioned them as the two finely dressed young women chatted and strolled the hallways, much like many other courtiers and ladies, until they wound through the palace to the king's presence chamber.

"Who are you?" a guard asked, peering along his nose at them.

"I am Lady Seraphina Winyard. Mage of England. If you try to stop me, I shall turn you into a toad." Seraphina held out one hand, where a ball of spinning swamp-green light hovered above her palm.

"Umm..." The guard swallowed and glanced at his companion.

At that moment, a tall, thin courtier bustled forward. "Duchess, we have been expecting you. Do come this way." He gestured to the room beyond, crowded with people.

The guards stepped aside, and Sera dissolved the spinning orb as they followed the courtier within. The rectangular presence chamber had white painted walls and gold embellishments around the cornicing and wainscoting. A large marble fireplace to one side contained flames with no heat—or perhaps it was merely the size of the space that rendered the embers useless. Life-sized portraits of former monarchs looked down as they passed.

"There is Lady Abigail, with those women," Kitty whispered and pointed with her chin to a group halfway along the chamber.

Sera sought out her friend and smiled when their eyes met. Abigail must have alerted the courtiers to expect her and provided a friendly face among the sea of strangers.

As they neared the end of the chamber, Kitty let go of her arm and Sera continued on alone. She stood before the rich red brocade hangings. The golden lion and unicorn rampant stood on either side of a silver shield on the rear wall. In lush red velvet chairs sat King George and Queen Charlotte. Clustered to the right and by the large window, several of the queen's ladies were clad in matching yellow gowns.

To the left of the royal couple, two mages stood with heads bent together. The younger of the two, at less than ten years older than Sera, was Lord Tomlin. He was a serious man with prematurely thinning hair and a weak chin, and she'd had little to do with him.

The older mage she knew all too well—Lord Branvale. Her former master narrowed his eyes as she approached, and his lips tightened into a thin line.

The courtier leading the way bowed low and rapped his staff against the floor. Conversation fell to whispers.

"Your Majesties, may I present your newest mage, Lady Seraphina Winyard." He swept to one side, revealing Sera behind him.

Remembering everything Abigail had taught her, and painfully aware of all the eyes boring into her, Sera executed the perfect deep curtsey and kept her gaze focused on the floor in front of her. She must be bidden to rise or commit a breach of etiquette. Silk rustled and a silver gown glided into view. A gloved finger was placed under her chin, and her face was raised to that of the queen.

"How extraordinary to finally set eyes upon our woman mage. You did not tell us, Lord Branvale, that she had grown into such a striking woman. Not pretty like so many ladies, but almost as though one senses the magic coursing under her skin, it demands your attention," Queen Charlotte said.

Sera rose as the queen returned to her seat. She clasped her hands lightly before her and set her shoulders straight and her head high. The court scrutinised her every move and if she clutched at herself too tightly or curled her posture, they would read her uncertainty and pounce like hounds on a wounded fox.

She paused for only a moment before addressing the royal couple. "King George, Queen Charlotte, having reached the age of eighteen, I present myself to you as one of England's mages. I stand before you to claim what is now due to me—a property and an allowance, in return for my devoted service to England."

Silence fell across the throne room, apart from a few startled coughs. Lord Branvale stepped forward and cast her a withering look before he turned to the king. 'She is not ready, Your Majesties. Her mind struggles to retain spells and her efforts are...lacklustre. I have the agreement of the Mage Council that she must remain under my tutelage for at least another ten years."

Sera drew a quick breath and swallowed her anger. 'With all due respect to my former guardian, he does not know what I am capable of now that I have reached the age of maturity for a mage."

Branvale huffed a laugh. 'She is a mere girl, and everyone knows a man must govern the weaker sex for their own good."

"The Mage Act clearly states that *all* mages are entitled to accommodation and a stipend on attaining the age of eighteen. By what authority does Lord Branvale withhold what I am legally entitled to and extend his guardianship?" Sera's anger turned cold in her veins. His arrogance would be his downfall. Only the two of them knew how he'd stifled her magic with the bracelet. She met Branvale's gaze. No more would he pull her strings like a marionette.

He waved a hand and chuckled. 'A mere oversight in the legislation. We cannot allow a feeble girl to fritter away the Crown's limited resources, just because she can cast a few basic spells."

"Feeble girl?" Seraphina breathed out the words while inside she screamed them. No more would she be underestimated and cast aside.

She clapped her hands together, and as she drew them apart, a blue sphere of sparks and bolts appeared. The sphere grew larger, swirling as lightning struck across its radius. When it reached half a yard in diameter, she threw it at Branvale. The ball knocked him off his feet, and he flew backward and upward in the air.

Lord Tomlin gasped and cast a red-tinged spell of his own at the sphere holding Branvale aloft. Red and blue clashed and swirled purple, but the other mage could not disable her spell.

"No! How is she doing this?" Her master crafted balls of grey light that plopped to the floor and dribbled along like heavy bowls thrown by a child.

Power surged through Sera, fed by years of anger, resentment, and despair. At last, Branvale danced to her command. What would she make her puppet do?

HUGH MILES STOOD against the wall, rather like a shark on the fringes of a school of fish. Courtiers and ambassadors swirled across the presence chamber, each more extravagantly dressed than the last. Women wore gaudy colours and bright florals, their powdered hair piled high atop their heads with an assortment of dead birds and tiny ships as further embellishment. Men strutted like peacocks with elaborate metallic embroidery on their jackets and waistcoats.

He glanced down at his own unadorned navy wool coat and grey waistcoat. The items were well tailored, subtle, and, oddly, fitted his broad frame. Exactly why he had borrowed them from the cadaver. The dead man had no more use for fine clothing, and Hugh was expected to stand before royalty. How was a former street rat supposed to afford court clothes?

His mentor, teacher, and one of the king's physicians, Lord Viner, conversed with a group to one side. Heads nodded and wigs bobbed at the serious discussion.

A courtier led two women into the room, and the crowd parted around them. One captured his interest, and his heart thumped loud in his ears. She stood tall and slender, as though she, too, knew the gnawing pang of going days without food. Her dark brown hair was swept up off her nape in a simple style such as a country wife might adopt. Her gown was a bold deep green and white stripe in a sea of florals and filigrees.

She grasped the hand of her friend, they shared a nod, and the striking woman strode to end of the room behind the courtier. She dropped a curtsey that elicited murmurs of appreciation around him.

Conversation hushed. Hugh's heart climbed up his gullet and wedged in his throat. An anatomical impossibility, but there it was. The blood pounded in his ears, and the minnows in the room faded into flashing shadows. He saw only the young woman.

Lady Seraphina Winyard, someone whispered in front of him. The name scratched at his memory. He didn't follow the argument unfolding between the woman and a stuffy mage. Instead, he focused on the way her lips formed each word. The faint swallow between sentences. The blue vein stretching down one side of her neck. Long fingers laced over her stomach.

When she raised her hands and threw the blue orb at the object of her anger, Lord Branvale, Hugh's brain kicked into action. Another mage to the side of the room rolled up his sleeves and threw spells to try to release the floating prisoner. The screams of women and shouts of men brought soldiers running through the doors. They encircled the woman with flintlock rifles aimed at her.

Whether or not the woman possessed magic, a ball in the back would stop her.

Hugh pushed through the people, made easier by his size and their panicked flight, to the back of the room. Electricity danced over Lady Winyard's form. For once he was grateful for his size, because the only thing he could think to do was going to hurt.

He reached out and took hold of her left wrist, holding the lean bones firmly enough to tug at her attention, but not so tightly as to hurt her or leave a bruise. Touching the enraged magic wielder was like grasping lightning. The charge surged up his arm and through his torso. Then it shot upward and downward in one blast. At any moment, he thought smoke would fill his nostrils as his hair and stockings caught fire.

The soldiers paused, their rifles aimed at the woman, ready to riddle her body with holes.

Hugh shook his head. *Wait*, he willed them. They glanced among themselves, probably not sure what shooting a mage would do. Who wanted to fire the first shot, only to discover the ball ricocheted into them?

He gritted his teeth through the pain, and once he had control of it, Hugh asked in a soft tone, "I say, that's a nasty scar. Have you put anything on it? You don't want an infection getting under the skin."

She paused and the electricity rolling up his arm diminished, but still he kept his gentle hold on her. Startling blue eyes turned to him, and any pain he felt vanished as his heart whooshed from his body.

SOFT-SPOKEN WORDS CAME from beside Sera and warmth encircled her wrist.

"What?" An odd question had jolted her rage off track.

She glanced to the side, where a young man who must have been a pugilist, given the size of him, held her arm. His thumb rubbed the angry wound on her wrist. Shaped like a tree, lines radiated from a central trunk. The skin had closed over, but it had a bright red tone.

The sizzle of power continued to course through her limbs, but now she held it under tight control. Lord Branvale dropped to the ground, and Lord Tomlin rushed to his side to help him to his feet.

'I'm a surgeon. You don't want to lose this arm to gangrene. I can dress it for you, if you have a moment.' Interest simmered in his brown eyes, along with a flash of concealed pain.

Only then did she realise he had taken hold of her while the spell coursed through her veins. She had hurt him. Excess power surged over his flesh and made the muscles in his arms twitch, but his hold on her remained gentle.

'I scratched it on a piece of metal,' she murmured. Anger drained from her under his gentle touch.

'This woman has proven herself hysterical and should be confined before she hurts someone.' Lord Branvale pointed at her from behind Lord Tomlin's tall form.

Sera stiffened her shoulders and ground her teeth.

'Don't give them more fodder for their delusions,' the young man murmured under his breath, so only her ears caught his words.

With his head bent, he appeared intent on the unusual injury to her wrist. He continued to stroke her arm with his thumb, and the rage dissipated under his caress. Only when she released a held breath and nodded did he let her go.

'I am sorry, Your Majesties. I did not mean to cause alarm. I only wished to demonstrate that my magic is more than equal to that of any other mage.' Sera dropped a curtsey to the royal couple while she cast a smile at the young man who had rescued her from her anger.

King George leapt to his feet and clapped. "Well done, Lady Winyard. You bested Branvale here."

All the courtiers and nobles rushed to applaud her performance, and the tension drained from the room.

Branvale's eyes threw daggers at her. "She is prone to fits of emotion and could hurt someone when she lashes out. Such an outcome is too dangerous to allow her to remain at liberty in London."

Sera channelled her anger inward. All of London was safe from her fits of emotion, except for the man who had locked away her magic and treated her as one of the servants.

The crowd parted as the most stunning example of humanity Sera had ever seen stepped forward. Women and men alike sighed as he passed. Some reached out a hand to brush his clothing. His tall, muscular form, broad of shoulder and narrow of waist, was expertly displayed in his high-collared jacket. Well-turned calves were encased in cream silk stockings. His blond hair was like gold but among the strands were deep caramel tones, as though a master painter had highlighted them with a deft touch. Eyes the blue of a clear summer's day regarded her, lush, dark red lips made for languid days of kissing pursed as he smiled at her.

Lord Arwyn Fitzfey, the king's half-Fae bastard, bowed to the king and queen before speaking in lyrical tones. "This woman has committed no crime. We witnessed a young mage proving she is of age to take her place among the magical protectors of this country. You cannot lock away this woman for displaying the power you intend to use to benefit England. Lady Winyard should be given the opportunity to serve her country, and in turn, this country should bestow upon her what she is due by law."

He smiled at Sera, and she nodded her thanks. A woman farther back in the crowd swooned and was caught by her companion. Sera stopped herself before she rolled her eyes. Yes, the king's bastard possessed otherworldly beauty, but her mind recalled the gentle touch of the only man brave enough to approach her in the grip of rage. Where had the half-Fae been then? Safe somewhere behind all the soldiers.

Kitty stepped forward and curtseyed to the king and queen. "Your Majesties, I am Katherine Napier, friend to Lady Winyard. For centuries, a contract has existed between England and her mages. Our mages use their magic to protect these isles and serve its people. In return, England provides home and hearth for her mages. If England breaks her contract with Lady Winyard, then she is no longer beholden to this country and may take her person, and magic, elsewhere."

Murmurs and a few snorts of indignation broke out around Sera. Under her lashes, she glanced at Kitty. Well played, she thought. Kitty and her father must have spent many a night poring over the Mage Act and its attendant legal cases to ensure Sera could claim the same entitlements as any male mage. Her friend's words struck England at its weakest point—the fear the mage might leave to serve the French, or worse, those young upstarts, the Americans. That young nation had few mages and would welcome an English defector in its battle for freedom.

King George leaned forward on his throne, a sheen of sweat to his brow and a glint in his eyes. "Our mages serve England and no other!" he bellowed.

A secretary rushed forward, then stilled. He laced his fingers loosely before him and plastered a serene expression on his face. He appeared like an actor slipping into character, rehearsing his lines in his head before he spoke them aloud. "Of course England will meet its obligations to Lady Winyard, as she is expected to meet hers to us." His dark eyes drilled into her, defying her to announce her intention to leave England for that uncivilised place...*America*.

Sera tilted her chin to the secretary in equal parts defiance and acceptance.

"Since it is settled that Lady Winyard will remain on English soil to use her considerable power as our king directs, she is due both a house and a stipend for her service to the Crown." Kitty fixed the much taller secretary with a glare.

King George's eyes wandered in two different directions at once before focusing on Sera and Kitty. A confused look crossed his brow. "What house?"

"That is the question, Your Majesty. What house has been made available for your newest mage?" Kitty refused to let the issue drop and pushed her advantage before anyone asked who she was to be questioning the king.

Another secretary hurried forward—Sera assumed

an undersecretary to the current one, given how he bent his knees to ensure he was shorter than the other man. A hasty whispered conversation took place before the first secretary cleared his throat. "I believe a final decision has not yet been made, Sire. Although your secretaries have selected three possible locations for Miss—er, Lady Winyard."

The king waved a hand. "Well, pick one for her. We cannot have one of our mages out in the street."

Sera wondered how many weeks it would take for the secretaries to decide.

"Lady Winyard will keep us entertained while you finalise the details of her new home. You have an hour," the king commanded.

The courtier's eyes widened, then he bowed and shuffled backward the requisite three steps. His footsteps disappeared at speed along the hall, once out of royal view.

"You can entertain us, can't you?" King George asked.

Sera stared at Kitty. *Entertainments?* she mouthed.

Kitty shrugged. *Birds?* she silently replied.

A brilliant suggestion. She would stick with what she knew her hands did best. Nature.

"Of course, Your Majesty." Sera bowed her head and cupped her hands together. She considered what to conjure, then with an idea fixed in her mind, she breathed upon her hands. Red and yellow sparks shot from between her closed fingers as the spell grew and took shape. She peeked at it between her thumbs and, once satisfied, threw it into the air.

A brilliant copper and gold phoenix, no larger than a sparrow, flew around the king. Its long tail of curling feathers left a fiery trail behind it. The court gasped as the bird spun in slow circles.

Sera cast a similar spell and released the next bird, this one the colours of a peacock. Green and blue water spirals joined the flaming one, as together the birds performed an aerial ballet.

The rapt king clapped his hands. The phoenix alighted on his outstretched hand and the peacock balanced on the arm of the queen's throne.

"How marvellous, Lady Winyard. No other mage has produced such delicate entertainment for us," Queen Charlotte said with a pointed look at the petulant Lord Branvale.

Sera allowed herself a broad grin, directed at her former guardian. He narrowed his gaze and whispered under his breath. From between his lips shot tiny silver arrows, each no longer than two inches, and aimed directly at the hearts of her creations.

FIVE

Oh, no you don't, Sera thought. Drawing her hands through the air, she captured Branvale's arrows and worked a new casting over them. They dropped to the ground, points down, where they burrowed into the floor. Then, they sprouted back up tall as sunflowers, but with silver petals.

People gasped and clapped their hands. Arwyn picked a silver bloom and presented it to Kitty with a bow. "For advocating so fiercely on Lady Winyard's behalf," he murmured.

"Thank you, my lord." Kitty took the flower and threaded it through her hair. She turned to Sera and flashed a huge grin for a mere second, before her normally composed expression dropped back over her features.

Sera cast around, searching for the young man who had taken her wrist. She found him standing against the wall, his arms crossed as he watched her.

"Who is that? The large man in dark blue and grey over there," she whispered to Kitty as she crafted a green bird to add to the other two.

Her friend turned a slow circle, surveying the court without lingering too long on the subject of discussion. "I shall find out."

With a smile, she stepped into the crowd and sought Lady Abigail. The two young women conducted a conversation while Sera crafted magical flowers and butterflies to amaze the royal couple. Kitty returned to Sera's side, but before she could say anything, a secretary slid into the room and approached the king. He whispered in the monarch's ear and then straightened.

"Good. A house has been decided upon for you, young woman." King George waved his hand, as though that was the end of the matter. A butterfly perched on his finger when his hand remained outstretched.

"I assume a carriage will be provided to take her there, Your Majesty? Or will she be required to walk?" Kitty asked.

The king huffed and narrowed his gaze. Their entertainment value was wearing thin on his patience and nerves. But he nodded to the secretary before waving a hand and rising to his feet.

"Thank you, Your Majesty." Sera curtseyed as the king stalked from the room. She offered a silent thanks that the king had retained his lucidity long enough to sort matters. Now, she didn't care if her new home turned out to be a barrel on the docks. It would be hers, and Branvale could control her no longer.

The two women followed the secretary out into the hall. A gaggle of lower-level secretaries clustered to one side, all clutching different-sized pieces of paper. One even carried a tray bearing a quill and ink pot with which the others could make notations on the move. Another swung a set of keys from his fingers like some gaoler.

The shortest man among them cleared his throat and thrust a folded sheet at Sera. "This is the right of residence for the property. In return for the accommodation, you agree to serve English interests for so long as you live. Sign, if you agree."

'She doesn't sign until we have examined the contract." Kitty snatched the page and unfolded it, scanning the contents. She huffed, snorted, and sighed as she read.

'Pen." She held out her hand.

One secretary looked to another, who shrugged. Then he dipped the pen in the ink, scraped it on the side of the pot, and placed it in Kitty's hand. The secretary held the tray out on his outstretched arms.

Kitty laid the paper on the impromptu desk and paused for a moment before wielding the pen. Words were struck through and new ones substituted. After some minutes, she set down the pen and spoke to the first secretary. 'Now, Lady Winyard will sign it."

His eyes widened as he stared from the contract to Kitty to Sera. "You cannot change a royal contract like that."

"We can when you try to impose different clauses than those offered to *male* mages. Lady Winyard's contract is now exactly the same as the one signed by every other mage who joins the council. Do you want her to sign, or shall I send for the American ambassador? I hear he is here somewhere. Lady Winyard would be delighted to talk to him." Kitty went up on her toes to glance about over the tops of their heads.

Sera held her silence, but her heart swelled with gratitude for her friend and her father.

"Yes, well, umm...the contracts must have been mixed up. Thank you for pointing out the oversight." The secretary stared at his associates and was met by shakes of the head. One fixated on his shoes and refused to make eye contact.

With the matter resolved, Sera took up the pen and signed her name to the contract. "I'll take my copy, thank you."

A secretary stepped forward with a slender wooden box. He opened the lid to reveal a sheet of paper. The ensorcelled paper was the exact duplicate of the one she had just signed, complete with all the amendments Kitty had made. Sera took the papers and rolled them up, muttering under her breath as she did so to remove the spell over the pages. Now, they could not be altered again. Then she handed one back to the secretary.

They were shown through St James's Palace to the cobbled courtyard. The Napier family carriage was gone, but was hopefully not too far away. Another vehicle was waved over, and Sera smiled at the attending secretary. "Thank you for your assistance."

He passed her a brass key with a length of green silk cord tied to it. "The house is number twenty-three, Lady Winyard. It has been my pleasure to be of service."

When the door shut and the carriage moved off, she let go of a long, pent-up breath and embraced her friend. "I could not have done this without you. Thank you."

"Friends stick together. Lady Abigail has to stay behind and attend the queen with the other ladies, but I can pass on one piece of intelligence. The man who stopped you from electrocuting Lord Branvale was Hugh Miles. Apparently he is a surgeon of some note and is mentored by the king's physician, Lord Viner."

"A surgeon? Is he an aftermage, that he is attending at court?" Sera rubbed her wrist. The healing wound itched and served as a reminder of what Branvale had done to her.

"No. Which apparently makes his skill even more remarkable. Given the size of him, I can't see him stitching anyone up. He has the arms of a publican used to throwing kegs or men, likely both at the same time." Kitty pulled aside the curtain to stare out the window.

"Indeed," Sera murmured. The footmen Branvale kept were lean. Only the tradesmen who came to the kitchen courtyard came close to a similarly broad physique.

After some time rattling along the roads of London, the carriage came to a halt, and they were handed down. While they stood on the cobbles, the driver cracked the whip and the horses trotted away, almost as though the man had been told not to remain.

Kitty glanced at Sera, then around them. Her eyebrows shot up. 'I see either the king or the Mage Council are sticking to the letter of the contract, rather than the spirit."

The newest mage to serve England took possession of a terrace house wedged in the middle of a row, in an area that clung to the label *respectable* by its fingernails. Her neighbours were probably either tradesmen on the rise, or nobles sliding backward into ruin on the outskirts of Soho.

'It's a home, and I am free of Branvale's control. I would rather be far away from him, even if it pains my heart not to be close to you." Sera steeled her spine and marched to the front door. She turned the key in the lock and flung the door open.

Both women coughed as a blast of cold, musty air rushed past them in its haste to escape.

'Smells like the last mage died in here and is still mouldering where he fell," Kitty quipped as they stepped inside and pulled the door shut.

They explored the small town house. On the street level were a drawing room, a modest dining room, and a study facing the desolate rear yard. Upstairs were two bedrooms of identical size and a third, smaller room that could serve as a dressing room or a maid's room. Below the street hunkered the kitchen, storeroom, and a chilly room for washing and laundry. A few furnishings remained, draped in sheets, but the floors were stripped bare of any rugs, the walls devoid of any paintings, and nothing ornamental provided a flash of beauty in the gloom.

"You cannot stay here alone. It would be akin to leaving you in a crypt. You must come back to Mayfair with me," Kitty said when they finished their tour and returned to the small entranceway.

Sera shook her head. "I am a mage. I will be fine. After you leave, I will cast a spell so no one may enter." There was one piece of useful information she'd learned from Branvale—a mage could stop any unwanted intruders from entering their home but must never seek to make it airtight. A mage had once suffocated his entire household when he removed the air from the rooms.

"It's your birthday. You should celebrate with us tonight." Kitty pursed her lips.

"Tomorrow night, I promise. Tonight, I need to be alone." Sera took her friend's hands to ward off any argument. "Besides, we have much to arrange—from furnishings, to my wardrobe, to finding a few staff I can trust. We can discuss all that over supper tomorrow."

Kitty arched one eyebrow. "And what do you intend to do about your supper tonight? You cannot wander the streets in a court gown."

There were spells to change clothing from one form to another. A temporary illusion would give her fancy gown the appearance of something more practical, so as not to attract too much attention. "I can alter my gown, but you cannot walk home. I shall come with you to find a hired carriage, and purchase something to stop me from starving in the interim."

A sigh escaped from Kitty. "Very well. But you cannot stop me from worrying about you."

Sera hugged Kitty, and tears welled up in her eyes. "I would not be standing here, if not for you and your father. Thank you for all you have done. You would make a formidable solicitor."

Kitty laughed. "Father thought they would try something like that, so we spent many hours finding and analysing mage contracts."

Before they left the house, Sera cast a small enchantment to mask their gowns and clothe them in simpler robes. Not far from the row of terraces, they found bustling streets, shops, and vendors pushing carts laden with goods for sale. Sera purchased a loaf of bread, a small wheel of cheese, and two apples. Then she saw Kitty into a carriage.

"Until tomorrow. We will set your new home to rights," Kitty promised.

Sera waved to her friend and then walked back to her new accommodation. She stared up at the house, crammed between its neighbours. Noise rolled from the street, children played, women shouted from windows, and men yelled at one another. She embraced all of it. If the Mage Council thought to break her, they would find her made of much sterner stuff. Placing her in the little town house didn't crush her spirit. Rather, it grew taller and expanded. Finally, she had the room to inhabit her own form and become who she was meant to be.

"Might as well make a start." Sera marched to the modest dining room and pulled the sheet from the table. The surface bore the wounds of many a dinner, as though the residents dined without plates and cut directly into the timber. She patted the wood, and thought how it reminded her of herself—scarred, but enduring.

Room by room, she removed sheets and examined what her service to England earned her. Very little, apparently. But then, she had yet to prove herself. As her reputation grew, her coffers would fill and she could afford better furniture or even another house if she so wished.

Upstairs, she pulled the dusty covering from the bed, the mattress bereft of any bedding.

"No, not tonight," she said to the solemn room.

Heading back downstairs, she fetched the basket containing her supper. Her explorations revealed an airing cupboard containing a few woollen blankets. Sera draped one around her shoulders and returned to the hallway.

"Where are you?" she muttered. She released a small spell that resulted in a piece of trim emitting a squeak. Pulling on it revealed steep and narrow stairs that led to the attic.

Tucked under the roof, she discovered two tiny rooms with single cots. She picked the one with a rounded window that peered out over the street below. Then she cast a warm glow to make up for the lack of a fire. With care, she stripped off the silk gown and removed her stays. Clad only in her chemise and stockings, Sera curled up on the cot and tucked the blanket around her. Leaning against the chill wall, she ate her small supper.

"Happy birthday to me," she murmured before biting into an apple.

Night fell outside the window. Sera rose and stood on her toes to look out over London. Lights winked off and on in the distance. Whispering under her breath, she wrought a spell that would keep out any intruders and ensure the doors and windows remained locked.

Only then did she lie down and pull the blanket over her. Exhaustion swept her into welcoming arms and carried her away to the land of Morpheus.

A TAPPING at the window awoke her early the next morning, as pale pink ribbons of sunrise danced over the clouds. Clutching the blanket around her, Sera rose from the cot to find a curious crow on the windowsill, rapping on the glass. Morning light rippled on its black features, giving the bird the appearance of being cast from metal.

Sera kept hold of the blanket to ward off the chill and reached out to lift the latch. "Good morning," she said to the creature as she opened the window.

The bird croaked around something in its mouth, silver glinting on an object trailing from both sides of its beak.

"What do you have there?" She stretched out her hand, and the crow draped a length of silver ribbon across her palm. "Thank you, my friend. You are the first of my neighbours to welcome me. I'm sorry I have nothing to offer you in return."

The bird pecked at her hand, not hard, more like an admonishment for not reciprocating the gift.

"I still have some bread left, if that would be acceptable?"

The bird tilted its head to regard her with one serious eye, then it emitted a caw.

She took that as agreement. Retrieving the loaf, she broke off a chunk and held it out.

The crow grabbed the piece of bread, croaked again, then took flight.

Sera leaned out the window and stared at the street stirring into life below her. A rumble from her stomach reminded her of all she had to do—the first of which was to procure clothing. She had only the court dress; her rough linen frock had been left in Kitty's bedroom.

She chewed a piece of bread and made a mental note of her priorities for the day—clothes, food, and bedding.

A heavy knock on the door made her look down, but the angle of the roof obscured her view.

"Coming!" she called out. Then, clutching the blanket around her shoulders, she raced down the narrow stairs.

A man stood on the front doorstep, dressed in plain trousers and a brown woollen coat. A large trunk sat at his feet and a crate balanced atop that. Out in the street, a placid horse snoozed before a cart. The man slid the cap from his head as she opened the door and twisted it in his hands. "Pardon me for banging on the front door, Lady Winyard. Miss Napier sent me and said no one would hear if I hammered on the kitchen door."

"That's all right, and Miss Napier is correct. There are no staff in the house as yet."

Relief flashed across his ruddy features. "Shall I take the trunk below stairs?"

"No, bring it in here, please." Sera silently thanked her practical friend for whatever she had dispatched.

The man placed the crate inside the door, and then the larger trunk. A delicious aroma wafted from the crate, and when Sera peeled away the covering cloth, two crumpets with a polished glaze of melted butter sat on top. Her stomach rumbled.

At that point, she realised the man was waiting for her to tip him. She had no coin, Kitty having purchased her supper the day before. "I'm afraid I don't have any coin. Could I offer a spell instead as a thank-you?"

The man screwed up his face. "I don't have much need for magic, milady."

Her gaze snagged on the hole in his boot. "Perhaps I could fix that for you?"

He nodded. "That would be handy, milady. I do hate wet socks when I stomp through a puddle."

She knelt, placed one hand over his boot, and murmured to the leather, encouraging it to stretch, grow, and cover the hole. When she lifted her hand, the boot was restored to near new condition.

The tradesman wriggled his toes. "Thank you very much, milady. I won't have to worry about the rain now."

Once he had gone, Sera rummaged through the

trunk. It contained undergarments, two practical gowns, and a pair of boots. The accessories included two shawls, two jackets, and a large hat decorated with feathers. Beneath the crumpets, the crate held fresh bread, cheese, salted meat, tea, and a jar of relish.

Sera decided on the soft green countrified gown, so called because of its simple lines. Then she selected the darker green redingote jacket, modelled after a man's riding coat. She changed in the parlour—rather than dragging everything up and down the stairs—and used her magic to tighten the laces on her stays and fasten the hooks on her gown.

Once dressed, she carried her box of supplies down to the kitchen. She needed to find someone to take charge of the house, and she knew exactly whom to poach for that task. A thumping at the door echoed through the house as she contemplated lighting the fire in the hearth.

The noise became more insistent as she hurried along the hall, wondering what it could be this time. She pulled the door open to find Kitty on the step, wringing her hands.

"Lord Branvale is dead!" she exclaimed. "They are saying it is murder."

SIX

Sera drew her friend into the house and shut the door. 'Dead? Are you sure? We saw him only yesterday and apart from ruffled feathers, he appeared healthy."

Kitty paced the short length of hall before the stairs, one hand pressed to her forehead. 'We heard the shriek this morning when the young maid, Vicky, found him. Honestly, I thought *she* was being murdered, from the fuss she made. Father went to investigate and found Lord Branvale dead in his bed. Father said that from the look on his face, he died in great agony. The Bow Street Runners and the magistrate have been sent for to investigate, and I came straight here."

Sera's first concern was for the servants—there was little point in being worried about Branvale now. 'Vicky has always been nervous, and screams murder if a mouse runs across her foot. While I appreciate being informed, Lord Branvale's death is of no consequence to me. I did not harbour any great affection for him."

Although objectively, it meant his powers were now reborn in another form somewhere in England. Boy or girl?

Kitty stood before Sera and took her hands. "You don't understand, Sera. You had an altercation with him in front of the entire court only yesterday, and the morning newspaper is full of reports about it. Today he is dead. What if some suspect *you* of murdering him?"

She snorted. "I would say they don't know me at all, if they think I would kill someone in their bed." Then another idea occurred to her, and she fetched her hat from the parlour. "I shall return to Mayfair with you. I need to find Rosie."

Kitty narrowed her gaze and appeared to be on the verge of saying something. Then, given the determined set of Sera's shoulders, her friend changed her mind. Instead, she held out a slip of paper. "Lady Abigail sent you a message at our house. She wishes to call."

Sera placed her hat on her head and then took the sheet. She read the brief message and then sent it flying to a table in the parlour. "Marvellous. I need Abigail's counsel. I shall send your man to tell her to come here this afternoon."

Kitty opened the door. "After you, Lady Winyard."

The Napier family carriage took them back to the borders of Mayfair. Sera hopped down unaided outside the grand homes. "I'll go talk to the servants. You see if your father has learned anything."

Worry pulled at Kitty's eyes, but she held her own counsel and merely nodded. "You know where to find me when you are done."

A few men in deep blue coats huddled on the pavement, and from their worn features, Sera assumed them to be Bow Street Runners. Curious women stood across the road, whispering and gesturing. There was nothing like a scream of murder early in the morning to rouse everyone from bed.

Sera took the stairs from street level down to the servants' entrance. Then she rushed along the dark corridor and burst out from the empty kitchen into the courtyard. The staff clustered around the edges, standing in the shadows cast by the walls. Vicky sat on a bench pushed under the kitchen window, her shoulders heaving in silent sobs. Rosie looked up and hurried to Sera.

'Sera! I mean, Lady Winyard.' Her friend came to a wobbly halt and then bobbed a curtsey.

Sera snorted and reached out to hug the worried older woman. 'Don't start with that nonsense. We are family.'

Rosie patted Sera's cheek with a gentle touch. 'We've been ever so worried about you, slipping out like that early yesterday without so much as a word.'

'I'm sorry to leave without saying goodbye, Rosie, but I had to get out.' To be fair, she'd had no idea she could escape until it happened, and as she crept through the house, she couldn't spare the time to leave a note. Nor would she mention the odd bracelet she had worn most of her life and its roots that spread through every part of her, sapping her power.

'Where are you living? Did the Napiers take you in?' A frown pulled the cook's auburn brows together.

"King George has kindly allocated me a modest home in an even more modest neighbourhood on an outer edge of Soho." She didn't care that the house was far beneath that given to the other mages—it was *hers*.

Rosie stared at her with wide eyes. "Fancy putting a mage like you somewhere like that."

Sera shrugged. If the location of the house was supposed to unnerve her, it failed. She much preferred the company of common folk. While she adored her odd family, she hadn't returned for a reunion. "Now tell me everything that has happened, starting from the beginning."

She pulled Rosie to the other bench in the sheltered yard. The footmen all stood, as though unused to sitting. From a glance, it appeared the entire staff had assembled in the yard while the house sat empty except for their dead master.

"Well, poor Vicky found him. She crept into his room early to lay the fire. She said there was a terrible smell...he had shat his bed, you see." Rosie lowered her voice as she shared that last piece of news.

"How did she know he was dead?" Sera didn't bother directing her questions to the maid in question. With her face as pale as a freshly laundered sheet and the way she hugged herself, Sera doubted anyone would get a sensible reply from the girl for some time.

"Vicky crept closer to ask if he was all right. Her lantern cast enough light to see his eyes were wide open, and he had the most terrible expression on his face." At this point, Rosie contorted her face, stuck out her tongue, and turned her hands into claws.

'Oh. I assume it was at that point that Vicky screamed?" Poor mite. While the other girl was only two years younger than Sera, the age difference seemed much greater in the way they reacted to adverse events in the world.

Rosie nodded. 'Jake came running first. He had been asleep in the master's dressing room. His lordship came in late last night, and can't have been in bed more than a few hours when Vicky found him. Mr Napier heard the kerfuffle, and it was him that sent for the Bow Street Runners and a doctor. Aren't mages supposed to disappear when they die?"

'Our magic is transferred to a new soul on our death, but our physical body remains." Sera knew less about medicine than she did about magic. They had yet to confirm Branvale had indeed been murdered. From what her guardian had taught her, the murder of mages was highly unusual. Not that it took much to imagine someone wanting Branvale dead. He didn't exactly inspire love or warmth in his staff or others he encountered.

The altercation she had witnessed in the entrance hall replayed in her mind. Had that disgruntled customer indeed made Branvale sorry for his failed spell?

'Will his family take over the house now?" Rosie asked.

Sera pursed her lips and dug into her memory. Lord Branvale had fathered two children to ensure a trace of his magic flowed through successive generations, but he did not live with their mother. Instead, he continued his life as a bachelor—which made it even more odd that he had taken a five-year-old girl mage under his wing. 'I imagine his children will be notified. If he owns the house, it becomes part of their inheritance. If the Crown holds title, it returns to the king."

"Either way, we're all out on the street." Rosie wrapped her apron string around her fingers.

Noise from the street beyond washed over them as they sat in the weak sunlight that penetrated the servants' yard. Since employment preyed on Rosie's mind, Sera took the opportunity to broach another issue. 'Perhaps I might tempt you to come work for me, Rosie. Kitty is ensuring I don't starve by sending me food parcels, but I would rather trust my household to your capable hands."

Rosie raised her round face to Sera, tears misting her hazel eyes. "Truly? You would want me?"

Sera huffed a short laugh. 'Of course I want you. Now, more than ever, I need people I can trust around me. Besides, we both know that Branvale always treated you abominably, and I know your true worth. And since, as you already said, you are now without an employer."

"What about Vicky?" Rosie cast a glance at the young maid, who at least had stopped crying after her traumatic morning.

"Vicky, too. I will also need a footman." A man in the house would be a visible deterrent to any would-be thieves who might think a woman alone an easy mark until word spread that a mage resided there. Three staff seemed excessive, but she only wished she had the resources to employ them all. "Perhaps Elliot would be a good fit?" She glanced to where the rangy footman in question stood. While he possessed good looks and an easy charm, that wasn't what made Sera decide on him. He had a depth of loyalty to his friends that she admired, and a larcenous streak that might prove handy.

Rosie stuck out her hand. "Very well, a deal."

The two women shook. Sera leaned her head back against the stone of the house. Having a few staff she could trust was one weight off her mind. Branvale, with his insistence that she continue as his ward for ten more years, had removed himself as another potential problem.

She snorted under her breath. Ridiculous. Hopefully, the Mage Council wouldn't seize the idea to force another guardian on her. She would ask Kitty's father to examine the legalities of that, in case they tried. What she needed now was days alone in the mage library, soaking up the knowledge formerly denied to her. And to find out what spell Branvale had cast over the copper bracelet.

"Lady Winyard? What are you doing here?" a familiar soft-spoken voice asked.

She opened her eyes to find Hugh Miles's bulk filling the kitchen doorway, and her heart skipped a beat at his reassuringly solid presence. Today he wore a dark grey jacket with patches on the elbows that had seen better days. His brown hair was ruffled and sticking out at odd angles. Perhaps he hadn't expected to be called away from his surgery.

"Doctor Miles. I came to see if there was anything I could do to assist. This was my home until yesterday." She smiled at him.

"You know my name?" His brows pulled together, but his eyes sparkled.

She couldn't resist a mischievous laugh as she waggled her fingers in the air. "Of course I know who you are. I possess magic."

"With all due respect to your magical abilities, I must make one slight correction—I have no claim to the appellation of doctor. I am a self-taught man and not a noble who has completed training at a medical college. I am fortunate in that Lord Viner gave me a private education and paid for me to attend some anatomy classes." He bowed as he paid the compliment to his absent mentor.

Sera's heart warmed toward the surgeon. They both had to find their own way to educate themselves in their particular abilities. "That makes you even more extraordinary, Mr Miles. But what are you doing here?"

He waved to the house behind him as he stepped into the yard. "I happened to be at the Runners' station when the lad came in and said Lord Branvale had died under odd circumstances. I offered to attend."

Sera rose from the bench and approached him. "Was he truly murdered?"

He glanced around at the gathered staff. "His symptoms do not seem consistent with natural causes. It will require further investigation before making any definitive statement about how he passed, but I shall have to seek royal permission to do that since this involves a mage."

A commotion beyond the gate to the mews halted their conversation. The wide gate creaked open, and a face appeared in the gap before disappearing as they pushed it open wide. More men walked into the yard, and Sera recognised Lord Ormsby, the Speaker of the Mage Council. Lord Pendlebury, another of the senior mages, trailed behind him.

"Is the physician here?" Lord Ormsby demanded of them. As he aged, the mage grew larger. Never possessing great height to begin with, his body expanded outward, which only seemed to make him appear shorter. In his sixties, he now resembled a caricature of himself. Sera hoped no one would mistake him for a keg of ale and roll him into the wine cellar.

"I am the attending surgeon." Mr Miles inclined his head to the mage. "I have conducted a preliminary examination of Lord Branvale's remains and can confirm he died less than ten hours ago."

Lord Ormsby harrumphed. "We'll take matters from here. His body is to be moved to the mage tower." Then he swung to Sera and narrowed his pale gaze. "Is it true that you did it?"

Before Sera could muster an answer, Mr Miles stood between her and the stout mage. "It's rather premature to be making accusations. I have not yet ascertained the cause of death."

"Everyone knows she tried to harm Branvale yesterday. The whole of London can talk of nothing else. She attacked him in an unprovoked manner in front of the entire court and amply displayed why women aren't suitable vessels to contain our magic." Lord Ormsby could barely conceal his contempt.

Sera curled her hands into fists. "Lord Branvale called me feeble. I merely demonstrated that I am not, and that I am ready to assume my duties. How odd it is that despite my being so deficient in magic, neither he nor Lord Tomlin could unravel my simple spell holding him aloft."

The surgeon glanced at her and his lips quirked in a brief smile.

Ormsby waved a dismissive hand. "Tomlin said he let you win, to give a good show for the king."

Let her win? Oh, no, he hadn't.

"Now is not the time to discuss this," Lord Pendlebury interjected with the voice of reason. Somewhere in his late thirties and of average height and slight build, he had a harmless air about him, rather like that of a bookkeeper or librarian. "Our concern at this moment is Lord Branvale, and discovering the truth of what happened to him."

Sera liked Lord Pendlebury. He took a practical approach to matters. When she was trotted out like a show pony to perform for the council and others sought to depreciate her efforts, Pendlebury always argued they had no idea how power might present in a woman due to the lack of comparative examples. Now she could show them all that, like a rare flower, she would bloom all the more magnificently for taking her time.

"As I was saying earlier, I will need to examine the

remains to determine how Lord Branvale died." Mr Miles edged closer to Sera, sheltering her at his side. Or protecting the two mages from her temper, she wasn't sure which.

'No one is going to rummage around inside Branvale." Lord Ormsby's nostrils flared.

Lord Pendlebury interjected before Lord Ormsby could continue. 'We have arranged for the removal of our fellow mage's body. The king and then Branvale's family must be informed. Then we must determine where his powers have been reborn."

Sera wanted to bombard the men with questions, since they were before her. When would she be admitted to the council? Who were her parents? The questions must have swirled across her features.

Lord Pendlebury cast her a kind look. 'We have much to discuss, Lady Winyard, but perhaps that could wait a day or two, if you don't object? More immediately, we need to deliver your communications box. Will you be here today if I have a man bring it to you?"

'I will be next door at the Napier home until midday, most likely. If it could be delivered there I would be most grateful." A communications box of her own! The ensorcelled container allowed mages to send instant letters to each other around the world, and the Mage Council would use it to dispatch her tasks.

Lord Pendlebury inclined his head while Lord Ormsby stared at his fingernails and ignored her.

The Bow Street Runner emerged from the kitchen and glanced around. His eyes nearly crossed trying to determine whom to address. 'Men are here to take him away.'

Lords Ormsby and Pendlebury followed the Runner into the house to oversee the removal of their fellow mage.

Before the surgeon turned to join them, Sera placed a hand on his arm. 'I want to thank you for what you did yesterday. I am sorry that I hurt you when you were only preventing me from making an even bigger mistake.'

He placed a large hand over hers. 'Fortunately, I am solid enough to absorb the excess magic that flowed from you, and I now have a much better understanding of the principles of galvanism.'

That made her laugh.

'Now, if you'll excuse me, I must attend upstairs. But I hope our paths will cross again, milady.' He nodded to her and ducked through the doorway.

Sera didn't realise she had been staring after him until Rosie slipped an arm through hers. 'He's rather handsome, that one. You'd expect him to be all sharp and angry given his size, but he seems as gentle as a lamb.'

'He does seem to possess a kind heart.' There was little more Sera could do or learn about Branvale's death, so she turned her mind to life instead. 'Why don't you pack your belongings? I will ask Mr Napier if one of his men may drive a cart for you to my new lodgings. Be warned, though, they are rather shabby and not as grand as this house.'

Rosie barked a short laugh. 'I'd rather have shabby

and working for you than that horrid man and this lovely house."

Sera left the cook to organise Vicky and Elliot and the possessions they would need to take with them. The door to the Napier house opened as she approached along the footpath. The butler showed her through to the front parlour, where Kitty paced before the window. No doubt she had spotted Sera emerging from Branvale's home.

"Did you learn any more?" Kitty asked.

"Very little. Branvale died during the night, but the surgeon, Mr Miles from court yesterday, does not yet know how he died." Sera swept aside her skirts and dropped to the settee.

Kitty took the seat next to her. "I have a bad feeling about this."

So did Sera. It did not bode well that the Speaker of the Mage Council believed her capable of murdering one of their fellow members. Had she escaped Branvale's leash only to find a noose placed around her neck?

S era used her morning with Kitty to decide
what her new home needed. She had no intention of wasting her allowance in a frivolous
manner. "Only the bare essentials, Kitty. I don't need a
fancy home for entertaining."

The king, or the Mage Council, had done her a
great favour with the house they had allocated her. Any
visitors to the neighbourhood would be close, personal
friends only, so she had no need for lavish furniture and
draperies.

Another thought occurred to Sera. "I will also need
a riding habit."

"Will you be wanting a horse, then?" Kitty dipped
the pen into the ink and held it poised over the list they
were making at the dining room table.

"No. The riding habit is for practical reasons. Men
may wear trousers or breeches, but I cannot. Yet I am
still expected to work and wield my magic to assist the
people of England. A habit of plain and sturdy

construction will be more suitable for whatever situation I might find myself in." The Mage Council could barely cope with a woman mage. If she adopted trousers, they would most definitely rush to burn her as a witch.

"Excellent idea. As an interim measure, Abigail might have an old one that will fit you." Kitty wrote *riding habit* in her neat hand on the sheet.

They were nearing the end of their task when the butler appeared in the doorway and coughed discreetly into his hand. "A man is here to see Lady Winyard."

"Excellent." Sera rose from her seat and followed the butler out to the tiled entranceway.

A man in the deep purple and gold livery of the Mage Council clutched a box of polished rosewood with brass corner protectors. He bowed as she approached. "I am to hand this only to you, Lady Winyard."

Sera took the box from his outstretched hands. Despite its solid appearance, she found it rather light. "Thank you."

She ran a finger across the top. A plain brass circle inlaid in the wood waited for her to add her personal symbol.

"How does it work?" Kitty asked after the messenger had been shown out.

Sera placed one hand over the latch and let her magic touch the metal. The lid popped up a fraction, and she lifted it open. Within were a few sheets of paper, inscribed with names and displaying each mage's symbol.

"When I add my symbol to the lid, my details will appear on the list of mages. To send a message, I place my correspondence inside, touch the brass plate, and visualise the symbol of the mage I wish to communicate with." She lifted the pages, but found nothing underneath and so closed the lid again.

Kitty tapped the smooth brass circle. "What will you choose?"

Sera recalled the moments before she entered the court. A peacock had crossed her path and gifted her a single feather that she had added to those in her hair. One of the birds she had conjured to entertain the king had been a peacock, too. "A peacock feather entwined with my initials."

The clock behind them struck one, reminding Sera of other engagements for the day.

"You had better be on your way. You don't want to leave Lady Abigail standing on your doorstep. I shall miss having you next door and our chats over the wall." Tears misted Kitty's eyes.

Sera hugged her friend tightly. "You have not lost me. Now that I am of age, I shall craft you a mage silver ring so we can talk whenever you want."

Kitty nodded and blinked away her tears. "Good. Otherwise it will cost me a fortune to have boys run you messages a hundred times a day."

"I will be back at dusk, for a belated birthday supper with you and your father. Then in the morning, I will send a message so you know I have survived another night." Sera made a joke of it, even as worries nibbled at the edges of her mind. A burglar she could keep out of the house, but what if the Mage Council turned against her?

With a promise to return later that evening, the family carriage deposited Sera back at her new abode on the south side of Soho. The door swung open as she walked up the stairs, opened with a grin by Elliot Bryn, the personable (and handsome) footman formerly employed by Branvale. "Welcome back, milady."

"Elliot, I'm so pleased you could join my little household." In his late twenties, he was tall and well formed, with sun-bronzed skin, dark hair, and near black mischievous eyes. He was a rogue, but hopefully a useful one.

He closed the door and shrugged. "Rosie says there might not be too much to do, which suits me just fine."

"You will need to be adaptable. There will be many tasks that I might need you to undertake for me." Sera stripped off her gloves and pulled the long pin holding her hat in place.

"I've served one mage. I can't see you being any more odd than he was. Even if you are a woman." He winked, then held out his hands to take her hat.

Sera glanced into the mirror on the wall and smoothed a strand of hair. She would have to do. Abigail was due within the hour. "Is Rosie downstairs?"

"Yes, milady. She and Vicky are giving the kitchen a good scrub." Elliot hung her hat on a hook in the hall where she could retrieve it readily.

Down in the kitchen, she found the two women busy cleaning. Rosie looked around from wiping down the bench. "Nearly done, Sera. Miss Napier placed orders with the butcher, grocer, and the dry-goods store and everything should be delivered later this afternoon."

A roof over her head, a full belly, and friends around her. What more did she need? "Thank you, Rosie. Lady Abigail will visit soon. Is it too much to ask for a pot of tea?"

The cook nodded and gestured to a tea service sitting by the sink. The cups and pot were newly washed and dried. "We'll be able to rustle up something. I'll send Elliot out to find cakes from the bakery around the corner."

With one more task taken care of, Sera returned upstairs to examine the small parlour. It possessed a settee, two armchairs, a low table, and a desk. The floors were bare boards and shadows on the walls hinted that paintings had been removed. With no books on the shelves or waiting to be read by the chairs, the house seemed to be missing its soul. How she longed for a library of her own, one she could fill with volumes she discovered along her journey.

"This will have to do," Sera muttered to the room.

She moved the ensorcelled box from the side table to the desk. Resting one hand over the plain brass insert, she conjured her symbol in her mind—a peacock feather with the letters *S* and *W* entwined over the middle. Her palm tingled as the magic engraved what her mind created.

Eventually she would find furnishings for the small study at the rear of the house, but until then the parlour would serve both for entertaining and for conducting business.

A small gilded carriage clock, borrowed from Kitty and placed on the mantel, chimed three times. As the third chime faded, a rap came at the door. Sera stood and waited while Elliot showed her visitor in.

Her friend crossed the threshold, stared around, and then sneezed. She pressed a handkerchief to her nose, her eyes widening. "You cannot stay here, Seraphina."

"I can, and I shall." She took Abigail's hands in greeting and led her to the settee with its faded fabric that might once have been red, but seemed more the hue of rust now.

"You will be murdered in your bed," Abigail said as she seated herself. As she stripped off her hat and gloves, she realised her *faux pas* and stared at Sera with concerned eyes.

Elliot returned bearing a tea tray and set it on the table beside the two women, then disappeared on silent feet.

"You mean like Lord Branvale, who snored his last in his comfortable Mayfair home?" Sera murmured as she poured tea.

Abigail perched on the edge of the settee. "Yes, well, I chose my words poorly, but the sentiment remains true. The odds here are surely stacked against you. This neighbourhood is home to...*tradespeople*."

Sera offered a cup to Abigail, then took her own and leaned back in the armchair, which proved surprisingly comfortable despite its shabby appearance.

84

'Surely I am now a tradesperson? I will labour as directed by the Mage Council and the Crown, working to earn my keep. Given it is a lifelong commitment, I could be considered a type of indentured servant."

'Don't be silly, Seraphina. Of course you are not a servant." Abigail pursed her lips and shuddered. Then she glanced over her shoulder at the window. 'I hear there are...Unnaturals living in this area. What will you say if you encounter one on the street?"

'I shall say *good day*, as I do to every person I meet." Many people thought Unnaturals weren't human. Which she supposed they weren't, really, or not entirely. While she had not encountered one directly, if they were civil to her, she would respond in the same fashion. She certainly would not hunt lycanthropes for their skins, like some nobles had in centuries gone by. Or enslave goblins to do her housework.

Abigail shifted on her seat, uncomfortable with the discussion. 'This accommodation is beneath someone of your status. You are the equal of a duchess and should not forget that. With such a rank come certain expectations. I shall talk to Papa and see if you can visit with us until somewhere better is found."

'Yet this is the accommodation the king made available to me. I know you have my best interests at heart, dear Abigail, but I am quite content where I am for the moment." Sera found much to appreciate in the lively surroundings, the children playing in the street, and the raucous conversations of the women chatting by the roadside.

Let the other mages tend to the needs of the upper

classes. She saw much to be gained in making a friend of the common man. A lesson French nobles might do well to learn, if whispers on the wind were true.

"I had hoped to have the support of my friends as I embarked on this journey." Her magic marked her as extraordinary, and she intended to pursue what that meant. Male mages were given certain freedoms. Why could she not also embrace those liberties? Beginning with living alone.

Abigail's shoulders tensed. "Of course you have our support. It is exactly because we care about you that Kitty and I worry so. We want to see you flourish, truly, but we also want to see you somewhere safe."

Who needed more than two friends when they were such protective ones as these? "Give me a little time to try living alone first. That is all I ask."

Abigail selected a sliver of cake and placed it on her saucer. "Very well. But in return, I insist you attend an evening I am hosting. You must be introduced to proper society. Have you given any consideration as to whom you will marry?"

Sera spat tea into her cup, and only a wave of magic saved it from shattering on the floor. She dabbed at herself with a handkerchief and wiggled her fingers to create a spell to sop up the tea from her dress and the floorboards. "Marry? I haven't even spent two days on my own and have given no thought whatsoever to marriage. I don't even see that such a state is necessary or even possible for a mage. Many of the mages remained bachelors."

Abigail set down her teacup on the table with a

rattle. "You cannot buck every single expectation of society, Seraphina. A man may marry or choose to remain a bachelor, and no one raises an eyebrow. But a young woman, particularly one elevated to your new rank, is expected to make an advantageous marriage. There will be many fine English nobles who will see the advantage of possessing a wife who is a mage. You might even find some European royalty will try to woo you away from our shores."

Possessing a wife. Seraphina poured more tea into her near empty cup. "I cannot imagine anything worse than being paraded about like a novelty for men to bid upon." Now that she thought about it, she doubted any of them were brave enough to court her. In a chamber crammed with nobles and courtiers, only one man had had the courage to take her wrist while she sparked with power.

Abigail heaved a sigh and picked up her cup and saucer. "How many hours did we spend in each other's company as I tried to make you a civilised lady? To think I laboured for years in vain." She drew out the words, dripping with mock despair.

Seraphina laughed. "All right! I shall attend your evening and you can show me off like some curiosity acquired abroad. If any of the men are intolerably boring, may I turn them into toads?"

"No. You may not." Abigail sipped her tea, and the silence stretched between them. "Oh, very well then, but just the one. And do ensure it is the most boring of the young bucks at the table."

"Will you sing?" Her friend's songs could move you

87

to tears, or laughter, or send you soaring from despair to the happiest moments.

'Father says I may, but there will be no other opportunities for at least a month." Sadness tinged Abigail's words.

Her father ensured Abigail's performances were few and far between, so that invitations were highly sought after when rumour spread that she would sing at an evening. His daughter's voice became a currency with which to trade favours with other nobles.

To think that at the beginning of the week, Sera had been little more than a scullery maid, and now she was to attend society evenings, a duchess in her own right. 'I will need a gown appropriate for the evening. Which reminds me, do you have an old riding habit I might use?"

A frown pulled at Abigail's delicate brow. 'An old riding habit? Surely you will want the latest fashion if you intend to ride Rotten Row?"

Sera chewed the cake and swallowed as she waved away the idea of riding out just to be stared at. 'I won't be riding. I want one for working. I doubt you will want to read in the scandal sheets of my wearing breeches as I perform whatever tasks the Mage Council will set me?"

This time it was her friend who most politely nearly choked on her cake. 'Breeches? Good God, Sera! Most certainly not. I do happen to have an old one in a trunk that will fit you. I shall have my maid air it out, hem it up, and send it over."

"Thank you." She really was blessed in her friends.

Although a tendril of mischief wanted to know exactly how Abigail would react if she donned men's fashion to stride out in the streets and fields.

After their visit concluded, Sera waved goodbye to Abigail from the front step. Another carriage pulled up in the street and a footman jumped down from the rear, carrying an envelope.

"Whatever will the neighbours think of me, with all these fine carriages coming and going?" she murmured to Elliot as she waited for the courier to climb the stairs.

"That you are running a bordello, most likely." Elliot held out his hand and took the envelope before presenting it to Sera.

Slitting it open, she found a summons to appear at court. "It appears I am much in demand. The king and queen require my presence, no doubt as the afternoon's entertainment."

She heaved a sigh. All during her time under Lord Branvale, she had dreamed of what she would achieve once free. Of how she could use her abilities to bring about real change in the lives of ordinary Londoners. She imagined using her magic to help crops grow faster and stronger, or sheep with fluffier wool. Instead, she was offering up amusing tricks for jaded nobles. Perhaps she should have joined the theatre, where she could perform her tricks on stage and heat the hot chocolate afterward.

Elliot took down her hat and handed it to her with an amused glint in his dark eyes. "While you're out, I might find a red lantern to put in the parlour window. I hear that's what bordellos do."

"Don't you dare." Sera pointed her hat pin at him.

The royal footman helped her up into the carriage and Sera waved to her gossiping neighbours as they departed. She needed to think of something to do for them, to show her commitment to her new community. And to prove she wasn't running a bordello. Once the locals saw the advantages of having a mage in the neighbourhood, frowns and stares would turn into smiles and conversations.

At court, Sera was ushered into the royal presence. She curtseyed and waited to be acknowledged. The moment stretched out, but she was no stranger to waiting. With eyes downcast, she considered how to deliver an enchanted evening for her neighbours. Unicorns would delight the girls—young and old alike. What did boys prefer? Boats, perhaps. She would put on a performance involving both.

"Lady Winyard, we are advised that your guardian has died under most unusual circumstances," Queen Charlotte said at last.

Sera straightened from her curtsey and considered what to say. The queen regarded her with curious eyes. The king sat sideways on his throne and dangled one leg over the arm. Every day, rumours grew about his mental state. Perhaps the queen should concern herself more with her husband, and less with Sera's former guardian.

"As I, too, have been informed, Your Majesty. It is a great loss for England." And an even greater blow for the local wine merchant, but Sera kept those words rattling around inside her own head.

The king seemed bored, and to ensure he stayed out of the conversation, Sera crafted a golden fish with one hand and sent it darting toward the monarch. He gasped and began waving at it like a child trying to catch a butterfly.

The queen drew breath to speak when a commotion erupted at the door. A finely dressed noble swept into the presence chamber and bowed to the queen. A man of average height and rotund build, his pale hair was powered almost white. He wore a jacket of deep purple with silver embroidery that contrasted sharply with the red tone to his rounded face.

Then he levelled a finger at Sera. "This is the murderous witch. Seize her!"

EIGHT

S oldiers edged into the room behind the
intruder and loosely arrayed themselves in a
semicircle.

Sera didn't recognise the finger pointer, which
meant he was no mage and therefore of no consequence
to her. Rolling her hands together, she created a shark
and set it to swim lazily above their heads and disturb
the golden fish, which had split into two and multiplied
every time the king poked one.

The queen glared at the newcomer. 'Lord Ketley,
what is the meaning of this? How dare you speak
before you are acknowledged in our presence!"

Now Sera recognised the name. A duke. Aged in his
late fifties, he possessed a very eligible and attractive heir
who was long overdue to select a bride, from what she
recalled Abigail telling her.

'I am here on behalf of your concerned subjects,
Your Majesty. This ungrateful witch has murdered her
guardian, Lord Branvale." Diamond clips sparkled on

his shoes. From top to toe, the noble was the epitome of fashion.

Sera swiped her hand and the shark swam over to hover above the duke's head.

'Before you rudely interrupted this court, we were discussing that exact topic." Queen Charlotte stepped forward to stand before Sera and Lord Ketley. King George appeared oblivious to the conversation as he tried to capture a school of tiny luminescent minnows.

'I am curious, Lord Ketley. How exactly did Lord Branvale die?" Sera asked with wide-eyed innocence. When she'd spoken to Mr Miles that morning, he'd said an examination would be necessary to determine what had caused the mage's death.

'Murdered," Lord Ketley huffed. He lowered his hand and fussed with the lace at his cuff.

'If I might offer an expert opinion, Your Majesty, murder is not a cause of death." The crowd parted with a twitter of laughter to reveal Hugh Miles. The young surgeon looked down at Sera's accuser from his far greater height. 'Do you know what precipitated his death, Your Grace?"

'No." The duke frowned and stared at the soldiers. His eyes bulged as though he sought to use mental powers to make them do his bidding.

'If you do not know the cause of death, how did you determine he was murdered?" Mr Miles had an open and curious expression on his face, and Sera rather enjoyed how he made the duke squirm.

'It is obvious that the ungrateful witch caused his death." Ketley spread his arms wide and turned to the assembled courtiers, as though seeking confirmation among them that if a nobleman cast an accusation, that was as good as any proof.

"Yet by your own admission, you don't know how he died. How can you accuse anyone without a single shred of evidence? Or does English justice rely on mere rumours now?" Mr Miles raised his voice to ask his question of the assembled courtiers.

That made them shuffle from foot to foot. The English loved their reputation for fairness and justice, even if that justice was swayed by the status and wealth of the victim or guilty party.

"Our learned medical friend is right. There will be no baseless accusations in this court." Queen Charlotte stared down Lord Ketley. No one argued with the queen when she narrowed her gaze and pursed her lips. Not even a duke.

The duke cast around him, his gaze seeking out someone within the assembly. "Surely an aftermage with a medical gift can discover what killed Branvale? That should conclude the matter."

The queen smiled and batted a minnow toward her husband. The tiny fish spun through the air and circled above the distracted king. "How fortuitous that we have at our service a surgeon whose skill is akin to magic. Mr Miles, did you examine Lord Branvale this morning?"

He nodded, and his gaze slid sideways to Sera. "Only a cursory examination, Your Majesty. My preliminary finding is that his condition does not seem to fit any natural illness. However, Lord Ormsby arrived and removed the body to the mage tower before I could investigate fully."

The queen returned to her velvet throne. "There is a simple way to resolve this issue. We charge Mr Miles to discover how Lord Branvale died. He will act on our behalf in this matter."

Sera met the surgeon's gaze and, once again, was grateful for his stepping forward. A ripple through her bones assured her that he would act honestly and find the truth of the matter. Determining cause of death would be easier than figuring out who might want to harm the dead mage. Lord Branvale had possessed a talent for creating enemies, from the servants under his roof to the people misled by his potions and spells. Any of them could have sped him on his way to the afterlife.

Lord Ketley's outburst altered the court's mood. Courtiers gathered at the edges of the room and whispered, casting glances at Sera. Fortunately, the queen dismissed them after the king ran off chasing a minnow. Sera drew a breath and schooled her face into an impassive mask. There were more sharks circling the room than the ones she'd crafted to entertain the monarch.

She navigated treacherous waters with few friends at court. The Mage Council had yet to reveal its intentions for her. Would she be welcomed as the newest mage to sit at their council table, or shackled like an unpredictable beast?

She walked through the state rooms, hoping to find Abigail. Had her friend also been summoned to court?

Sera had spent years waiting for others to decide her fate. Now she would seize the initiative for herself. To one side, Sera spotted her friend. Abigail separated from the group of women and linked arms with her. They left the presence chamber and strolled the wide corridors of the palace, stopping to gaze at portraits when others ventured too close.

"There is a group insisting you are responsible, and that you poisoned your guardian before you left his household yesterday," Abigail murmured, while she tilted her head to study a painting of a Restoration woman with an enormous portrait collar of lace.

Sera bit back the instant retort that surged up her throat. Of more immediate concern was learning that more people than Lord Ketley wanted to finger her for the crime. "Who? Aside from Ketley."

They strolled to another painting and waited for a cluster of secretaries to pass. "I do not know yet. Someone within the council, most likely."

"More than one of them, I suspect." When Sera had removed the bracelet from her wrist and shattered Branvale's barrier keeping her tethered to the house, she'd thought her battle to be free was over. Now, she discovered it was but a skirmish in a much bigger campaign.

She couldn't sit and wait for Mr Miles to determine how Branvale had died and by whose hand. There had to be a way to take an active part in proving her innocence. Starting with discovering who the dissatisfied customer was who had declared Branvale would be sorry if the purchased spell didn't work. An odd, dark red vial scratched at her mind, too. What potion had it contained and to whom had Branvale personally delivered it? For answers, she would need to search Branvale's records. Somewhere in his ledgers would be an entry detailing the spell.

"My soirée is in two nights. Do tell me you will attend?" Abigail said in a louder tone for those approaching. A group of women strolled toward them and her friend would be called back to their side.

"Of course. I wouldn't miss a chance to hear you sing." Sera smiled at her friend and let her go, to drift back to her world of courtiers and ladies-in-waiting.

How many allies did one need to survive in society? Sera hoped that with Abigail and Kitty, the three of them would prove formidable enough to see her through the early days of her voyage. Once Sera had established herself, the waters would offer smoother sailing.

Having been dismissed from court, Sera returned to her modest home to change before her dinner with the Napiers. She paid the hired carriage driver and stepped down. A young girl of no more than five years, with a dirty face and clutching an equally dirty doll, watched her with wide eyes. She had been no older when men had taken her away and thrust her into Branvale's care. At least this girl clutched a companion—more than Sera had possessed.

"Hello." Sera approached and knelt down to the girl's level. "Does your doll have a name?"

The girl's eyes widened, and she swallowed. "Sarah," she whispered.

"Hello, Sarah," Sera addressed the doll. Her dress was worn through in places and her hair a tangle, but the intense hold of the girl spoke of her love for the toy. 'I was wondering if you would like a new dress?"

The girl thrust out the doll and squeaked, "Yes."

What sort of outfit would suit the doll for the adventures ahead? Something practical and hard-wearing, like the riding habits Sera would wear to fulfil her duties to the Mage Council. With a picture formed in her mind, she rubbed her hands together and then cupped them around the doll. She whispered the words of the spell in a language known only to mages and that ran through her blood.

A green sphere enveloped her hands and the doll. Silver sparkles glinted within it and then it dissolved into mist and fell away. The little girl gasped. Her doll now wore a deep green riding habit in a simple cut, with a tricorn hat perched on her perfectly coiffed head. The girl jumped forward and kissed Sera's cheek, then ran off, waving the doll and calling for her mother.

"You're welcome," Sera muttered to herself with a smile.

As she walked up the path, the front door swung open to reveal Elliot. "We going to be a modiste now, milady? Because you'll have every little girl in the street lined up here with their dolls by dark."

'Dolls I can manage. Let's hope their mothers don't go getting ideas." Sera swept into the house and removed her hat. How she detested current fashion and longed for a simple gown, something with Grecian lines. Perhaps she might start a new trend. Everyone already thought her an abomination, anyway.

AFTER LEAVING THE ROYAL PRESENCE, Hugh paced the corridors as he waited for a royal warrant and for his mentor, Lord Viner. The warrant enabled him to examine Lord Branvale's remains, but his noble mentor was needed to smooth the way into the mage tower.

It was nearly two hours later that a chill washed over Hugh's skin as they passed through the gate in the wall surrounding the mage tower at Finsbury. Magic infused in the stones kept the unwanted out. Hugh had heard rumours of other such places, hidden from view by magic, that contained things the mages didn't want walking free in the world. His curiosity paid attention to those rumours. One day, he would discover their secret stronghold and learn what they hid.

Dry, packed earth surrounded the tower, and close to its base, a small patch of muddy green, scraggly grass attempted to grow. Built of a drab grey stone, the tall, circular tower looked somewhat like a chimney with no obvious windows. A solid oak door set at ground level was the only way in or out. Or the only visible way.

Lord Viner stared at the door, which had no knob or knocker.

"I assume they learned of our arrival when we passed under the gateway," Hugh murmured.

The hairs on the back of his neck prickled.

Someone watched them, even though the circular yard appeared deserted.

The eight-foot-tall door swung open on silent hinges to reveal Lord Pendlebury. He wore a deep navy robe draped over his clothes, tiny silver stars winking against the fabric. 'Lord Viner, Mr Miles. I am obliged to say that the council has lodged a formal protest at this barbarity you would conduct against our fallen brother.'

Lord Viner nodded to the mage. 'We are, of course, sensitive to your loss. However, an accusation of murder has been made. Our monarch and justice both demand that we ascertain the truth of such a charge. No one knows how Lord Branvale died. My associate Mr Miles and I will treat Lord Branvale's remains with the utmost respect during our examination.'

Hugh kept his hands behind his back, and his mouth closed. This matter could have been resolved without anyone picking up a scalpel if the mages would simply use their magic to discern how Branvale died. But they concerned themselves with more material acts of magic, not with ailments. Nor did he know of any aftermage who could diagnose after death with any accuracy.

As the surgeon, Hugh would conduct the autopsy. Physicians took pulses and felt foreheads, but they didn't dirty their hands. Society drew clear lines between the work of surgeons and that of physicians. It always struck Hugh as odd that physicians were held in such high regard, when they did very little except dispense tonics to cure the ennui that plagued the upper classes.

It was the surgeons who set bones and stitched up wounds. Or, in cases such as this, conducted a conversation with the dead. Perhaps it was the nature of what surgeons did that repulsed people. The population shuddered at the idea of being cut open and their innermost secrets revealed. Hugh's relationship with Lord Viner served them both well and behind closed doors, they shared their knowledge with one another. The court physician treated Hugh as an equal.

"Of course I understand the necessity of your actions. The truth must be ascertained." Lord Pendlebury gestured for them to enter.

Hugh stepped over the threshold and gazed upward. A staircase clung to the inside of the tower, spiralling above until his eyes could no longer focus on it. The walls were smooth and covered in brightly coloured tapestries depicting key events in mage history. Light spilled through windows that didn't exist on the outside of the tower.

"You are a conundrum, Mr Miles. You give the appearance of being Lord Viner's guard, rather than his student." Lord Pendlebury led the way to the staircase, but instead of ascending, they trod downward.

Hugh had always been more interested in the aftermath of a fight rather than in throwing punches. He had joined a boxing gymnasium at an early age to learn how to defend himself from those who thought to take down a bigger lad. That had grown into his passion to learn how to patch up the bloodied fighters.

'Mr Miles is the finest surgeon in London. While he is not descended from a mage, he has a magical touch in his large hands." Lord Viner's voice swirled around them in the narrow stairwell.

Hugh lost count of how many steps there were. Every inch of enclosing wall looked like any other. After some minutes, the stairs opened into a hallway with a slate floor. Lights gave a steady yellow glow with no visible flame. Along the hall, Lord Pendlebury stopped at a door and placed a hand on the wood. At a whispered word, it swung open.

Another word, and the light hanging from the ceiling burst into life, revealing a circular room with a table set in the very centre. A body draped with a sheet rested on the table, one foot jutting from the bottom corner. A curved bench was built into the wall. The opposite side was covered in shelving and a variety of bottles and containers. The light hanging over the table resembled a tree branch with various limbs, each holding a glowing yellow orb at its terminus.

'Do you require anything?" Lord Pendlebury asked.

Lord Viner glanced at Hugh and left him to reply. 'We have most of our equipment with us, but if we could impose upon you for hot water, towels, and some bowls? That would assist our endeavour."

Lord Pendlebury nodded. 'I will send down water and towels. You may make use of the containers on the shelves. They are all empty and have been cleansed. When you finish, do not leave this room. Cover Branvale and wait by the door until you are fetched."

Hugh unpacked his bag and laid out his equipment on the bench. Next to the scalpels, saw, and clamps, he placed a journal and a pencil for his notes. Then, he examined the containers on the shelves and selected an array of bowls and a handful of smaller wide-mouthed bottles for any evidence they found.

A young man knocked on the door and carried in a stack of towels and a large pitcher of water, a curl of steam wafting from the spout.

"Shall we begin?" Lord Viner said, even though his role was mainly supervisory.

The two men took a side of the sheet each and folded it up. Both doctors examined the dead mage, as every inch of skin needed to be scrutinised.

"No visible signs of injury or any defensive wounds," Hugh murmured as he inspected the mage's hands with their perfectly manicured nails. "The grimace would indicate some pain preceding death." With nothing more to be learned from the mage's exterior, it was time to take the quest to the inside.

Hugh removed his jacket, rolled his shirtsleeves above the elbow, and donned a thick canvas apron. He took up a scalpel and glanced at his mentor. Theirs was an unusual arrangement. Yet combined, their reputations grew for working miracles where other doctors merely shook their heads and recommended a visit to a priest.

Lord Viner had seen the potential in Hugh some years ago, when a chance encounter saw their paths cross. Hugh had set the leg of a young noble who had been thrown from his horse. That lad proved to be

Lord Viner's son, and saving the boy's leg opened a new world of opportunity for Hugh.

"Proceed, Hugh. I shall observe." Lord Viner waved him on.

Hugh made quick, sure incisions. Setting aside the scalpel, he pulled back the skin and layers of muscle. Only a slight shudder ran through his mentor's frame as Hugh cracked the ribs and prised open the chest to facilitate an examination of the heart and lungs.

"Well, this is unusual," he murmured.

NINE

"There are lesions on his liver, but not the kidneys." Hugh removed the organs and placed them in two bowls. Greenish-red blotches, appearing somewhat like rust in its effect on metal, covered the larger organ. In places, the blotches had eaten through the outer layer.

Returning his attention to the torso, he found that a dark, congealed mess stained the internal cavity. "He bled out from his liver, and that might have been what killed him." He couldn't be sure yet, not until he had considered and disproven every possibility.

"What of his heart and lungs?" Lord Viner leaned in a fraction, curiosity overwhelming his distaste for the task at hand.

"They appear healthy. Whatever attacked the liver acted quickly and left the other organs unaffected." Hugh left the heart in place, but held aside the ribs to show his mentor.

Next, Hugh turned his attention to the stomach.

With a few slices, he removed the entire sac and placed it on what appeared to be a serving platter. A dull, greenish-black liquid oozed out in places. A theory formed in his mind, one that was soon confirmed when he opened the stomach.

More of the thick fluid, somewhat like melted tar, remained in the stomach. Lesions like those on the outside of the liver appeared on the inside of the stomach, though only in one or two places had they pierced the stomach lining.

"What is that?" Lord Viner gestured with one hand and held the other to his nose. The liquid emitted a sour, rank odour.

"I don't know, but I shall take samples to examine later." The mages were quite adamant that Lord Branvale was to be left intact. Any organs removed for examination were to be replaced afterward. Hugh could take only the samples he required for a diagnosis.

"There are the remains of a meal here, which confirms the valet's story that Branvale had dined out that evening, returned late, and died sometime during the early hours." Hugh used a metal prong and tweezers to sift through the stomach contents.

"I do not know of any disease that results in such lesions to the stomach and liver." The older physician tapped his chin and stared upward in contemplation.

"No. But there are poisons that, once ingested, would spread through the blood to the liver and possibly cause such a rupture." His stomach heaved, not at the work he undertook, but at finding an unknown hand had caused Branvale's end. Had the hand responsible also discharged excess electricity when he'd grasped it?

Damn it. He wanted to prove Lady Winyard's innocence, not deliver her death warrant. He closed his eyes for a moment and drew a deep breath. He needed to remain impartial. Only that way could he obtain justice for the dead mage, and for the one with the bewitching blue eyes.

Lord Viner stared at the contents of the serving platter and bowls. "Arsenic, perhaps? Although the damage is not what we would expect to find."

"There is a mushroom that causes acute liver failure, but I will need to test the substance in the stomach to confirm its presence. However, it does not cause lesions such as we have found." Hugh continued the autopsy in a slow and methodical way. At each step, he noted his findings and any abnormalities.

Then he turned his attention once more to the internal organs. Each was weighed and measured. He drew sketches of the liver and its lesions. Samples were taken and placed in vials. After some hours, and copious pages of drawings and notes, he was ready to return the displaced organs to their correct location in the torso. The finishing touch was a row of neat stitches that formed an upside-down T.

He scrubbed his hands and arms clean and packed his samples into his satchel, while Lord Viner draped the sheet over the victim once more. Their duty complete, the two men waited by the closed door.

Within minutes, it was opened by Lord Pendlebury.

"Gentlemen. Did you learn how our colleague died?" the mage asked.

"My preliminary finding is that Lord Branvale ingested something that caused rapid, fatal damage to his liver." Hugh doubted the mage wanted to know about the bleeding lesions that had created that black mass in Branvale's stomach cavity. Death would have been incredibly painful as the liver haemorrhaged and the heart, not knowing of the damage elsewhere, continued to pump blood.

"He was poisoned? There will be those who will say it was Lady Winyard's parting gift to him." Lord Pendlebury led the way back up the spiral stairs.

Lord Viner spoke to the mage's back. "We make no accusations, only seek to determine the cause of the internal damage."

"I have taken samples of the fluids we found," Hugh said. "I should be able to identify what Lord Branvale may have ingested that caused his death."

Hugh had seen Seraphina Winyard lift Branvale off his feet and pepper him with tiny shards of lightning in front of the royal court. While he didn't know her that well, what he had observed suggested she was a woman who would come after you while your eyes were wide open. She was no stealthy poisoner. If she truly sought Branvale's death, she would have done it in a magnificent and undeniable fashion—like quartering him at a busy crossroads in the middle of the day.

The sky had darkened to night by the time Hugh and Lord Viner returned to court to deliver their preliminary findings. King George, in a moment of lucidity, leaned forward on his throne and took an interest in the death of his mage. No one could recall the last time a mage had been murdered. They tended to die either from terrible accidents...or natural causes.

"What did you discover?" The king's eyes shone a little too brightly.

Hugh clasped his hands behind his back before answering. "Lord Branvale ingested an as yet unknown substance that claimed his life."

"It was indeed murder?" A frown pulled Queen Charlotte's brows together.

Hugh kept his expression noncommittal. He could only state what had taken the mage's life, not by whose hand the poison found its way into his body. "I must perform some tests to determine the nature of the poison. There is the possibility that Lord Branvale may have ingested it willingly, perhaps believing it to be something else."

"That's how poisoning generally works," someone behind him muttered, to a titter of laughter.

"Where's that military chap?" the king called, and he craned his neck to peer around the court.

The crowd parted, and a man in a bright red uniform strode forward. He snapped his heels together and nodded his head. Tall and possessed of broad shoulders, he had the most amazing curling moustache and pointed goatee.

"This is Lieutenant Powers. The queen thought Branvale's death might prove to be foul play, and asked the army to loan us a man to oversee the investigation. They rate Powers quite highly in this sort of matter, and we want it resolved. Can't have people going around murdering our mages. We only have twelve of them and it takes eighteen years before a new one is of any use to us." The king waved his hand in dismissal and then fell back into his throne.

Hugh raised his eyebrows at the lieutenant, who gestured with his head. He and Lord Viner fell into step beside the other man as they exited the presence chamber. They kept walking the length of the corridor until they reached a quiet spot.

"Do you have any suspicions as to the type of poison used?" The lieutenant leaned against the wall.

"One derived from either arsenic or the mushroom *Amanita phalloides*, and, if my theory is correct, some sort of magical process to accelerate its action." That was the bit that bothered him.

"How do you know it was accelerated?" With one finger, Powers stroked the swirl of his dark moustache.

"Two lesions on his liver had ruptured, resulting in internal bleeding, which caused his death. But here is the anomaly. The lesions should have taken days or even weeks to form before they perforated. Branvale would have experienced pain during that time and should have displayed symptoms, which his staff would have noticed. However, the mage showed no signs of discomfort or pain until that evening. When I spoke to him, his valet said Lord Branvale went to bed grumbling about an upset stomach and they assumed something he had eaten at dinner had disagreed with him." How ironic that the mage had been correct. The disagreement in his stomach had ended his life.

Powers had a keen glint in his eye as he considered the information. "Do you think it was something he ingested at dinner, or could he have consumed it earlier in the week?"

Any hypothesis Hugh could come up with needed to be tested to find the correct course of events. "Impossible to tell without knowing the rate of progression of the poison, or if there is any delayed start to it."

"Which means Lady Winyard could still have been under Branvale's roof when he was poisoned. As a mage, she had the ability to concoct the fatal potion." Lieutenant Powers moved from his moustache to tugging on the point of his goatee as he thought.

"There are aftermage apothecaries who could have brewed such a potion. It does not require the talents of a mage." Hugh narrowed his eyes at his partner in this investigation. Why was everyone intent on finding Lady Winyard guilty? "Granted, Lady Winyard has drawn such attention to herself as to make it easy to point a finger at her. But what of her past history with the mage? Would anything there have led to such hatred as to poison a man in such a painful way? But even if it had, why now? Why on the very eve of her presentation at court? It doesn't add up."

The lieutenant laughed and slapped Hugh on the back. "Excellent. You are challenging my theories. Between us, we shall unmask the murderer. Let us tackle the preferred suspect first. Tomorrow morning, we will talk to Lady Winyard. Then we will interview

Branvale's staff and those he dined with on his last night."

"Of course, Lieutenant," Hugh murmured. He would grasp with both hands any opportunity to be close to the young mage again.

THE NEXT MORNING, Sera sat at the desk in her drawing room. From the window, she watched a group of children cluster around the girl whose doll wore a new dress. Occasionally, one would stare at her house, no doubt trying to work up the courage to tap on the door. A carriage pulled to a stop outside, and scattered the girls back to the sides of the road. Two men stepped down and gazed about them at their surroundings.

"So it begins." Sera set down her quill and sorted the papers into a pile.

Elliott's voice came from the entrance hall, and then he knocked on the drawing room door. "Lady Winyard, a Mr Miles and a Lieutenant Powers to speak to you."

She composed her face before rising from the chair at the desk. "Show them in, Elliot, and then ask Rosie to send up tea, please."

The men stopped inside the room and bowed.

"Gentlemen, please be seated before you begin your interrogation. Am I allowed to know how Lord Branvale met his end, since the accusation of murder has been levelled at me?" She gestured to the armchairs and swept her skirts to one side before sitting on the settee. With her knees together, she sat ramrod straight, her hands loose in her lap. Abigail would approve of her posture.

"Poison. A particularly nasty one that caused him a great deal of pain before snatching his life." Mr Miles sat, and the chair creaked as though to emphasise his muscular bulk.

"Where were you the night he died?" Lieutenant Powers asked before he had even taken his seat.

Maintaining her calm exterior, she turned to face the military man. "Here."

"Can your staff verify that?" The lieutenant sat and pulled a notebook from one pocket and a pencil from another. He began scribbling far more on the page than her one-word answer.

"No. I spent my first night in this house alone. I did not acquire my staff until the next day." If she had done as Kitty insisted and returned to the Napier home that night, would she have prevented her accusers from marshalling against her? Most likely they would have taken her proximity to the Branvale house as proof she'd done it.

"You mean the day Branvale died?" The lieutenant glanced at Mr Miles, who nodded.

"Yes. I would have preferred to poach his staff while he lived, but I offered work to a few once he passed." Sera congratulated herself on keeping her tone light and her temper under control.

Conversation paused as Elliot entered, carrying a

silver tray. He set it on the low table before the settee and arched a questioning eyebrow at Sera.

She gave a small shake of her head. She could handle her guests and did not need his assistance.

Mr Miles leaned forward in his chair, his intent gaze on her. "You were alone that night, after all the court saw you lift Branvale off his feet and send bolts of lightning at him. You must see why people are whispering."

"No. I wonder if they saw events clearly at all. I confronted Branvale head-on. I don't lurk in shadows to strike while someone's back is turned." Her hand curled into a fist around the teapot's handle.

Mr Miles smirked and swallowed a laugh. "I have made a similar remark to a few people."

She held out a cup of tea, met his warm brown stare, and placed an innocent smile on her lips. Did his bravery extend to taking tea from someone others would accuse of poison? "Tea?"

"Thank you." His hands brushed hers and laughter simmered in his eyes.

She watched the large surgeon, her attention drawn to his arms and hands as he downed his tea in a few gulps. He had the upper-body strength of a winning pugilist, and from his appearance, one would expect him to be drawing pints in a tavern. When he spoke, it was with soft, measured tones. He confused and intrigued her simultaneously.

He replaced the empty cup on the tray, then leaned his forearms on his thighs to lace his fingers together. He glanced at her. "Do you have a question, Lady Winyard?"

Sera appreciated a direct approach. There was only so much subterfuge a person could stomach. She waved her cup away, and it drifted to the table and settled next to its companion. "Why are you a surgeon?"

"Why are you a mage?" He threw back without pause.

What an odd question. Her destiny had been decided when a mage drew his last breath as she took her first. "I was born with this ability."

He sat up and tapped his chest. "As was I."

Mentally, that rocked her back on her heels. Magic coursed through her veins, waiting for her to call upon it. She could not imagine a normal human experiencing a similar compulsion to follow a particular path. "You are not an aftermage with a gift for medical matters."

"No." His hands clenched together. A sore point, perhaps?

A slow smile spread over her face. She liked him. He gave no quarter in his quiet way. Most people didn't have the spine to challenge a mage. "You have the appearance of someone who uses their hands in a rather different fashion."

"When you are the size I am, you have to learn to defend yourself. People think that knocking you over is a goal to accomplish. But I found I preferred to mend the fighters, rather than be one. That was how I learned I had a gift for setting their bones and stitching them back up." A smile tugged his lips to one side.

Lieutenant Powers cleared his throat, having watched the exchange while he savoured his tea. "Perhaps we could return to our purpose here. Lady

Winyard, please describe your relationship with Lord Branvale."

Sera swung her gaze to the army man. He cut a smart figure in his regimentals, and his impressive curled moustache and goatee. She suspected he took longer in front of a mirror fussing over his moustache than a noble lady would about her toilette. "The Mage Council placed me under Branvale's guardianship when I was five years old. He used me, kept me ignorant of what I should know, and treated me no better than the servants—whom he treated with indifference."

Not to mention the magical bracelet he had clicked around her wrist as a child. It had inhibited her abilities, but why?

Sera watched the glances exchanged between the men. From his questions, she gathered the lieutenant rather liked the simplicity of naming her the culprit, whereas Mr Miles appeared to be acting in her defence. Could a mage even be charged with murder? Hopefully, Kitty's father was already deep in that research.

The lieutenant frowned. 'Lord Branvale was your mentor and guardian."

She scoffed. 'Did the Mage Council write that down for you? I grew up under his thumb. I know exactly how he treated me. His lessons were deliberately opaque to prove me deficient. I was punished for not completing tasks he didn't even set for me. He kept me imprisoned in the house and only half the garden. I slept in the attic in a servant's room. What more do you wish to know?"

'All, by your account, a strong motive for murder.

Did you poison him?" The lieutenant leaned back in his chair, but his keen gaze never left her face.

She barked a laugh at that question. "No. Although I suspect you will find that I had both the opportunity, being much in the kitchens, and the motive, due to his callous treatment of me."

"You also threatened his life in front of the entire court and your king," the lieutenant reminded her.

Sera shrugged. She had no regrets about her actions. For a single moment that day, Branvale had realised how much power coursed through her. For a single moment, he had been afraid. "Many people probably wanted to kill him. Only the day before, I had seen a confrontation with a customer whose spell did not work. The man demanded his money back or, he declared, Branvale would regret crossing him."

"A convenient story." More notes were scribbled in his little book.

"One you can confirm with his staff. Elliot, my footman, admitted the man that day, and I'm sure I wasn't the only one to hear the shouting."

The army officer leaned back in his chair and tapped his fingers against his thigh. "The Mage Council is most insistent that you are their primary suspect."

The surgeon observed her in silence, any thoughts on the matter kept behind a calm facade. She knew little of his involvement except that the king had asked him and his mentor to determine what had killed Branvale. That information was kept confidential, meaning it would circulate throughout the entire court by the end of an afternoon. Perhaps she ought to call on Abigail to find out.

'Rather convenient for them, isn't it? I have slipped their leash and they wish to replace it with a noose," she murmured.

TEN

Sera refused to sit by as the Mage Council built its fictitious case against her. 'I would like to offer my assistance in identifying the poison. I have studied herbology—in that, at least, Branvale ensured I had skills he could use.' She addressed her offer to the surgeon.

'The Mage Council has already assigned someone to study a sample and determine what, if any, magic was used to alter the effect of the poison.' Mr Miles shifted in his chair and a frown appeared on his forehead.

'Someone who will no doubt find that an unusual touch was used, one originating from a female mage. You surely cannot expect me to do nothing as they construct evidence against me? Let me assist, at least to balance the vitriol they pour into your ears.' She curled her hands into fists to contain the temper that wanted to set fire to the threadbare drapes. The council sought a way to remove her from the playing board, but she would fight to the last.

'I see no harm in having another opinion to balance the scales." He tugged on the cuff of his jacket, but to no avail. This garment cut somewhat shorter than his long arms required.

The lieutenant stroked his goatee. 'Very well. You are correct, Lady Winyard, in that the Mage Council is most insistent that we only need to examine your movements. They are deaf to any recommendation to cast a wider net to see who else might have borne ill feeling toward Lord Branvale. Luckily, I do not respond to the commands of the Mage Council, and will conduct a thorough investigation as I see fit."

"Thank you. You may speak to Elliot if you wish. He will recall the agitated man." Sera closed her eyes and crafted the soft *ding* of a bell above Elliot's head, where he lingered unseen in the hallway.

Within a few seconds, he materialised in the doorway. A smile quirked on his lips. 'You rang, milady?"

"Yes. Do you remember the man with whom Branvale argued the day before I left his household?" Sera asked.

The footman rubbed his hand over his nape. 'I know the one. Right upset he was, and Lord Branvale used his magic to blast him out the door like he was a leaf in the wind."

'Do you recall this wind-blown gentleman's name?" Lieutenant Powers' pencil was poised above the paper.

'Mr Harvey Sloane. Bit of a regular customer, with a warehouse down by the docks. His lordship used to send me or one of the other lads to deliver parcels to

Sloane occasionally." Elliot gestured with his hands as he spoke.

The lieutenant asked his next question without looking up, his attention on his notebook. 'Do you know where Lord Branvale dined the night he died?"

Elliot shook his head. 'Not me, sir. But Jake Hogan will know. He's Lord Branvale's valet. Or was. I suppose he'll be looking for a new position now."

Sera rose to her feet, and both men jumped to theirs.

'With your co-operation, Lady Winyard, I will speak to the staff under your roof who also worked for Lord Branvale," Lieutenant Powers said.

'Of course. Elliot can show you down to the kitchen, where you will find Rosie and Vicky." She nodded to the footman.

Mr Miles paused at her side, and a large hand hovered near her arm. 'I will ensure you receive a sample of the poison to examine."

'Thank you. Then perhaps we can compare notes as to our findings?" Sera figured society's strictures didn't apply to her and she could spend time alone in the surgeon's company if she wished—which she did. Not that she gave a fig what anyone thought. Except for Abigail. Already she could hear her friend's indrawn breath at the idea of Sera in a man's company, unchaperoned.

'I would like that." A slow blush spread over his cheeks and he ducked his head, which, due to his height, did little to hide his reaction.

She was still staring after his broad back some

minutes later when Elliot returned and snapped his fingers in front of her. "You have the same look on your face that Vicky gets when the coal lad winks at her."

"You do understand that I am a powerful mage, and could turn you into a frog for saying something so out of line?" She rubbed her hands together and created a ball of greenish pond water between her palms.

He grinned and swept his hands down his body. "If you did that, you wouldn't get to look at this every day."

Sera laughed and threw the water ball toward the ceiling, where it disappeared. She liked Elliot. He was cheeky, loyal, and would flirt with man, woman, or item of furniture. But he was most definitely not her type. She was learning that she rather preferred slow and quiet men. Thoughtful, intelligent ones.

An hour later, after the surgeon and lieutenant had finished interviewing her staff and had gone, Sera walked out the front door and sat on the bottom step. A cluster of girls had assembled across the road, clutching a variety of toys. Her ensorcelled box remained empty of any instructions from the council, so she would create her own work. What better place to start than by spreading a little joy in the shabby neighbourhood?

One girl glanced at her friends and then crept across the road. In one hand, she gripped a wooden doll—its paint almost worn away from the constant rubbing of small fingers. The child thrust out the toy. "You gave Em's doll a new dress, milady. Can you fix mine?"

Sera took the carved image and cupped it in her palms. "Let us see what can be done."

Some patient father had carved the doll. Her simple dress was made of wood, but the workmanship made it appear like fabric, with folds and pleats etched into the wood. Even a basic pattern had been scratched on. The doll's face was hauntingly blank, her hair worn almost silver. All the toy needed was a refresh. Sera imagined a new colour scheme and held it in her mind. She let the magic flow through her hands and over the toy. When she opened her palms, the little girl clapped with delight. The doll now wore a gown of painted brocade of iridescent blue and gold. Its hair was restored to a lustrous brown and the face expertly painted with rouged cheeks and a tiny beauty spot beneath a blue eye.

A crowd had gathered while she concentrated on the doll and Sera found herself surrounded by excited children, each clutching their greatest treasure. Women assembled across the road to watch, each smiling and nodding as her child presented a toy for a magical transformation.

The day lengthened, and fatigue had taken up residence in Sera's bones by the time she had finished them all. Magic took a toll, and while one small doll didn't present any real drain on her ability, dozens of the tiny patients did. The children danced and sang in the street and had to be collected by their mothers and herded home.

"Thank you, milady," a group of women and children called out, and they all waved.

Sera returned the gesture. "You're most welcome."

A morning well spent, she thought, as she used the railing to stand, and shuffled back inside. What she wouldn't give for a bath.

Her stomach rumbled.

And something to eat.

AFTER THEY LEFT HER PRESENCE, Hugh stood outside and stared back at Lady Winyard's house. Part of him was reluctant to leave the young mage, and would leap at the chance to become her champion. Should she require it of him.

With a sigh, he glanced at the lieutenant. "What now?"

Powers gestured down the street, and the two men fell into step together. "We hunt down Jake Hogan, the valet, and speak with this Sloane fellow."

Hugh had no experience in investigating murder. His expertise lay in the examination of physical matters. "The valet was the man closest to Branvale, but it does seem rather obvious that the cook might have slipped poison into his meal."

"A murderer uses what opportunity they find. It only needs an unobserved moment and a steady hand to pour the potion into a drink or over food. Given that Branvale dined out that evening, his cook is unlikely to be behind it, unless the poison did not act immediately."

At a crossroads, the lieutenant hailed a hired carriage to take them to their next call at the docks.

Hugh pondered how he had turned from surgeon to assistant in a Crown investigation. He should have bowed out once his part was done in determining the cause of death. But a face kept swimming before him. One with sharp cheekbones, rich brown hair, and piercing blue eyes.

"You think Lady Winyard did it." Hugh settled into the foul-smelling conveyance. He tried to avoid a large stain on the cushion that looked...sticky.

Powers stroked his goatee. "I keep an open mind. She certainly had a strong motive. But it would appear Lady Winyard was not the only person who had an unfortunate experience with Lord Branvale. She is simply the one who vented her anger in front of the entire court."

"The other staff appear to have been ambivalent about him." Hugh had watched as Powers questioned the cook and maid.

The cook openly voiced her disdain for her former employer, but was adamant she'd had no hand in his death. The maid, a nervous thing with darting eyes, paled at the mere mention of poison or the possibility of her being involved. Neither had struck Hugh as murderers.

"Time will tell, but I believe them as honest in their replies to me as their new mistress," Powers said.

The carriage decanted them near the docks and the busy industrial area of London. It took little work to find the warehouse owned by Mr Sloane—the name SLOANE & CO appeared in two-foot-high letters on the side. The red paint was worn by the action of the weather and water thrown from the river by high winds. Double barn doors stood open as men unloaded crates, kegs, and chests from a moored vessel and carted them up to the warehouse.

Inside, the dim interior had the musty, exotic aroma of spices and woods from warmer climates. Powers tapped a man on the shoulder. "Where will I find Mr Sloane?"

The chap gestured to a set of stairs in one corner that wound to a mezzanine floor. "Upstairs."

Each step creaked and complained as they passed, more so under Hugh's heavy tread. At the top was an open area with a balustrade that looked back over the expansive warehouse. The space accommodated an empty desk and vacant chair that commanded a view over the busy floor below. Next to the desk was a closed door. Powers rapped on the door with the backs of his knuckles and then pushed it open without waiting for an invitation.

Within was what appeared to be a storage room. Kegs were stacked four high in one corner. A few bolts of exotic coloured fabric leaned against them and mingled with rugs tied with cord. A desk the size of a single bed stretched before the only window. A man hunched over the strewn papers, muttering under his breath as he worked. One wall housed shelves stuffed with ledgers on the top half, the bottom half formed by square drawers such as solicitors used for documents.

"What do you want? If it's an invoice, leave it on the front desk for when my secretary returns." Sloane didn't even look up from the paper clutched in his hand as he tallied numbers in a ledger. His bent head revealed a large bald spot from which a shaft of sunlight bounced; the rest of his shaggy brown hair clung around his ears.

"I want to talk to you about Lord Branvale," Powers said, stopping before the desk.

That made the pen pause for a moment. "Don't know him."

"Do you suffer from memory problems? He's a mage. Or was. Someone murdered him recently, and his staff say that not only were you a regular customer, but that you had an altercation with him just before he died." The lieutenant pulled out his little notebook and pencil.

Sloane tossed the pen toward its holder, missed, and it fell to the desk, where the nib created a blue blob on the paper under it. He scrubbed his hands over his face. "Oh. Him. Wasn't no *altercation*. I asked for my money back, plain and simple."

"I hear he blew you out the door and you promised he'd be sorry for crossing you." Uninvited, the lieutenant seated himself in a wooden chair before the desk.

Hugh walked to the window and leaned on the frame, where he could both observe the interview and watch the bustle of activity below. Men swarmed over ships where cargo was hauled out in nets on boom arms, and placed on carts. He wondered where the vessels had been. India, perhaps. Or as far as America?

"It was business, nothing more. He sold me something that didn't work, and I'm due my money back," Sloane said.

"I'd appreciate a little co-operation about exactly what business you had with Lord Branvale. You must appreciate how bad it looks for you. You argued with him, threatened him, and he turned up dead not long after." Powers spoke with a measured tone.

Sloane leaned back in his chair. "I don't have to tell you nothing. I didn't see him again after that, so go bark up another tree."

Powers made a noise in the back of his throat. "Well, it is unfortunate you've chosen that route."

"Why? Is he your muscle, here to beat me up if I don't answer?" Sloane huffed and gestured to Hugh.

"Not at all." Powers balanced his notebook and pencil on the edge of the desk. "My friend there is a surgeon. He's going to try to patch you up after I shoot you."

"What?" Sloane's voice went up an octave.

Hugh turned back to the interview, his curiosity aroused. He considered what supplies he had on him, should he indeed have to remove a ball and stitch the wound. He might need to improvise. He always carried a small kit with catgut and needles. The bigger problem would be fossicking out the ball, depending on where it lodged. If Powers hit an artery, though, the merchant might bleed out before Hugh could stem the flow.

Powers reached under his red jacket, removed a pistol, and laid it on the desk. Then from another pocket, he pulled the necessary supplies to load the weapon. "You have until I ready my pistol to tell me what spell Branvale supplied for you."

The merchant coughed and glanced from Hugh back to the officer. Hugh shrugged. He had no idea whether the other man was bluffing. Given the lieutenant's relaxed manner as he measured powder, Hugh would guess it was no bluff. He patted down his jacket to reassure himself the small medical kit still sat in his pocket. The desk was large enough to be an impromptu surgery table. Another concern would be infection.

"Do those barrels contain alcohol? I will need some to cleanse the wound." Hugh pointed to the stacked kegs.

"Now, let's not be hasty. You can't go around shooting people on their own premises." Sloane pushed the chair backward, and the legs grated over the wood. Then he rose to his feet and glanced around.

"Actually, I can. I have been charged by the king to investigate the murder of one of his mages, and can use whatever methods I think are appropriate. You might want to stand still, so I can aim at something like an arm or a leg. If you insist on fleeing, I might inadvertently shoot you somewhere important." Powers finished loading the pistol and stretched out his arm, aiming at the merchant's shoulder.

Sloane gulped and held up his hands. "It was a poxy

spell that never worked, anyway. It was supposed to let me see my competitors' ledgers and what they wrote down. Helps, you see, if I know what prices they are paying and what cargo they have coming in."

Powers eased his finger off the trigger but kept the pistol raised. "Not exactly sporting, spying on your fellow merchants and learning about their businesses with the use of magic. How was this spell supposed to work?"

Sloane gestured to a small ledger to one side of the desk. "That book is blank. Branvale said if I read the spell over it, it would show me everything my rivals wrote in their ledgers. He said I got the words wrong, but I reckon the parchment he gave me was a sham and he knew it wouldn't work."

Hugh wondered how the ledger would know what his rivals wrote in theirs. From what he understood of such magical communication, it required *both* parties to possess a book or piece of paper with the same enchantment over it. For the spell to work, Sloane would have had to break into his competitors' offices and whisper the spell over their ledgers as well.

Why had Branvale omitted that part of the process, or had Sloane omitted it from his story?

"Where were you the night Branvale died?" Powers placed the pistol on the desk and put away his kit.

"Here, working. We had a ship going out on the tide, and we had to get her loaded in time. Ask anyone downstairs." Sloane waved his arms out the window and then to the floor below his feet. Then he wiped his sleeve across his sweaty forehead.

"I shall ask your men as we leave." The lieutenant returned the weapon to its spot under his jacket.

Hugh wondered that he didn't accidentally shoot himself if he were jostled in a crowd with a loaded weapon about his person. Downstairs, Powers stopped a few men and asked them about their master's movements. They all confirmed that they had worked past midnight to get the vessel under way. Then the two men walked back along the docks.

"They all confirm Sloane's story. Although he could have instructed them to say he was at the warehouse all night if anyone asked. I shall dig a bit deeper." Powers set a brisk pace, perhaps to put distance between them and the foul odour rising off the water.

"Branvale's spell was one-sided. It was never going to work," Hugh said as they turned down a street and away from the docks. He had a smidge of sympathy for Sloane, but only a tiny bit. He was trying to spy on his competitors, after all.

Powers raised his hand at a hired carriage and the driver acknowledged them. "Yes. Both ledgers would need to have the spell cast over them. Do you think he passed on that information and Sloane failed to enact it, or did Branvale simply fail to mention the other step necessary to make the enchantment work?"

"I suspect the latter. Perhaps he intended to charge double for the missing step." Hugh glanced at the officer. "Are you not worried about injuring yourself, with a loaded pistol on your person?"

Powers laughed as he stepped into the carriage. "I didn't tip any powder in and palmed the ball. I knew from the look of Sloane that he would talk with a little encouragement."

"Well played," Hugh muttered. Who else was bluffing, or concealing the truth, and he hadn't yet seen through their facade?

ELEVEN

After her interview with Lieutenant Powers, and drained of energy from repairing an almost endless stream of toys, Sera spent a quiet afternoon reviewing documents Kitty's father had sent over. The solicitor had set the process in motion to ensure her earnings were not only protected, but on a path to grow. He outlined several different investment options for her to consider. Shipping provided an excellent return, but also presented the greatest risk by far. She wondered if she could craft a few spells to help a vessel cross a turbulent sea, to ensure her investment didn't end up at the bottom of the ocean.

When she'd imagined her future as a mage, she'd thought there would be more time casting magic, and less time assessing stocks and bonds. Life as an independent adult entailed more paperwork than she'd expected. She set the paper aside and closed her eyes, giving her weary mind a break. A rattle came from beside her, and she cracked one eye open. The rose-wood box emitted a faint yellow glow that pierced the gap between case and lid. Sera flipped the catch and opened it. Within rested a single sheet of paper—a communication from the Mage Council.

Your presence is required at the mage tower.
A carriage will collect you tomorrow morning at ten o'clock.

Finally, they acknowledged her. A tingle down her spine warned that she would need her wits about her. That required a good night's sleep. After an early supper, Sera climbed into her bed. Sleep claimed her as she rehearsed what she wished to say, and how she would respond to their inevitable verbal barbs.

The next day, Sera dithered over what to wear from the small selection hanging in her armoire. A riding habit seemed too businesslike and grown up. For her first time in the mage tower as an independent woman, she wanted the council to view her as naïve and in need of guidance. She would not reveal too early that she intended to break their rules and control, and stride along her own path. Although she had to admit that lifting Branvale off his feet in front of the king might have indicated to the council she would be trouble.

Sera selected a gown with an embellishment of sweet peas, the blooms embroidered in various hues of pink, from a pale rose to a deep cerise. The charming floral work made her appear younger than her eighteen years, especially when she feigned wide-eyed innocence.

What Sera might lack in years, she had gained in a certain life experience from below stairs. Not to mention what she'd learned from Mr Napier—when playing cards, never reveal her hand first. In the game with the Mage Council, she intended to keep her cards firmly clutched to her chest. Let them make the opening move. Then she would consider her response.

A somewhat tired carriage collected her at the appointed hour. Sera waved to the assortment of children out in the street and they, and their toys, waved back. Then she leaned against the threadbare seat and clasped her hands. Anxiety swirled inside her and she sought to control her emotions. She drew deep breaths as the carriage hit every bump in the road.

The mage tower squatted at one end of the artillery range in Finsbury Fields. The city advanced ever outward, and a pretty new development called Finsbury Square was under construction, and would be the tower's newest neighbour. The terraced town houses were being built around a central garden, rather than staring at the unattractive tower with its surrounding wall.

Another tower for the mages soared from the ground at the army base in Woolwich, and was used for military applications to serve the protective needs of England. The Finsbury Fields tower housed the library and was where the council sat for its meetings. It also possessed a fine observatory in the turret room. The carriage rolled under the portcullis and across the barren earth. From the outside, no windows broke the plain grey stone of the tower. The construction seemed more prison or place of foreboding than the seat of magic in England.

While the driver unfolded the steps, Sera composed herself. Emerging from the carriage ready for whatever awaited, she crossed the dusty earth to the massive oak door. Twice the height of a man and six feet wide, it had no visible handle. But no mage needed one. As she approached, Sera held out one hand and then flicked her wrist, operating an invisible catch.

The door swung open on silent hinges. Lord Pendlebury awaited her on the other side, a fine navy cloak around his shoulders, the fabric embroidered with glistening stars. She had expected Lord Ormsby, as head of the Mage Council, to greet their newest member. Not that she minded his absence or that of his haughty contempt of her.

"Lord Pendlebury," she murmured, and dropped a slight curtsey.

"Lady Winyard, let me welcome you to the mage tower as our newest sitting member." He swept out his arm to indicate the grand circular entrance room. Light spilled from tall and narrow lights that were invisible from the outside. A spiral staircase of a golden stone emerged from the floor and curled upward to the turret room at the very top.

She had been here many times before as a child, but now she entered as an equal and would finally have a voice on the council. "I look forward to finally being able to serve my country, as directed by the council."

"Your skills will be most appreciated. The needs of England are many and never-ending." He tilted his head, as though measuring her reaction. He gestured across the tower to a set of large iron-clad double doors. "The others await you."

A man in the purple and gold mage livery grasped an iron ring as they approached and swung one door open.

Within, England's mages met in a room more fit for a sultan's palace. Soft orange silks draped the walls. Around the edges of the room, sofas in forest green were piled with vibrant blue cushions. A round table dominated the centre of the room, inset with a mosaic of cream, grey, and sage green. Within that was a clock face ten feet across. Twelve high-backed chairs encircled the table, each sitting at an hour on the clock. Inlaid in silver, the numbers were of the Roman fashion, rather than Arabic.

One of those chairs would now seat Sera. Four of the chairs were occupied. Lord Ormsby sat in a chair before the symbol for twelve. Draped across his shoulders, a bright purple robe emblazoned with golden runes indicated his rank. Lord Tomlin leaned one elbow on the clock face at the ten, a single large X. He wore a splotchy brown jacket and his short hair was dishevelled as though he had been pulled from labouring in a field and set directly at the table. Lord Gresham, clad entirely in black like some storybook villain, examined his fingernails at three. Lord Dench, resplendent not only in a blue cloak decorated with stars, but also a matching pointed hat, stared at her from beside the Speaker, with deep frown lines on his brow, tugging his eyes and lips downward.

Sera breezed in and, for the last time ever, made a slight curtsey. Never again would she treat them as better than she. "Gentlemen," she murmured.

Lord Pendlebury rested a hand on the back of a chair at number six. "This is your chair, Lady Winyard, and has always been the seat of your line."

Her line. He referred to her magic and how it passed from one mage to another upon death. For centuries, the magic flowing in her veins had occupied this very seat; only the vessel containing it changed form. She stroked a hand over the dark wood. A peacock feather carved into the wood ran up one side and arched across the top. How fitting that her council chair displayed her symbol.

She took her seat and rested her palms above the Roman numerals.

Lord Ormsby cleared his throat from directly opposite her. "This is a most unusual situation. Never has a woman sat at this council table."

Sera stared at the mosaic clock face. The soft greys and greens reminded her of pebbles in the bottom of a shallow river. Tracing a pattern calmed her thoughts and stopped her blurting out a scathing comment about the Mage Council's policy that deprived girl mages of their power—and their lives.

Instead, she chose a different tack. "Time marches on and the world changes as we become more enlightened. I may be the first woman to sit here, but I am sure I will not be the last. Perhaps one day, England will have an even number of men and women at this table."

Lord Dench made a startled choking noise, and his

hat lurched to one side with the movement. Once he finished spluttering, he glared at her. "Would you murder us all to make that happen?"

"Whatever you may think, I had no hand in Lord Branvale's demise." Her temper flared and the power coursed in her veins, ready to answer her call should she want to lash out.

She drew a deep breath as a soft voice whispered in her mind. *Don't give them more fodder for their delusions.* Hugh Miles had taken her wrist and warned against acting from a place of anger. Any such display would be labelled as feminine histrionics. Second by second, the clock ticked and her rage ebbed.

"I'm sure the council will find some minor tasks for you to perform that are within your limited range." Ormsby rapped his nails on the glass.

"Limited?" It took every ounce of self-control she could muster to hold her temper in check.

Lord Pendlebury, an apologetic look on his face, folded his hands into the sleeves of his robe. "I believe my fellow mage refers to how you have been tested twice a year and failed to meet the standards set for male mages."

There was a reason for that, but she would hold her tongue until she figured out Branvale's motives. "Perhaps girls are later to bloom. I did, after all, perform a casting before the king that neither Lords Branvale nor Tomlin could undo."

Tomlin's hands slapped down on the clock face. "A mere performance to entertain the court. I cast empty spells to give you the illusion of superiority."

Laughter surged up her throat, but she swallowed it down. That day she had seen the sweat bead on Tomlin's face. He tried, but could not match her. "Perhaps we could engage in such a mock battle again, to take our monarch's mind from more weighty concerns?"

"A fine idea, Lady Winyard. There is to be a state banquet soon, when we entertain important Austrian dignitaries. This council always puts on a display to amaze the guests. You and Lord Tomlin, as our youngest members, could be the star performers." Lord Pendlebury waved his hands, and a journal materialised before him and plopped itself open on the table. Then a pen and inkwell dropped from the ceiling and he caught them with an outstretched hand.

"A fine idea, Pendlebury," Lord Ormsby said. He narrowed his gaze at her and rapped his fingernails on the table. "This council is concerned that a young and naïve woman is living alone. We are discussing whether you would be better placed under another guardian."

"No other mage has continued his apprenticeship past the age of eighteen." She bit the words out. Let them try. Their magic was no match for the English legislation that ensured her freedom.

Lord Dench cleared his throat. "You are a woman and require the direction of a husband or father. It behoves this council to fulfil such a role until a suitable match is found."

Under the table, she clenched her hands into fists. *Count to ten, Sera, before you say something you cannot take back.* "I will, of course, seek the council's advice and be guided by your wisdom...should it be required."

Lord Ormsby pushed back his chair and rose to his feet. "Lady Winyard has officially taken her place on this council and will be directed as to how to use her abilities. The investigation into Branvale's death continues. Should we find her responsible, this council will have no alternative but to incarcerate her in the Repository."

The Speaker nodded to her and strode from the room. Lords Gresham and Dench muttered their welcomes and hurried after him. Only Tomlin and Pendlebury remained. The younger mage stared at her and clenched his jaw.

"What is the Repository?" Sera asked.

Lord Pendlebury made quick notes in his ledger and spoke without looking up. "The Repository of Forgotten Things is a rather peaceful place where time flows differently. Dangerous magical objects and Unnatural creatures are securely housed there, away from the general population."

"It's a prison, where any inmate serves an eternal sentence." Lord Tomlin's stony face revealed nothing behind his hard eyes as he leaned back in his chair.

"Then it is fortunate I am innocent, and have nothing to fear from such a place." Somehow, she doubted the council would let her linger for decades in a magical prison. Not when an execution would see her powers transferred to a new *male* vessel.

"I will consider what would be a fitting display for the state dinner and send you my preliminary notes,

Lady Winyard." Tomlin rose to his feet and offered her a slight bow.

She inclined her head to him and watched him leave the chamber. He might have been handsome if he smiled occasionally. "There is one other matter, Lord Pendlebury, before we conclude here. I require the names of my parents."

He set down the pen and his open look faltered for a moment, as something darker flashed behind his eyes. Then the serene expression returned. "Of course. We are all curious as to our origins. The information will be delivered to your correspondence box."

She had waited thirteen years to learn more than a faded memory of her mother. Finally, she could stand before the woman and ask a thousand questions. Odd that when she cast back in her mind, she could not conjure even a vague outline of her father. "Thank you. I would also like admittance to the locked portion of the library."

He closed the ledger and placed the writing set on top. "Of course. I can well understand your eagerness to dive into the centuries of wisdom contained in the mage library. Shall we adjourn to the yard now?"

All mages, regardless of age or gender, had access to one part of the library that contained dull histories, faded herbologies, and dry stories written centuries ago. The sorts of books used to educate youngsters in the basics, but lacking any of the vibrancy or excitement of the tomes whispering from behind the wrought-iron gate. To gain entry to the locked portion of the library, a mage had to plant and grow a single blade of grass in the yard outside the tower.

On the face of it, it struck Sera as a stupid test. Why one blade of grass—why not ask them to blanket the ground in lush grass, or roses, or a mighty oak? The answer lay in the scale of the test. Firstly, it required precision to craft and then place a tiny seed. Then most mages struggled with the fiendish difficulty of growing anything in the barren earth. It took immense concentration and a large amount of magic to make a blade appear, and survive, in the barren wasteland around the tower.

With the older mage at her side, Sera strolled back through the tower, leaving the silent interior for the harsh exterior. Mentally, she prepared to draw on her magic for the task at hand.

"Whenever you are ready." Lord Pendlebury gestured to the sad patch of grass to one side.

Sera walked closer, then closed her eyes and imagined a bright green blade of grass. When she had it firm in her mind, she called on her magic to place the blade in a spot not too far from the other scrappy bits. Hers burrowed its roots into the ground. She fed it more magic as it wiggled to the slight breeze...and promptly turned brown and shrivelled up. To add insult to injury, a puff of wind blew it across the compacted earth.

"Oh," Lord Pendlebury murmured. He seemed genuinely disappointed for her. "You can try again another day, if you wish."

Of course she'd try again. And again. And again. Until she succeeded. The knowledge she needed resided in the private area of the library and she needed a wretched blade of grass as the key to get in. On second thought, it really was a stupid test. That she possessed power at all should be sufficient to access their dusty old tomes.

"I am rather tired from the events of today. Of course I shall return for another attempt." Digging deep, she kept a hopeful expression on her face.

Lord Pendlebury glanced around, then leaned in closer to her. "Lord Ormsby was nearly twenty before he succeeded. Do not think it says anything about your abilities that success in this pesky test eludes you."

"Thank you, my lord." She meant it. He was the one person on the council who gave her hope.

"You will receive regular communications of any tasks the council assigns you, and will be expected to attend the meetings of the council when you are summoned. Otherwise, you may spend your time and ability as you see fit, so long as such activities do not bring this council, or England, into disrepute." He walked her to the waiting carriage and waved her off.

While she had failed in her goal of gaining access to the locked library, the day had revealed other snippets. Ormsby pushed to extend her guardianship, and she would make sure Mr Napier continued to block their efforts to change the Mage Act. Tomlin sought to save face by claiming he'd feigned countering her spells. Had he told them of her unexpected strength, or kept that secret? The council planned to inter her at this Repository should they succeed in their false accusations. A plan she would ruin by discovering the true murderer.

Ormsby had been twenty before he'd grown a blade of grass. *There* was a piece of intelligence she couldn't wait to drop into conversation.

The council appeared to give her the liberty she craved, but they did not fool her. Like a deer in a clearing, she sensed the wolves circling through the trees. The only thing she didn't know was from which direction the inevitable attack would come.

TWELVE

O ver the course of that day and into the next, Hugh trailed the lieutenant as the man hunted down Branvale's valet like a blood-hound after a scent. He idly wondered whether Powers possessed a trace of Unnatural—lycanthrope, perhaps —or simply had a knack for this sort of work. Their first problem was finding the remnants of Branvale's staff. Apart from those snatched up by Lady Winyard, the rest seemed to have scattered faster than autumn leaves before a winter wind.

From the scant details one footman provided, Powers focused on a particular working-class neigh-bourhood. The army man would stop someone and ask a quiet question, to be pointed down a narrow lane, or into a darkened alley. At times, Hugh rolled his shoul-ders to prepare his body for a fight. He expected at any moment to be set upon from behind as the shiver of being watched washed over him.

Their search ended at a flat-roofed, four-storey building crammed with families. The front doors stood wide open, admitting the weather. Wallpaper peeled back in the entrance, and the procession of feet had worn the stair runner threadbare. An argument erupted behind one door as they passed. Eerie weeping drifted from another. They stepped over playing children in the corridors as they made their way to a fourth-floor door. A young woman with sickly grey skin that almost matched the hue of her red-rimmed grey eyes answered their knock.

"Yes?" she whispered, her fingers curled around the wood.

"Is Hogan here, my dear? I need a quick chat with him." Powers smiled.

Hugh tried to look less intimidating by hunching his shoulders, which probably increased his resemblance to some mad creature shuffling around a laboratory.

The woman frowned and glanced back into the room. As her hand slipped from the door, Powers jammed his boot in the gap and opened it farther. They stepped inside and Hugh pressed the door shut behind him. He leaned on the wood and surveyed the room. They entered a combination parlour and kitchen with furniture that appeared worn but clean. An open door on each side of the space offered a glimpse of two smaller bedrooms.

"What do you want?" a man sitting at the table asked, playing cards arrayed before him. He paused with the deck in his hands. The man possessed an eerie pale grey gaze that seemed to penetrate straight through Hugh.

The woman returned to a sagging sofa and sat at one end. She dragged a blanket over her knees and pulled her feet up under her. Coughing came from the partially open bedroom door, and Hugh ran through a list of ailments that might plague the residents.

Powers strode over to the table and pulled out the chair opposite. "I need a word about Branvale."

"He died and left me without a reference. Do you know how hard it is to find work once word spreads your master was murdered?" Hogan's pale eyes flashed and his fingers tightened on the cards.

"Unfortunate, to be sure, and more difficult when your family relies upon you." Powers drew out the ever-present notebook and pencil.

Hogan nodded. "Got the word out and my ear to the ground for any work to support my ma and my sister."

Powers rolled the pencil between his thumb and forefinger. "What do you remember of the night Branvale died?"

Hogan dealt a card and stared at those already laid out on the table. After the valet sat immobile for a minute, Powers tapped the four of clubs at the end of a row.

Hogan placed the dealt three of hearts in the indicated spot. "He went out for the evening. He came in about one in the morning, complaining of a gut ache. Once I had him settled in bed like an upset baby, I crawled back into my cot. Next thing I knew, Vicky was screaming the house down."

"Who did he dine with?" The pencil scratched over the paper.

Hugh's attention turned to the young woman. She had the same unsettling pale eyes. He wondered if brother and sister had inherited the genetic trait from their mother or father. The breath struggled into her lungs, each exhalation accompanied by a dry cough. He suspected another woman with a similar condition lay beyond the bedroom door. Disease could spread through the tenements like wildfire, and those who most needed a doctor could least afford one. His attention shifted back and forth from Powers' conversation to assessing the woman.

"Some woman. Client, I think, as he used to mutter about mixing business and pleasure. He was a right cagey one and not inclined to talk to staff. He was a mage, after all. I was just the man shining his shoes and fetching clean underdrawers." Hogan dropped the deck to the middle of the table and rested his knuckles on them.

"Did he take anything for his stomach complaint before retiring?" Powers asked.

Hugh's attention swung back to him at that question. There were many things that could ease a stomach complaint, from ginger to milk thistle extract.

Hogan shook his head. "Not that I remember. Said he ate too much, and that he would sleep it off."

"Did you like your employer?" Powers asked without looking up, as he made notes on the tiny page.

The valet laughed. "Did anyone like Branvale? It was a job, and it earned me enough to help me look after my family. If you're asking if I poisoned him...then no. Why would I kill the man paying my wages?"

"Why indeed?" Powers leaned back in the chair and stared at the ceiling.

Since there was a break in proceedings, Hugh decided to conduct his own examination—of the obviously sick woman. "That's a nasty cough. Do you mind if I have a listen?" He approached and knelt on the floor before her.

Hogan shoved his chair back and leapt to his feet. "Stay away from my sister!"

Hugh held up his hands. "I'm a surgeon, and I'm concerned about her. I might be able to help."

She pressed herself farther into the corner of the sofa and glanced at her brother. With one hand, she clutched the blanket more tightly around her thin shoulders.

"All right, then, if you can help. I hate to see her suffering with that cough. Ma has the same one and the two of them are awake all night with it." Hogan nodded, and the girl let the shawl fall away.

"May I listen to your breathing? I need to put my ear to your chest." Hugh lowered his tone.

Her eyes widened, but she nodded. Hugh leaned forward and rested his head against her torso. Ignoring the noise filtering to his other ear, he focused on the unique thrum of her body, as her heart beat and her lungs drew air. Her heart reminded him of butterfly wings beating against glass, and a distinctive rattle from her lungs suggested a fluid buildup.

'She's congested, but there is a potion that will help it disperse and ease her breathing," he said.

Hogan rested his knuckles on the table as he lowered himself back into the chair. 'In case you forgot, I don't have a job anymore. There's no money for fancy potions."

"You don't need to pay for this. I have an understanding with a particular apothecary, and he will dispense the tonic free of charge. If your mother suffers from the same ailment, this will help both of them." Hugh patted down his pockets. In one, he kept a few slips of paper with the details of the apothecary on it. In another pocket, he found a stub of pencil.

At the table, he swept away a row of cards to place the slip on a flat surface. He wrote concise instructions to the aftermage who brewed remedies for the working class. Then he added his neat signature. 'The address is on here. Harvey will look after your family and ensure they have the medicine they need."

Hogan glanced at the paper, then stared at him with narrowed eyes. "Why would you do this for us?"

'I am fortunate to have a patron who gives me the freedom to do what I can to ease the suffering of those who cannot afford a doctor." Hugh held out the prescription. His patron, Lord Viner, settled the apothecary's bill every month.

"Thank you." The valet took the piece of paper and stared at the address. 'I can go there this afternoon."

"Who would know where Branvale went the night

he died? Did he keep his own carriage?" Powers asked, capitalising on the softening of the valet's attitude toward them with Hugh's actions.

'No, too stingy with his money for that. He hired one from the mews behind the house. The lads there will know where he went." He gathered up the playing cards and pushed them back into the deck.

"We'll not detain you any longer, so you can attend to your sister and mother." Powers rose and nodded to both of them.

'Let me guess—we now head to the mews to find out who Branvale dined with," Hugh said as they trotted down the tenement's crowded stairs.

'Indeed. I shall make an investigator of you yet." Powers grinned.

Hugh considered himself an investigator already— of the human condition. Like the lieutenant, he used questions and observations to diagnose a problem. His findings could also determine life or death for his patient. Would someone dangle at the end of a noose when Powers told the king what he had discovered?

The lieutenant hailed them a hired conveyance. 'Any advance yet on when you think Branvale most likely ingested the poison?"

'I tested the stomach contents on an unfortunate mouse, who died within the span of a few hours. I am making calculations of body weight to an approximate dosage. I want to ensure I haven't made some mistake and accidentally overdosed the poor thing. Apart from my observations, we will need a mage to discern what spell is lingering in the samples." The mouse had not suffered for long. Hugh despised the necessity of taking the creature's life and wished there were another way to obtain the same result.

Powers made a noise in the back of his throat and stroked his moustache in a way that Hugh discovered meant he was deep in thought. 'If the poison acted within hours, that suggests Lord Branvale must have either ingested it at his home, or during dinner with the unknown companion."

"The timing suggests those possibilities, rather than squarely in one location or another. It also places Lady Winyard elsewhere." His heart lightened at the thought that the mouse's sacrifice would clear the young mage.

'But it does not absolve her. She had friends under Branvale's roof and might have placed something in his path that night. Or as you have observed, there might have been a spell on the poison that delayed its effect until she was well away. She still might have ensured Lord Branvale drank it while she was still under his roof." Powers dropped his hand to his thigh to drum his fingers on his breeches.

'I will take a sample to her, and then we can compare the findings of two different mages." How he wanted to believe that the Mage Council would act honourably and deliver a truthful finding. But the knot in his gut suggested they would do otherwise. He hoped Lady Winyard's findings would balance those of the council. Odd that he placed more trust in the young and untested woman. Or was he simply falling under her magical spell? He should be careful lest his personal feelings intrude on his impartiality.

The carriage rattled to an abrupt halt in the lane by the mews. The lieutenant paid the man, and they walked down the lane to the busy stables. Horses were led out to be hitched to carriages owned by those living in the surrounding houses. Others were taken from harness and returned to their stables for a well-deserved groom and feed. A few stood to one side, waiting for a blacksmith to fit new shoes.

Powers stood in the open doorway and drew a deep breath. "Ah! How I miss the bustle of men working with horses."

"You're a cavalry man?" Hugh moved to one side as a groom led a high-stepping chestnut past them.

"Indeed. There is something about closeness to a horse that feeds a man's soul. Do you ride?" They ventured inside, Powers stopping to run a hand over the rump of a horse waiting in the tie-up.

"Only when absolutely necessary." Hugh admired the beasts, and they were handy for getting from one location to another, but he didn't have the obsession with them that consumed others.

"I say, my good man, who took Lord Branvale out on his last trip?" Powers tapped a man in livery on the shoulder.

"Ask Fred. He's in the office at the end. Keeps a record of every horse and carriage taken out." The man gestured to an end stall that had had walls and a window installed to convert it to an office.

The door stood open, and a man sat hunched over a pile of papers on a desk. Sacks of grain were piled in one corner and a mouse scurried from the grain to a knothole in the wood. A ginger cat leapt off the top sack and landed on the floor a second too late. Its quarry escaped. The man at the desk glanced up and sighed, as though dreading another interruption to his day. Hugh remained in the barn aisle, so as not to crowd the already overstocked office.

Conversation within rose and fell as he watched the grooms go about their business. One horse evacuated its bowels on the cobbles, and a lad rushed forward with a wide shovel to scoop the steaming pile up and carry it over to a waiting wheelbarrow.

Powers emerged a few minutes later and slapped him in the stomach with the diminutive notebook. "We close in on our mysterious dinner companion. The address is not so far away, if you are up to a walk?"

"Of course." He should be tending patients, not strolling Mayfair and its surrounds. But a need to remain involved in the investigation kept him at the lieutenant's side.

They walked for some twenty minutes, crossed the street, and made their way through a green square. On the other side, Powers led the way up a short path to a deep red front door. He lifted the brass knocker and rapped sharply.

Hugh stared at the windows. The drapes were pulled back, but the windows were shut tight. No movement passed beyond the lace net that allowed light inside, but afforded a small measure of privacy from nosy neighbours.

At length, the door opened, and a sombre butler

with clipped grey hair stared at them with muddy brown eyes. "Yes, sirs?"

Powers rocked on his toes. "I am Lieutenant Powers, and I'm investigating the death of Lord Branvale. I understand he dined here three nights ago? I need to talk to his dinner companion."

While they had an address, they still didn't know who had entertained Branvale.

The man didn't blink. "The Contessa Ricci is not presently at home."

"When will she return? It is most urgent we speak to her." Powers leaned on the door frame and crossed his booted ankles. While he adopted a casual stance, he stared over the top of the butler's head and scanned what little he could see of the interior.

The butler narrowed his gaze and huffed. "Tomorrow afternoon. She is away visiting with friends outside of London."

"Then I shall call on her tomorrow." The lieutenant nodded, handed his card to the butler, and trotted along the path to steer Hugh across the pretty square. "A temporary delay in our investigation, but we shall return."

"An Italian noble. Do you think Branvale's dinner was business or pleasure?" Hugh glanced back at the silent house, but unlike people, the exterior gave no clue as to the happenings within.

"Given he died not long after, one would hope he had a pleasurable evening first." Powers chortled to himself as he led the way to a busier street.

THIRTEEN

Sera had never imagined that a single blade of grass could practically drain her magic. Or more likely, it combined with the mental exertion of reining in her temper and maintaining an even expression on her face to deplete her resources. Once back at her humble home, she stretched out on the settee with a hot cup of tea in her hands. The day had left her exhausted, and she would sleep soundly when she eventually sought her bed.

A rap on the door was followed by two familiar voices. One belonged to Elliot, the other to a particular surgeon who often occupied her thoughts. Before she could decide whether she ought to move her feet off the settee and find her shoes, the surgeon had crouched beside her.

He stretched out a hand with a frown pulling his brows together. "Are you unwell, Lady Winyard?"

She should have waved his hand away, but she let him press his knuckles to her forehead first. "Simply drained, Mr Miles. I undertook a task at the mage tower today that has left me exhausted. Exercising magic is somewhat akin to undertaking physical labour."

He dropped his hand to his side and rose to drag a chair closer to her. "I had heard that magic takes a toll upon a mage. Does it deplete all magic users at a similar rate?"

"I have no idea, nor have I ever tested my limits before. Would you like me to keep notes for you?" She wriggled her stocking-clad toes against the faded brocade.

Interest sparked in his eyes, then he dropped his gaze to stare at his hands. "You mock me, milady."

"A gentle teasing, Mr Miles, no more." Despite all her lessons with Abigail, Sera struggled with the lines of propriety. She found comfort in the surgeon's presence and spoke to him like he was someone she had known for many years.

"Teasing is for friends." He clasped his hands and glanced at her with one eyebrow quirked.

"Do you think you could be friends with a woman mage? I hear it's not for the faint-hearted." Sera sipped her tea and studied him from under lowered lashes.

"Then I am fortunate that my heart is as sturdy as the rest of me, but I would appreciate it if we could leave the lightning for special occasions or holidays," he murmured.

Sera snorted at the idea of special occasions that might necessitate electricity between them. Mr Miles moved with speed to catch her falling teacup even before she could wrap a tentative strand of magic around it.

"Before I forget entirely why I am here, I brought you the poison sample." He placed the teacup on the low table with one hand, while the other dived into his jacket pocket.

Sera swung her feet to the floor as he pulled out a vial with a greenish-black blob inside.

Mr Miles kept hold of the vial. "I'm sure I don't need to tell you to treat this with the utmost care. It is poisonous and I cannot yet say how much is a fatal dose."

"I promise to take care of myself and my staff." Some other day, she would revisit their conversation about special occasions and electricity. The idea made a current ripple over her skin in an unexpected, but not unpleasant, fashion.

He nodded and placed the vial in her hand, wrapping her fingers around it. His touch lingered before his hands dropped away. "I shall leave you to rest and recover your magical resources."

"I hope you will return, so that we might discuss my findings?" she said as he prepared to leave.

He smiled, and it tugged at her heart. "Of course. As soon as you are ready."

Elliot hovered in the doorway and showed the surgeon out. When the door closed, the footman returned to the parlour. "I give it a month."

Sera frowned. "A month for what?"

"Before he works up the courage to kiss you." Elliot's shoulders heaved in silent laughter.

'Impertinent scoundrel," Sera muttered, and waved him away. 'Go tell Rosie I'm ready for dinner before I give you the jowls of a bulldog.

'A month," she whispered to herself as he went out, laughing. That seemed such a long time. Assuming, of course, that she even wanted to kiss the man for any reason other than curiosity. But a whole month...?

Shaking aside the idea of how to speed up time, she held up the vial. 'What are you?" With her magic exhausted, she could detect only a faint trace from the contents. Any further investigation would have to wait until she was recovered. Until then, she placed it in a box that could only be unlocked by magic. 'That is a job for tomorrow. I need dinner before I tackle this evening's task."

LONG AFTER DINNER and while the neighbourhood slumbered, Sera tucked her hair up under a cap and turned to Elliot. 'Will I pass muster?"

He stared at her and narrowed his eyes before blowing out a sigh. 'No. Even a blind man wouldn't believe you're my younger brother. You look like a woman in trousers. Which, funnily enough, is exactly what you are."

She stared down at her legs, her trousers tucked into a pair of laced boots. Fortunately, she could do something about adding a familial resemblance. Sera studied Elliot's square face and then whispered into her palms. A quiet afternoon and a substantial dinner had done much to restore her. With the spell in mind, she washed her hands over her face and down her neck.

Elliot stared. "That is..." The footman shuddered.

Sera frowned. A simple glamour should have masked her features. "Did it not work?"

He shook his head as though trying to clear his vision. "Oh, it worked, all right. I just don't like seeing my face staring back at me from atop your body."

Sera grinned. Every day her power grew, as did her confidence in tapping into the magic that flowed in her veins. If she imagined the spell she needed, the words to call it forth tumbled through her mind. "Come on. It will do for the task at hand."

"Will we be stopping for a pint on our way back?" Elliot called after her as she headed out the front door.

There was an idea—a chance to see what exactly men got up to in a tavern after dark. But it would have to wait for another night. They walked for a distance through the quiet streets, then hailed a conveyance at a busy crossroads. They alighted a block away from their destination. As they passed the Napier home, Sera considered that she could have visited Kitty and slipped over from her friend's home, but she wanted to keep her friend ignorant of her nighttime activities.

A crow fluttered to the railing, and Elliot paused. "Hello, girl," he murmured, and stroked the ebony head.

"Friend of yours?" Sera asked. She wondered if it was the same crow who had welcomed her on the first morning in the Soho townhouse with a gift of silver ribbon. But there were many such birds soaring above London.

'More like a relative. Off you go—we have work to do." His tone softened as he spoke to the bird.

The creature tilted its head to Sera and cawed before taking flight, its midnight wings disappearing against the nighttime sky.

Farther down the road, Sera's home for so many years sat in darkness. The staff had moved on with undignified haste the day after Branvale died. Down the spiral stairs, Sera and Elliot crept toward the staff entrance. Sera stroked the lock with a gentle touch until it gave with a click. She grinned in the dark and pushed the door open. Once inside, she handed a jar to Elliot. She had created two small glow lamps from two jars she'd found in the back of the larder at her house. The jars had short wire handles looped over the top. She tapped the sides, and a swirling mist in each jar emitted a pale blue light.

'What are we looking for?" Elliot whispered as they headed along the corridor to the narrow servants' staircase.

'Ledgers of Branvale's clients, in which he used to record spells and potions he made for them. Also, any letters, diaries, anything of a personal nature that might have been overlooked," Sera said as they climbed the narrow stairs.

'Didn't the Mage Council take all the magical stuff away?" Elliot huffed from behind her.

'They did, but we're looking for what they left."

The Mage Council's men had descended and seized anything with a whiff of magic, and Branvale's children had cleared out anything of value. What she sought was neither of those things. Sera cracked the door open on the first level and crept along the silent hall. She would start with the more obvious locations first—study, library, and bedchamber. While she had glimpsed the book he kept notes in, she'd never once seen him place it on a shelf. The only time she recalled seeing it, he either carried it with him clutched to his side or it sat on a corner of his desk waiting to be picked up. Otherwise, the ledger had been nowhere in sight.

They crossed the wide hall to the library. The house was eerie in its silence, even though they both knew every inch.

'But if that lot left anything behind, doesn't that mean it's not important?" Elliot asked.

Sera stopped in front of the double doors to the library. She resisted the long-ingrained urge to knock and wait to be allowed within. 'Rather, the opposite. If a mage wants to hide something, using magic is the obvious way. But to other mages, the magic used acts as a beacon, alerting us to whatever you want to hide. The best way to hide something from a mage is *without* magic."

Elliot grasped the handles and pushed them apart. He cocked his head, his dark eyes were curious, and reminded her of the crow. 'So if a mage has something important to hide, they don't use magic, but make it look like something worthless."

'Sort of. A ledger is still a ledger. If Branvale had

used to magic to turn it into something else, like a teapot, the council would still have taken it away." Sera followed Elliot into the library. The shelves had been emptied and any magical tomes removed. Personal items were gone, claimed by his children. The desk likewise sat empty. The two groups had picked over the house like hungry carnivores cleaning a carcass. "Flick through what books are left, in case any conceals a ledger."

They started at opposite ends of the shelves and worked their way toward each other, but none of the limp volumes that remained concealed a ledger. Next, they moved to the small study at the rear of the house. That room was likewise devoid of belongings and furnishings. Even the rug had been rolled up and carted away. Only the large desk remained with its ornately carved, high-backed chair.

Frustration built under Sera's skin and battled the certainty that *somewhere* Branvale hid his ledgers. "You are a footman. Did you not see him pull anything from a hidden spot?"

Elliot stared at the ceiling and pursed his lips. "No. He was always a suspicious bugger."

Given that her guardian had been murdered, it seemed his suspicions were not without foundation. "Let us assume *you* were a suspicious bugger. Where would you hide something you wanted to keep an eye on?"

Elliot walked around the desk and sat in the chair. He leaned back and stroked an imaginary beard as he adopted the role of their former employer. Then he clasped his hands before his face and narrowed his eyes. His gaze darted around the room before settling in the left-hand corner. 'Somewhere I could see it, but someone who came into the room couldn't."

Sera considered the spot. The door sat off centre in the study wall, being more to the right when viewed from the desk. On the left-hand side, a built-in shelf ended a foot before the wall, where a tall and narrow corner unit used to sit.

"Someone has removed the curiosity cabinet that used to be here." The cabinet had a lead-light front in a diamond pattern, and Branvale had kept a range of objects in there that he had acquired on his travels. As a child, she had delighted in staring at them, but had been told off if she dared put grubby fingerprints on the glass. 'If they were in the cabinet, they are gone now."

Blast. Outwitted by his family, who had carted off anything they could sell. She was surprised the desk had been left behind. Then again, most likely it had proved too awkward to shift. As she cast her light across the floor, a shadow caught her eye and she bent down to look more closely.

"One board sits higher than the others." She ran a hand over the wood. In the very corner, a length of board rose fractionally above its neighbour. Possibly whoever moved the cabinet had caught it, or the shifting of the weight above had jostled the timber.

Elliot joined her and set his glow lamp down on the bare floor. He pushed on the board. It depressed with a squeak and bounced up again under his fingertips.

'Do you think there is something under it?" This was Sera's first time committing burglary, and she found it exhilarating.

'Let's find out." He pulled a pocketknife from his jacket and eased the blade under the board. With a soft pop, it lifted. 'Cunning old bugger. This sat under the cabinet. He could have lifted the board from inside the bottom of the cabinet, and we were all none the wiser."

They pushed their lamps closer together to reveal the cavity beneath, and saw the distinctive shapes of books. Sera pulled out two fat ledgers. A quick scan revealed names, dates, and a brief description of the magical service they had required. 'Got you."

Brilliant. She gathered them all up and handed them to Elliot, who shoved them into a satchel he carried over his shoulder. They put the board back in place, but she remained on the floor. The odd niggle that there was something *more* wouldn't let her go.

'What do you think he was involved in, Elliot, that someone murdered him?" Regardless of her feelings for the old mage, no one deserved to die in such a hideous and painful way.

The footman picked up his glow lamp and shrugged. 'We'll never know unless he wrote it all down in one of these."

Sera took the offered hand and stood. The idea of some conspiracy sounded ridiculous when said out loud. Most likely, it was as simple as a client who didn't get the spell they paid for and lashed out in revenge.

'Although, if I were a paranoid old magical geezer up to no good, and I just happened to keep a note about it because I was getting old and forgetful...I'd keep it where I spent most of my time." Elliot pointed upstairs to Lord Branvale's bedroom.

Sera stared at the ceiling and followed Elliot's meaning. "Under his bed. Brilliant idea, Elliot. I am glad Rosie and I agreed on you, instead of any of the other footmen."

"Why did you pick me?" he asked as they walked along the hall and then up the main stairs to the bedrooms above.

"Because you're loyal, and that's very important to me." Sera held her glow lamp up to the wall, stripped of its dour portraits.

"And I'm the best looking of the bunch," Elliot added.

Sera hid her smile. He was handsome, but he'd never hear that from her. His opinion of himself was quite high enough already. "And devious, which is the most important trait of all. I don't think any of the others would have joined me on a midnight escapade to break into a dead mage's house."

Like the rooms below, the master bedroom had been stripped of everything easy to carry. The enormous bed with its bare mattress dominated the space and could have held an entire working-class family in comfort.

"You take one side and I'll go the other." Elliot winked and slid under the bed.

There wasn't much head room as they lay on their stomachs and ran their hands all over the floorboards. Similar to the study, they found a single short board right under the middle of his bed that sat a fraction above its neighbours. Underneath was a small, slim cavity.

"There's only a blank piece of paper." Elliot reached in and pulled out their latest find. He held the sheet to the soft blue light.

Sera took the page from him and turned it over. A tingle brushed over her fingertips. "It's ensorcelled. He was communicating with someone and didn't want anyone else to know about it."

"Magic business?" Elliot's eyes glinted in the dark.

"We have our rosewood boxes for those dispatches." She considered the page. A spell enabled it to show what another person had written on their sheet of paper. Could a different spell reveal those words, even after they had been erased? A restorative, perhaps? She folded the page and tucked it into her jacket. "Let's go before someone notices our lights bobbing back and forth. There's nothing more to learn here, and I need to examine the ledgers."

They crawled out from under the bed and retraced their steps. Sera locked the staff door again and cast one last look at the house. *What were you up to?*

But not even a crow replied.

Back at her little terrace house, Sera crawled into bed with the ledgers, since reading didn't require magic. She hid the ensorcelled paper between the pages of a novel on her bedside table, needing a clear head and daylight to tackle that mystery.

One by one, she opened the ledgers and ran her fingers down the columns of names, potions, and amounts paid. One potion that Branvale brewed monthly niggled in her brain, and she was determined to learn what client warranted a personal delivery from her guardian. She stifled a yawn, determined to find one answer before she gave in to her body's need for sleep.

A line jumped out at her—*Hogan, suppressant*. Had Branvale brewed something for Jake Hogan, his valet? Usually, the staff had to go to the local apothecary for remedies for sickness or injury, or Sera attempted to make a potion. Had her guardian made an exception for his valet? Tucking that snippet away, she kept reading.

The second ledger yielded the information she sought with the label *Ruby potion*. That had to be it. Nothing else listed created the dark red liquid. In his neat hand was an address and a name—*Contessa Ricci*.

Tomorrow, the contessa would receive a visitor. Sera hoped she would learn the answer to one nagging mystery, at least.

FOURTEEN

The next morning, when Sera checked the
wooden box on the desk, she found a
scrawled sheet within. Her first Mage
Council assignment—how exciting! Until she read the
brief. An obstruction in the East End hindered traffic
flow and required her skills. An aftermage at the scene
proved insufficient to clear it away. What could that be
—did not men manually clear such things? Perhaps a
building had toppled, and they needed her help to
move bricks and timbers at greater speed. Or a
rampaging wild beast from the king's menagerie needed
to be subdued with a gentle magical lullaby.

She shook out the plain riding habit and donned it.

"Where to today?" Elliot asked as he handed her
both gloves and the tricorn hat with its curling feather.

"The East End and some form of obstruction." She
placed the hat on a slight angle and then reconsidered it.
She would be overdressed for the area. Instead, she
handed it back to Elliot and plucked a scarf from the

drawer of the side table, draping it over her head and tying it under her hair.

'Do you want me to accompany you?" A frown marred his forehead as he hung the hat on its hook.

For a moment, she considered taking him up on his offer. A young woman alone in the East End could meet many troubles. But she was expected, and her magic flowed fresh through her. If anyone tried to grab her from behind, they would find their limbs turned into flippers.

'I am to meet an aftermage there, and will try to stay out of trouble." She managed a smile to convince both herself and Elliot of that. The council wouldn't send her somewhere dangerous on her very first assignment, would they?

She chewed that over as she travelled to the eastern side of the city. From the window, she could see the buildings and tenements becoming shabbier. The people on the street seemed weary despite the early hour. Children with grimy faces held out dirty hands, begging for any spare coin from passers-by.

Up ahead, people milled, and carts were stalled in the road. Horses nipped at each other as they grew bored. She hopped out of the carriage and waved the driver away. The vehicle would only add to the chaos, and she would find her own way back. An odour tickled her nose and as she pushed through the crowd, it grew stronger. Bile surged up her throat, and she drew a handkerchief from her pocket and pressed it to her face.

Her boots splashed through a foul-smelling puddle,

but when she glanced down, it didn't have the consistency of water.

"What is causing this?" she asked a woman sitting on a set of steps.

"Blocked drain. We're waiting for someone brave enough to clear it." She let out a cackle that revealed missing front teeth, and waved to indicate it lay farther up the road.

People hurried along the cobbles, jumping out of the way of the slow-moving mass. A group of children huddled to one side with a stick, poking objects caught up in the foul-smelling river. Up ahead, Sera spotted a group of men waving their hands in the air, the watery sludge up to their ankles.

"Oh, dear." She hiked up her skirts and tucked them into her waistband out of the way. Her boots would be ruined, but there was little she could do about that. As she neared the group, it became more apparent what it was that bubbled up from under the road and spread out. Sewage.

Open drains flowed toward the Thames and over time, they had been covered with timbers to prevent citizens from falling in. In the fancier neighbourhoods, proper brick drains were built to remove waste from houses to the river. Some new, expensive homes were being directly connected to the underground network. Since the Thames was tidal, it had the added benefit of pushing water upstream twice a day. When the tide turned, it created a siphon to suck waste back along the network of drains.

Until, apparently, it hit an obstruction that wouldn't be moved.

Her stomach flopped at the chunky bits tapping against her feet. A finger appeared to wave from the brown ocean, before the press of more fluid shoved it along the road. First thing she needed to do was settle her stomach before she added to the disgusting mess flooding the street. Sera conjured to mind sweet peas with their gentle fragrance, and crafted a spell to waft their aroma under her nose and fight off the rotten stench.

Ignoring the dampness seeping into her boots, Sera surveyed the men. They seemed to be yelling instructions to a young man with sweat beading his brow. The gentleman stood in the middle of the road and, somewhat like Moses, had his hands raised trying to part the sea heading toward him. He repeatedly swiped his arms to one side, and the sewer made a sluggish curve toward the buildings.

Her lessons with Abigail had not prepared her for the etiquette of introductions while standing ankle-deep in waste. Sera decided on a direct approach and tapped the man on the shoulder. He was tall and angular, as though he hadn't yet grown into his body. 'I'm Lady Seraphina Winyard. The Mage Council sent me to investigate the blockage. Given the smell and sewage in the streets, I'm assuming something has obstructed the drain.'

The man's eyes widened for a moment, then relief flowed over his features and he dropped his hands. 'Oh, milady, thank goodness you are here! I'm Finlay

Mulvaney, third-generation aftermage. I usually deal with water, but this mess is beyond my abilities. Surprised they sent you, milady, if you don't mind my saying so. It's not a pleasant job."

"Well, Mr Mulvaney, I go where the Mage Council directs me." Sera smiled, but inwardly she suspected Lord Ormsby had chortled to himself as he wrote her name down for this particular task. She retied her scarf around her neck in a loop, where she could raise it over her mouth and nose if necessary. "Have you been able to locate the blockage?"

"Best I can determine, it's the side drain over there. There's one that crosses under the road and whatever it is, it's wedged tight. This muck is backed up on both sides." He used a handkerchief to wipe the sweat from his face and then waved to a point up the road.

A crowd gathered, keeping clear of the filthy water by standing on the steps of the surrounding buildings. More people hung out of windows and yelled not very helpful instructions, like "Show us your knees!" No doubt in reference to the way Sera had hiked up her skirts like a dairymaid, but propriety be damned, she wasn't ruining her habit by letting it be soaked in *this*.

Ignoring the surrounding distractions, she focused on the spot the aftermage had indicated and fixed it in her mind. Then she set free a swirl of magic, skimming over the road and then diving into a drain. Much like the way she attached her mind to a bird to fly high above the ground, now she used the water to convey her to where its path was impeded.

Through the pipe she squirmed, until she reached a

congealed mass hunkering in the dark. Liquid hit the object and then turned around, surging back the way it had come and flowing through the grates to the street. "I've found it," she said to the aftermage at her side.

"Can you shift it?" Mr Mulvaney asked.

"I shall try." This was her first official day of work as one of England's mages. How embarrassing it would be if she couldn't complete the task. It might be only clearing a sewer for the working-class neighbourhood, but she would give them the assistance they desperately required.

She couldn't imagine any of the other mages wading through the muck to help.

She considered the obstruction from a few different angles, then crafted a net to wrap around it, hoping to haul it out like cargo from a vessel's hold. Sera tugged, but the object remained firm. She pulled with more effort, and her net slipped through the fat greasing the ball's sides.

"Nothing's happening!" someone helpfully yelled from a nearby window.

What she needed was a different approach. Since the blockage had the consistency of butter, spikes might work better. Sera crafted magical paddles like those a cook used to shape the dairy spread. Then she gave them spines like nails hammered into a board. Working with her eyes closed and letting her gift guide her, she wielded the paddles to bat the lump. It shuddered and moved a small amount. Like a cat with a ball of twine, she experimented with different types of blows. If she hit it too hard, her paddles burrowed into the object. Short, sharp whacks worked best. Inch by inch, her magic propelled the mess closer to a drain.

'It's moving,' she muttered to Mr Mulvaney.

Sera stretched out her hands and wrapped more magic around the squishy lump. As the pipe opened out, she changed tactics and enveloped the ball in a magical net again. This time, she managed to encompass the obstruction. Gritting her teeth and digging deep, Sera called on a blast of air and sent it surging around the ball as she mentally yanked on the net.

A bang sounded as like a cannon ball as the obstruction cleared the pipe, burst through the grate, and flew through the air. People shouted and ducked as the projectile smacked into the side of a building. The squishy mass smeared down the side of the brick and dribbled to the road. People cheered as once again the sewage could gurgle down the drains.

'Oh, well done!' Mr Mulvaney said.

Working with the aftermage, the two of them soon swept all the waste back into the drains and gave it a push to send it toward the Thames. By the time she was finished, Sera was sticky with sweat, smelt worse than three-day-old fish left in the sun, and could not even contemplate what coated her boots. She sat on a step with Mr Mulvaney to survey their work.

'For you, milady.' A woman of a similar age approached with a tin mug of ale.

'Thank you.' Sera drank deeply to relieve her parched throat. She was filthy, exhausted, and triumphant. With her first task successfully completed, the Mage Council couldn't grumble about her ability or willingness to do as they asked.

Good humour erupted around her as people chatted and children waited for the fatty ball to fall from the side of the building. All the neighbourhood needed now was a good bit of rain and a stiff breeze to clean the road. She wiped her forehead on her sleeve and glanced up at the sky. There weren't many clouds, but she would send out a ripple to Mother Nature and ask for her assistance. Perhaps later in the evening she would oblige with a downpour.

"Thank you, Lady Winyard, for clearing that mess." Mr Mulvaney toasted her with his mug of ale. "Having worked beside you, I don't believe a word the Mage Council are saying about you."

She could well imagine what rumours filtered through to the aftermages and the rest of London. "Whatever you might have heard, Mr Mulvaney, I can assure you I am neither feeble nor hysterical. All I need is a little time and experience."

"I meant the other thing they are whispering. That you...you know..." He stared into his mug, unable to meet her gaze.

Ah. She could guess what particular rumour had reached his ears. "That I killed my guardian? A malicious rumour with no basis in truth whatsoever. Lord Branvale's death is being investigated, and I am sure they will identify the guilty party."

"Well, I don't believe it, and will correct anyone who dares repeat it in my hearing," Mr Mulvaney said.

The people gathered around them muttered in agreement.

Sera had won her first few supporters. An idea formed in her mind. Nobles might hold wealth and position, but if one had the support of the common man, a person could be unstoppable.

Once she had finished her ale and ensured the drains were working as they should, Sera turned her mind to how to get home. No driver, no matter how shabby his carriage, would want her as a passenger after her morning's work. In the end, a man fetched his horse and cart and offered her a ride back to Soho. Four children as dirty as she sat with her and chatted the entire way, regaling her with stories of what they'd found floating in the muck that had flowed down their road. Apart from body parts (and where on earth had *they* come from?) the children had found small trinkets they'd fished out with sticks.

In her street, she jumped off the cart and waved. Then she headed up her path. Elliot opened the door and barred her entry. "You are not coming into this house looking like that."

"I am mistress here." Having battled the muck for some hours, and with the help of her aroma spell, her nostrils had become accustomed to the odour. Looking down at herself, she admitted her appearance was rather...dishevelled.

"You smell like an overflowing chamber pot." He pinched his nose and pointed to her boots and the stained hems of her skirts.

"Which is exactly what I had to deal with, but on a

much larger scale. I'll go down to the kitchen and leave my dirty clothes there." Poor Vicky would faint at the state of her. Sera might send the habit out to be laundered to see if it could be saved.

A woman detached herself from a trio chatting on the pavement and walked across the road. "Pardon me, milady, I'm Bernadette Jackson. I could launder that frock for you. I'll soon have it as good as new. I have a wee talent for stubborn stains."

Sera thanked whatever entity had been listening in on her thoughts and responded so quickly to her needs. "Oh, could you? That would be so kind."

Only slightly older than Sera, the woman smiled with tired eyes. "You fixed my little one's doll and she talks of nothing else. I'd be pleased to help in return."

"It was a pleasure to do something for the children." An idea whisked into her mind. "I thought to hold a party for the street with food, music, and some magical displays, if you think that would be welcome?"

Bernadette's mouth made an O shape, and she glanced over her shoulder. "Oh, that sounds marvellous. The women around here would all pitch in with some baking."

Sera rubbed her hands together. Charm would win more people to her side than Branvale's prickly exterior ever had. "Now, if you have a moment, I will shed this habit and petticoats and you can take them away." Sera gestured for Mrs Jackson to follow and they took the stairs down to the kitchen, discussing the best night for the celebration in the street.

Rosie narrowed her gaze as Sera entered her

domain, huffed, and then set to boiling water. Sera stripped off the habit and bedraggled petticoats and handed them over to the laundress with a promise to pay her amply for the work. Vicky dragged out the copper bath and set it up in the scullery. Between their efforts and Sera's magic, the tub was soon full of steaming water.

Sera let out a sigh as she immersed herself and scrubbed her hair clean. While she worked at her skin with a brush and soap, Elliot spoke to her from behind a screen. Sera cast an enchantment over the paper-thin shield to stop the footman from peeking. If he dared, it would move.

"The neighbours have been making themselves known, and I've been keeping my ears open for any tasks bothering them that you can wiggle your fingers at." His voice came from behind the screen.

"Good. I'll do whatever I can for them." She wanted to build a loyal network around her of people she could trust.

Elliot paused before continuing. "There was one gent who approached me who asked if you lived here. Right odd he was."

"How so?" Sera examined her fingernails, making sure all the muck had gone.

"He dressed like a workman, but wasn't. Nails were too clean, and he spoke well." The footman waved his hands as he spoke and they cast shadows on the stretched fabric.

Sera stilled and wondered what it might mean. She trusted Elliot's assessment, which meant someone had tried to hide who they were with an ill-fitting disguise. "Who do you think he was?"

Elliot shrugged. "Don't think he was a noble. I would have spotted one of them. Might have been a noble's man, though."

Curious. She would consider an enchantment she could leave with Elliot to throw over the man to enable them to follow him. "Keep your eyes open in case he returns."

"I did a bit of snooping this morning and visited that address you found. The contessa is away and due back this afternoon."

At last, she might learn the purpose of the thick red potion. "Excellent. I shall pay her a visit and see if we can learn what business Branvale had with her."

Sera waited for Elliot to leave before climbing from the tub and pulling on a dressing gown. Then she walked up to her bedroom to consider her outfit for the afternoon. The gown with its sweet peas seemed too innocent for talking business with a contessa. Instead, she chose a *robe à l'anglaise* in navy with a grey petticoat underneath. Then Vicky pinned her hair up as best she could, since Sera refused to don a wig or additional hairpieces. To finish the look, they perched a wide-brimmed straw hat trimmed with navy ribbon on her hair.

Elliot whistled as she descended the stairs. "From guttersnipe to lady. You do scrub up all right." Then he sniffed and wrinkled his nose. "You sure you got all that muck out from under your nails?"

A moment of panic washed over Sera. Had she

missed a spot? She held her fingers to her face, but before she could inhale, the footman burst into laughter.

"Go find me a carriage, before I'm tempted to cast a stench spell over *you*." She waved him out the door.

Then once he had trotted off, she sniffed her fingers anyway. Just in case.

FIFTEEN

Elliot handed Sera up into the carriage and gave the address to the driver. Then he tapped the side of the vehicle and saluted her with two fingers as they headed off. She allowed herself a quiet moment of satisfaction at the way her staff had settled into their new roles. Rosie and Vicky kept their home maintained and all of them fed. Elliot...well, Elliot had evolved from footman into something far more handy. A man she could rely on, one who didn't blink when she asked him to help her break into a house.

The view outside her window changed to the grander homes on the edges of Mayfair. The horses trotted around a picturesque green square and rolled to a halt along a row of smart, pale stone town houses. An unusual, but not unwelcome, sight greeted her. Mr Miles and Lieutenant Powers stared up at the same address.

"Lady Winyard?" Mr Miles called, and stopped his

companion with a touch to the arm. The surgeon walked over to open the carriage door and held out a hand to assist her down.

"Good afternoon, Mr Miles. What a coincidence to find you here." Sera's curiosity sat up and took notice if the lieutenant's investigation had also led him to the contessa's door.

"Indeed. I am curious as to what brings you to this address?" He kept hold of her hand and tucked it into the crook of his elbow.

"Lady Winyard. Do tell me you have some information that has led you here?" Lieutenant Powers bowed to her as he joined them.

She studied the lieutenant and considered whether to share her information. The cavalry officer had a brisk but honest approach. So far, she had detected nothing about him that hinted at his being a lackey of the Mage Council, intent on curtailing her freedom. She would share, but not everything. "Perhaps this is a mere coincidence. But every month, Lord Branvale would brew an unusual potion and deliver it himself to this address. I admit curiosity brought me here, and a little personal financial interest. With one source deceased, the contessa might wish to continue receiving that brew from another mage."

"What sort of potion?" Mr Miles asked.

Sera shrugged. "That is what has made me curious —a potion with no discernible purpose apart from being a preservative. I had hoped to ask the contessa about the effects of the brew."

"Well, let us see what answers she may provide." Powers bounded up the path and rapped on the door.

The butler appeared in the doorway, his face set in a stern mask and his eyes narrowed. He appraised each of them before stepping aside to admit them.

"This way," he intoned and led the way to a tall panelled door painted a deep grey, the trim picked out in silver.

They entered a parlour with a sparse colour palette, but made all the more arresting because of that. Grey walls the colour of storm clouds were relieved by silver-embossed silk draperies. Against the hues of grey, the lush red velvet covering the matching chaise and settees provided a stark contrast.

The contessa reclined on the chaise, a book dangling loose in her fingers. She could have been plucked from a fairy tale, with raven black hair, alabaster skin, and lips of ruby red. Her pale grey gown, the same hue as her eyes, was covered in silver embroidery.

"Who are you people?" She arched one black eyebrow.

Lieutenant Powers stepped forward to introduce them. "This is Lady Winyard, the mage. I am Lieutenant Powers, and this is Mr Miles, the surgeon. We are here to discuss an associate of yours, Lord Branvale."

The contessa tossed her book on a side table and peered at Sera. "The woman mage. It was so novel of the English to finally allow such a rare flower to bloom.

I have wanted to meet you." She sniffed. "It should have been your card sent up, not his."

Sera tucked the woman's words away. What did she know of women mages? From Branvale, she had learned that in most European countries, on the rare occasions power transferred to a female, she was allowed to live. Although under rather strict rules, much like a troublesome noblewoman confined to a nunnery.

"Did you discuss me with Lord Branvale?" Sera seated herself upon the settee at an angle to the chaise.

A smile touched the other woman's lips, but her eyes remained cold and appraising. "At times, he would mention you and how you progressed."

If he complained of her feebleness, the contessa might not want Sera brewing her potion. Even though the previous failures had been no fault of hers, but due to Branvale's duplicity. "Since my former guardian is deceased, I thought to offer my abilities to provide for your needs." Sera chose her words carefully, to give the hint she knew what the potion did and, perhaps, to elicit more information.

"I may be interested in such a proposition. Do be seated, gentlemen." The contessa sat up and gestured to the settees.

Mr Miles sat next to Sera, the cushion bouncing up slightly under her as his weight sent his side down. Then he leaned on the arm and away from her, as though wanting to be next to her but not wanting to crowd her with his large presence.

Lieutenant Powers took the chair closest to the

contessa, and assumed control of the conversation. "I understand Lord Branvale dined here the night he died."

"Yes." The contessa extracted a black fan from under a pillow and snapped it open. With a lazy action, she fanned herself.

"What did you consume that evening?" The lieutenant extracted a notebook from a pocket and removed the tiny pencil hidden in its spine.

"I consume very little." She ran a hand down her slender torso. "But my chef will remember the dishes he prepared. My man will fetch the details of our menu that night." The contessa waved her fan at the footman stationed by the door and he nodded before disappearing through it.

Powers crossed his legs and balanced the notebook on his knee. "Was Lord Branvale a friend of yours?"

One black eyebrow arched. "I have few friends, and many associates. Does a person have to be an intimate *amico* to receive an invitation to dinner?"

The pencil tapped a page. "No. But it would help my investigation to know how you regarded him."

The fan resumed its motion and light glinted over a pattern painted in darkest grey on the black fabric. "I had not yet decided if he was a friend. Nor were we so close that I have shed tears over his departure from this earth."

Sera wondered if many shed tears at his parting. His family had decided on a private funeral and, given the suspicions cast her way, Sera would not attend. Afterward, she would pay her respects at his final resting place. Whatever her opinions of Branvale, he had still housed and fed her for thirteen years.

"What did you discuss that night?" The next question punctured the silence.

The contessa hummed as she thought before answering. "Many things. Politics. The care and maintenance of orchids."

Sera couldn't decide if the other woman was serious, or being facetious. Branvale had no interest in delicate house plants. Politics she could believe; he often voiced firm opinions about the working class of England. He believed them to be lazy, otherwise they would improve their lot in life.

Powers focused on the contessa's features. "How did the evening progress? Did you argue over anything?"

The woman's lush lips pulled thin for a moment. "You English see any disagreement as an argument. We exchanged opinions about a particular orchid, and such discourse turned...passionate."

Sera looked away and caught Mr Miles smiling at her. She did not want to think of her guardian and the word *passionate* in the same sentence. She hoped the contessa meant *passionate* in a different way, as in they argued violently. Otherwise, the images it conjured in her mind nearly turned her stomach. Imagining Branvale in an intimate embrace with the elegant woman struck Sera as unlikely as his becoming animated about a house plant. Sera had tended all the greenery in her former guardian's house. She doubted he'd ever known an aspidistra from a begonia.

Powers tapped the tiny pencil against the notebook. "What time did Lord Branvale leave?"

The contessa gestured in the air with a pale hand. "He dined early. Then, due to our disagreement, he left early. Around eleven, I believe."

"You're Italian, are you not?" Powers asked a rather obvious question given the contessa's title and her accent.

"Yes." The fan snapped shut against her palm.

The lieutenant glanced at the noblewoman as he scribbled a few words in his notebook. "Very clever poisoners, the Italians."

Contessa Ricci smiled and seemed to issue a challenge to Lieutenant Powers. "Yes. When we poison someone, nobody ever realises it. No student of Medici would be so careless as to use a detectable poison that resulted in an investigation."

"What would you use if you *were* so inclined?" Mr Miles leaned forward, his intense stare fixed on the contessa.

She laughed with a rich musical tone. "I cannot say. It is an old family secret."

The interview went in circles, rather like a formal dance. The footman returned and supplied a written menu from the night Branvale had dined under the contessa's roof.

They all rose, as though responding to an unheard cue. The contessa reached out and took Sera's hand with a surprisingly cool touch. "Perhaps we could discuss business another day, when the men are not present with their questions of poisons."

'I look forward to the opportunity to provide whatever you require," Sera murmured.

Laughter flashed in the older woman's eyes. "The potion will suffice."

While Sera pondered what that meant, the butler returned to show them to the door. Mr Miles extended his arm to Sera as they walked along the path.

"Well, that was interesting. We have an admitted Italian poisoner who argued with Branvale the night of his death. Can you match the stomach contents to the menu, Mr Miles?" Lieutenant Powers tugged on the hem of his jacket.

'I can try. We also need a better understanding of how quickly the poison worked to approximate when he ingested it." Mr Miles stared up at the house's exterior. "What I found most fascinating about the interview was the contessa herself. How long do you think she's been dead?"

"What?" Sera and the lieutenant said in unison.

"What do you mean, dead?" Powers also turned to stare back at the house, as though he could peel away the layers to reveal its occupant.

The surgeon explained his findings. 'She didn't breathe. The fan was excellent at making it harder to discern, and it took me several minutes to realise what struck me as odd about her. Then, I realised there was no rise and fall of her breast, nor did she draw any air into her lungs. Oh, she feigned a gasp at times when needed for dramatic effect, but she never exhaled it."

"She must be some type of Unnatural," Sera murmured. Then she looked over her shoulder. Unnaturals were excluded from society, and she didn't want to reveal the woman's secret to all her neighbours. She continued walking along the pavement, drawing the other gentlemen with her.

'Do you think she is recently deceased, that she has not yet rotted away?" Lieutenant Powers asked.

Mr Miles considered his answer. 'Decay follows death. It is inevitable, and how quickly it occurs depends on the weather. To stave off the natural process, she would have had to have died within the last few days. If so, she has adapted to her situation remarkably well. There was a pallor to her skin, but I am no expert in the use of feminine cosmetics. She might use powder or rouge to mimic a healthy skin tone."

'Of course!" Sera exclaimed and halted to turn to her companions. 'Branvale provided her with an odd potion, and I could never figure out its exact purpose. The other spells he brewed were obvious, such as erasing wrinkles or adding a sparkle to the eyes. This one had no other purpose except to *preserve*."

Mr Miles leaned closer to her with excitement burning in his gaze, and his unique scent, as warm as his personality, tickled Sera's nostrils. 'You think she slathers a preservative on her skin to stop the rot?"

'I cannot think what else she would use it for. Although it was such a small vial, hardly enough to smear over her entire body." Although they could only see the woman's face, who knew the state of her body under her clothing? Sera could brew a larger vat of the potion the contessa could bathe in to preserve her skin.

'If she is an Unnatural, do you know what sort?"

Lieutenant Powers dropped his voice, even though no one was within earshot.

Sera tried to recall what Branvale had taught her about Unnaturals and what little she had read in books. What type of creature was dead and yet remained ambulatory? Only one leapt to mind—the vampyre.

"Vampyre," Mr Miles murmured, reaching the same conclusion as Sera. "But they are immortal. They do not decay."

A horrible thought occurred to Sera, one that made more sense. "They dine on the blood of mortals. What if the preservative was not to keep her from decaying, but to stop blood from spoiling?"

Mr Miles rubbed the back of his neck. "Blood congeals once outside the body. She might make use of something to keep it fluid and warm. We could test the theory, if you could replicate the potion."

The lieutenant glanced from the surgeon to Sera. "While it is interesting that she is some sort of other-worldly creature, that is hardly proof of any involvement in Lord Branvale's death. Apart from the circumstantial facts we have ascertained."

"The contessa said she did not consume much. Being already dead, any poison lurking in a dish might have a negligible effect on her constitution. What better way to put your victim at ease than by eating from the same plate?" Mr Miles mused aloud.

An old memory niggled at the back of Sera's mind, but it hid when she tried to look directly at it. "Branvale harboured strong feelings about Unnaturals. He saw them as beneath the feet of the lowest Englishman.

What if that caused their argument and the contessa lashed out and poisoned his coffee?"

'If he held such beliefs about Unnaturals, is it not odd that he dined with one on a regular basis?" Lieutenant Powers fell into step on the other side of Sera as they continued along the street.

'Possibly he did not notice that she failed to breathe?" Mr Miles suggested. 'I only noticed because I have made a study of the human condition."

Sera combed through her memories for more about Branvale's prejudices against Unnaturals and the odd potion he brewed. The memory she sought would surface in its own good time. The more she tried to force it into the open, the more it burrowed under other memories. 'I suspect his dislike of Unnaturals was at war with his love of money. The contessa paid handsomely for her potion."

Once Sera established her reputation, similar opportunities would open up with which she could supplement her finances.

'You, my friend, have much to do," Lieutenant Powers said to the surgeon. 'I need to know if the menu matches what you found in Lord Branvale's stomach. If I might request Lady Winyard's help—are you able to replicate the potion he brewed for the contessa?" Powers gestured to a side road that led them back to the main thoroughfare.

'If I had his potion ledger, yes. But I suspect the Mage Council might have seized it." However, one of the ledgers she had retrieved with Elliot had, at first glance, appeared to be pages of nonsense. Lines of tight script in a sort of code made from symbols, letters, and numbers marched across each page. With time, she might be able to decipher it.

'I shall ask them if they hold such a ledger. Returning to another topic, dashed odd talk about house plants and orchids. What do you make of that?"

It had also struck Sera as unusual. 'Lord Branvale had no interest in flora or fauna. The plants and the sole orchid in his house were under my care. Creating a warm spell around the orchid was one of my first successes." It had delighted her to finally craft the exact humid climate the delicate plant required, and have the spell sustain itself. Her reward came when the plant revealed its luminescent white flowers.

'Perhaps it was a jest, or some private joke between them?" The lieutenant hailed a carriage and stood by the door.

Who knew? The dead told no tales. Or could Sera elicit more information from the contessa on her next visit? She needed more information about vampyres before then, but that required gaining access to the restricted area of the mage library. She wanted to curl her hands into fists. So much knowledge she required was held by the Mage Council, all of them maddeningly tight-fisted with it.

'Have you had a chance to examine the sample?" Mr Miles asked.

After her experience in the East End this morning, she needed to replenish her magical reserves to tackle that task. 'Not yet. I shall undertake that tomorrow."

'Once I know when Lord Branvale was poisoned,

the hand responsible will reveal itself." Powers stroked his goatee and looked back along the road. At least he hadn't stared at Sera when he said it.

'I look forward to discussing your findings with you." Mr Miles raised her gloved hand and kissed her knuckles as she climbed into the carriage and took her seat.

Sera rubbed her hand as she watched their retreating figures. Blocked drains, vampyres, orchids, and a chaste kiss. The day had proven rather eventful. Whatever would tomorrow bring?

'Blast!" Tomorrow was Abigail's soirée. In the rush of the last two days, it had quite slipped Sera's mind. 'What on earth will I wear?"

For her first foray into society, Sera wanted to meet her friend's high expectations. Luckily she possessed magic and would play her own fairy godmother to provide a suitable gown. A small tingle of excitement raced through her at the thought of the evening, followed by a sad note that Mr Miles would not be attending.

Although it would probably be better to discuss anything she discovered about the sample in private, rather than over dinner. Abigail would not approve of such a topic of conversation. Elliot would be able to find out where the surgeon lived. Then she could call upon *him* for a change.

SIXTEEN

Sera spent a quiet evening before an enchanted fire throwing blue and silver flames. She plotted with Elliot, Rosie, and Vicky about the evening she would hold to entertain her new neighbours. They divided up tasks. All she needed now was for Mother Nature to cooperate and not rain on their event. By the time she retired to her bedroom, her limbs were heavy but her mind light from all she had achieved.

The next day, Sera read aloud the lead article in the newspaper over breakfast in the cosy kitchen with the others.

LORD TOMLIN DELIGHTS *London with his Thames spectacle. The powerful mage transformed the river into a silver and purple road upon which the fish danced.*

. . .

SHE SNORTED and tossed the paper to the table. A pointless feat that had probably caused damage to the fish. To add insult to injury, the newspaper hadn't printed a single word about her unblocking the drain in the East End.

"The people know what you did, Sera. That spreads quicker and farther by word of mouth than any article printed that most folks can't read anyhow." Rosie collected the empty plates and carried them to the bench.

"I suppose you're right." Certainly those she'd spoken to yesterday were grateful for her efforts. But a little official recognition would have been nice.

Sera left the table to gather up a few items and then headed to the rear of her house. She delighted in one feature of her somewhat shabby town house—it possessed a strip of garden. Long, narrow, and neglected, it presented an opportunity to create whatever small oasis she wanted. Already in her mind, she imagined a rill of water running its entire length. Next, she would plant ferns and a spreading tree. In the shade would be pretty snowdrops, bluebells, and aquilegia in soft pink and deepest purple.

For today, she sat cross-legged on a blanket on the scruffy grass. As a priority, she should figure out a dirt-repelling spell to apply to all her skirts. Vicky sighed every time she returned to the house with grass stains on her behind. At least the friendship she'd struck up with the local women meant her laundry now went to the capable Bernadette, but if her gowns were impervious to dirt, the bill would be less.

In her lap were two items—a sheet of plain paper and a twisted length of fabric. She unwound the fabric to reveal the copper bracelet. Picking it up between two fingers, Sera held it to the light. Red flashes caressed the carved tree, and it seemed to shake its leaves at her.

"What are you?" she murmured as she considered it.

Whatever magic it contained had burrowed into her body and suppressed or drained her magic. Her ability had been wrapped in tiny silver shackles from the very first day of her apprenticeship. As she turned the bracelet this way and that, a blue line drifted across the surface and congealed where she held it. A gossamer thread, like that pulled from a spiderweb, wriggled free of the copper and waved at her fingers. Even now, it sought a way back into her body.

Sera used the cloth to change her hold, and the thread drooped like a sad puppy. Something about the bracelet bothered her—apart from the fact Branvale had snapped it around her wrist and it had grown into her body. It simply didn't feel like him. In fact, it hadn't felt magical at all. How had she worn it for all those years and never suspected that an ensorcelled bracelet sapped her ability?

Magical items emitted a faint resonance, similar to the way some items smelled. Whenever she was near a spell, mage, or enchanted object, a tickle would brush over her skin. But even as she watched the strands explore the edges of the metal, the bracelet gave off no emissions to hint at the spell cast over it.

She had lived under Branvale's roof for thirteen

years, and for most of that time had seen him cast on an almost daily basis. Each mage manifested their magic in a slightly different way. While her guardian had crafted a few amulets for clients, he had never displayed any affinity for working with metals. The spreading tree etched in copper had a delicacy to its branches and leaves unlike anything she'd ever seen Branvale draw. The more Sera stared at the bracelet, the more convinced she became that someone other than Lord Branvale had created it.

But who? And had they known it would be used on a child?

They must have, for it had grown along with her.

It seemed most likely that Branvale had acquired or purchased it from another mage. His assurance that it was a pretty piece to calm her feelings of homesickness was clearly a falsehood. He had known exactly what it would do once it came in contact with her skin. What bothered her was whether he had acted alone, or in concert with another?

"You are a mystery that I will uncover," she murmured to the bracelet as she wrapped it in the scarf again and tied the end in a knot.

Putting aside the scarf, she turned her attention to the blank piece of paper.

Breaking another mage's spells was tricky business. Whatever Branvale had been about, she would find the truth. Ideally she wanted the entire sequence of any secret correspondence Branvale had conducted. It would be too much to hope for each entry on the page to be dated. She needed a spell that would reveal the most recent impression on the page, and then work backward in time to give her both sides of the conversation.

Whatever Branvale's shortcomings, at least he had schooled her in the basics of casting—magic, mind, and matter. His process had failed Sera. Her mind and magic had rebelled against the shapes and rules followed by the Mage Council. She had to start over. Now that she and her magic were free, they had to find their own path.

As she sat on the grass, she found that nature whispered to her. Barefoot, having left her stockings and shoes inside, Sera wiggled her toes in the grass.

A tingle surged up her foot, as though she created a connection between her magic and the earth. Yes, this was her way, drawing on the surrounding elements to weave into her spells. Sera leaned on what Branvale had taught her, but adapted it. In her mind, she visualised what she wanted to achieve. Next, she considered the material she had to work with—the paper, which came from trees. Last, she whispered to the power coursing through the soles of her feet and into her veins, and asked for its help to bring about the desired result.

Words formed in her mind and she laid her palms against the paper, clasping it before her as she whispered, 'What has been erased will be revealed. I will discover what has been concealed."

The paper vibrated in her hand, but when she peered at it, the sheet remained blank.

'Blast." She had hoped for an instant result. She drew a breath and set aside any niggling doubts, any thoughts of failure. The spell would work, but she asked a complex task of her gift, and it merely needed time to unravel the ensorcellment embedded in the paper. "I shall put you in a safe place and check on you tomorrow."

Gathering up the items and shaking out the blanket, she returned to the house. Her safe place for the page was a locked box in the linen cupboard. She doubted many criminals would go fossicking among clean sheets and towels for valuables. While she trusted her loyal staff, she made no assumptions about her enemies and the Mage Council. For all she knew, her house had been chosen deliberately because of some secret entrance they could use to spy upon her. Nor was she so arrogant as to think no one could breach her wards, if they were determined enough.

Her next task was to discover what lurked in the greenish-black muck stuck to the sides of a small vial. She retrieved the glass container and took it to the study that overlooked the desolate garden. The room had a desk and chair before the window, and one wall held an empty built-in bookcase. Over time, she would transform the space, but it would serve her purposes for now.

"Doing witchy stuff?" Elliot stopped in the open door.

"Yes. I'm going to figure out what substance in this vial killed Branvale." She held the vial up for the footman's inspection.

Elliot screwed up his face. "Looks as nasty as him. Do you want some tea while you experiment?"

"Yes, please. Could I also have an old saucer and a knife that won't be missed?" She smiled to herself as she took a seat. Elliot continued to treat her like a kitchen maid, or his sister. Her elevated position made no difference to him. She enjoyed his company and thought that in the years to come, his manner would keep her feet on the ground. There would be no chance to develop an inflated sense of self with the cheeky footman handy to burst any illusions of grandeur.

To begin, she rolled the vial around as she held it to the light and observed how the thick matter moved and changed colour. Then she reached out with her magic and poked it with a gentle touch. While she had read about magical poisons in a book, this was her first actual experience with one. Mr Miles had suggested the main poison was either arsenic or derived from a mushroom. She would tackle that element first, then move on to discovering any spell infused with it.

She was still rolling the fluid around in the vial when Elliot returned with a tea tray, at one end of which was an old, plain saucer and a knife. "I'm never touching those again once you finish with them."

"Oh, Elliot, I would never poison you. Not when there are so many more interesting ways I could kill you." Sera grinned and put the saucer and utensil to one side.

He placed the teapot, teacup, and saucer on the opposite end of the desk. Then he tucked the empty tray under his arm. "I could have taken a job as a footman in a big fancy house, you know."

She furrowed her brow and nodded solemnly. "Yes.

202

Where you would stand around all day in uncomfortable livery and be treated like, well...a servant." She lowered her tone on the last two words and shuddered.

He huffed a quiet laugh and then waggled his eyebrows at her. "Do you need me to break into any houses tonight?"

"No. I need you to ensure we have everything necessary for our evening with our neighbours. Do you think you could find some musicians and order the ale?"

He grinned and tapped the side of his nose. "Leave it to me."

Elliot departed, whistling as he went.

Sera suspected the street would be turned temporarily into a tavern, but the entertainment would, hopefully, settle her into the neighbourhood. Alone again, Sera opened the vial, ensuring she pointed it away from her nose. Then she pushed the knife into the opening and caught a blob of the mess on its tip. Corking the vial again, she smeared the fluid over the bottom of the saucer, spreading it thin as though it were the last tiny bit of butter on her toast.

Next, she considered how to tackle the problem before her. One, or possibly two, substances comprised the base of the poison: arsenic or the death cap mushroom. Both were natural elements—the one found in rocks and soil, the other a plant.

"I can do this," she muttered. Mother Nature smiled on her only daughter among the English mages and would guide her work.

She closed her eyes and held out her hand over the saucer. For years, she had worked backward to pick out the ingredients of Branvale's potions. Rather like a cook tasting a meal, she relied on her senses to separate the elements that danced over her tongue. Or, in this case, across her palm.

"Aha!" She recognised a deep, earthy presence. Buoyed by her success, she focused on the other sensations tickling her skin. None had the solid, bitter signature of rock. Then she dug deeper. Arsenic could come from soil, and that would register as earthy as a mushroom might.

Among the fluid's ingredients, her magic brushed up against a single speck of earthiness, but of what type? Closing her eyes, Sera reached out again and let her magic flow around the dot, awaken it, and invite it into a conversation. After a few moments of concentration, an image burst into her mind that left her in no doubt as to the foundation of the poison—a tall, pale mushroom with a modest domed top.

"Death cap," she whispered as she opened her eyes.

Branvale had been poisoned with the same fungi that had taken the life of Emperor Claudius in Roman times and, far more recently, that of the Holy Roman Emperor Charles VI in 1740. Could Branvale's death have been a terrible accident, like that of Charles VI? The emperor had consumed a dish of sautéed mushrooms that had changed the destiny of Europe following his death. Mistaken for a harmless relative, the mushroom had led to the War of the Austrian Succession.

Innocent side dish or deliberate murder? To answer her question, Sera had to determine if magic had twisted the mushroom's toxicity in order to take her guardian's life.

"I can do this," she said out loud to encourage herself. She only had to figure out how to tease aside any magic in the sample before her. She took a sip of cooling tea to revive herself before starting anew.

Sera angled the saucer to allow light from the window to play over the smear. There was so little to analyse, but in that rested her advantage over the other mages. She delighted in working on a small scale, because little things underpinned bigger things. Most mages, in her experience, seemed to ignore the tiny elements in their spells to concentrate on the larger overall effect. Like turning the whole of the Thames purple.

She cupped the saucer in her hands and let the contents simmer in her magic as though it sat upon a stove. All the while, her gift danced over the scant amount of matter. With a light touch, she sought to peel back the layers to find anything darker hiding within.

A wisp of unfamiliar magic rose from the dish, and Sera encircled it with a gentle touch to guide the cloud into an empty vial. "Got you." She stoppered the vial and wrapped magic around the glass to keep the other spell contained.

Setting aside the saucer, she turned her focus to the second bottle. She had captured a tiny burst of smoke. Dark green, it spun in the container and brushed against the glass sides. Someone had ensorcelled the poison to alter its effect. But how, and would she discover something that exonerated her, or served to convince others of her guilt?

She turned the vial over and over in her fingers, noting that the green wisp danced in the opposite direction. Once again, she let her magic encircle it. Branvale had taught her that each mage's magic felt different. The spells they cast embodied a speck of their personality or physical presence that served as a type of signature. Over a period of years, she had become familiar with the unique essence of Branvale that resided in his castings and potions. Whoever had cast this particular spell was someone she didn't know. Not too surprising, since she worked only with Branvale.

That raised more questions in her mind—had a fellow mage poisoned Branvale, or had they merely supplied the potion mixed with his meal? That was something for Lieutenant Powers to determine. Sera focused on what type of spell the wisp represented.

Rather than forcing the mist to reveal its true nature, Sera instead invited it to dance with her. Her magic and the green wisp of smoke twisted around one another, forming shapes and contortions within the confines of the vial. As she worked, the green fog changed colour to a deeper shade of teal.

"I see you." Sera swallowed a gasp, disconnected from the swirl, and set it on the desk.

At its core, the spell contained an accelerant and an amplifier. An unknown hand had magnified the toxic effects of the mushroom, bending time so that effects that should have taken days occurred within a few hours. Relief flooded her and her head sagged over the desk. This cleared her of involvement. There could have been only a matter of hours between Branvale's ingesting whatever had contained the poison and his death.

She needed to tell Mr Miles of her findings. A flicker of warmth flared into life inside her at that idea. Sera picked up the teacup and slurped the remaining liquid, only to find it cold. The clock struck out in the hallway and reminded her of the passage of time. Her stomach rumbled, to further highlight the amount of time the analysis had taken—far longer than she had expected. Absorbed in the sample, she had failed to notice the sun moving across the sky. The time had come for her to begin the transformation from a kitchen maid into a noblewoman dressed for an evening of high-society company with Lady Abigail Crawley.

With a gesture, she collected the smeared sample from the old saucer and directed it back into its vial. Next, the knife and saucer would need to be disposed of in a way that didn't put anybody or anything at risk. Sera glanced at her fingertips. She also needed to bathe and scrub her skin, in case any trace of poison lingered from her work.

Abigail would never forgive her if she poisoned her other dinner guests.

SEVENTEEN

Making herself presentable took longer than teasing the secret from the poison. First Sera had to be scrubbed, again, in lavender- and rose-scented water. Then Rosie and Vicky layered her in a clean chemise, petticoats, and stays. Sera didn't yet have the resources to acquire an expensive gown. Instead, she would enhance the one given to her by the Napiers for her birthday.

With her gift, she wrapped the green striped silk in a climbing vine. The plant started at the hem and spiralled around the outer skirt. Leaves with a faint glimmer spilled over the fabric. On the stomacher and petticoat front, tiny pearl-like blooms nestled among the foliage.

Vicky piled her hair high in the current fashion and then placed a bract of vine among her locks. Both Rosie and the maid stood back to survey their work.

"Oh, you look like something from a fairy tale."

Rosie placed one hand on her chest and her eyes misted with tears.

"Right beautiful you are, milady," Vicky agreed.

"You exaggerate, but I thank you for the compliment." Sera glanced in the mirror. The gown suited her and enveloped her in a sense of confidence. She would never consider herself beautiful. Her face was too sharp and her temper too quick for such a word. But her overall appearance would reflect well on Abigail, and that was what mattered most.

She descended the stairs to find Elliot standing by the front door. His square jaw dropped a fraction.

"Do I look passable?" she asked as she brushed a hand over the skirt.

Elliot shrugged and held out her cloak to drape over her shoulders. "Hard to believe only yesterday you smelt like an open sewer and looked like a beggar who had been dragged backward through a hedge."

Sera smacked his arm as he held open the door. "Why do I keep you around again?"

"Because I keep you modest. Branvale had the biggest head, just like all them other mages. Think they're special just because they can, you know..." He wiggled his fingers in the air.

"I appreciate your ceaseless efforts to keep my sense of self under control." She peered out into the street at the waiting carriage. Abigail had insisted on sending one to collect her, almost as though she thought her friend might change her mind.

"I'm going to need you to increase my pay with all

these extra duties I perform for you. I'm not a charity, you know," he said as he escorted her to the carriage.

Good humour washed through Sera as the vehicle jolted when the horses set off. Day by day, she took control of her life and fashioned it into what she wanted for herself. Worries nibbled at the corner of her mind, trying to erode her contentment. What if the council managed to change the legislation and dragged her back under a guardian? Or worse, what if no one believed what she had discovered about the poison and they interred her at the Repository of Forgotten Things?

"Take each day as it comes," she murmured. Then she found a smile to place on her face. Abigail would be displeased if her student failed to shine tonight.

The carriage rolled to a stop outside the Crawley family home. A footman in livery opened the door and held out his hand to assist her down. Sera took a moment to take in the majesty and beauty of the house. Its simple lines oozed elegance. Every window was ablaze with light, no doubt courtesy of Abigail's mage grandfather, Lord Rowan. Sera knew little about the oldest mage except that in his late seventies, he had stepped down from his role as Speaker of the Mage Council to concentrate on his academic studies.

Taking a breath and steeling her spine, Sera walked toward the open door and her first foray into society. Kneeling at the feet of the monarchs didn't count. That experience had been more akin to a noble girl showing off a porcelain doll to her friends.

Abigail, clad in a cream silk gown that reminded

Sera of the understated elegance of the house, greeted her guest.

"Lady Winyard, how delighted I am to welcome you to our home." Abigail took Sera's hands and kissed her cheeks.

"Lady Abigail, it was kind of you to invite me," Sera murmured.

With their arms linked, Abigail escorted Sera through to the drawing room and the cluster of noble gentlemen and scattering of ladies. Abigail made the introductions, and names and faces swam before Sera's eyes. She took to invisibly crafting a label with the person's name that hovered above their head so she could keep them all straight.

"This is Lord Loburn." Abigail gestured to a tall, slender man with a bookish look about him. Before the individual could speak, Abigail swept Sera farther into the room. "He is a marquess. However, neither his title nor his fortune make up for the fact that he is frightfully dull. I had to include him this evening. Father insisted."

Sera didn't think anyone whose hands appeared bereft without a book could be dull, and Lord Loburn had flashed a shy smile before they diverted their path around him. They continued around the room, Abigail offering snippets about each person attending her soirée.

"Lord Mercer is a most excellent catch. His father is an earl and in poor health. He is well regarded in society and is rather fine to gaze upon," Abigail murmured in Sera's ear.

Sera stared at her friend. "You sound like a matron deciding at which man to throw your daughter."

Abigail beamed. "Why, of course! I have your best interests at heart. That is why I have invited a number of gentlemen who would be willing to allow you to fulfil your duties to the Mage Council. Others I had to discard as they simply baulked at the idea of a wife...*working*. But I do think we need to make an exception in your case, as repugnant as the idea might be."

Bile surged up Sera's throat, and she stared at the men around her with a different perspective. The evening was a thinly disguised marriage market, and she the prize exhibit. Would Abigail issue the men paddles with which to bid on her later in the evening?

How to gently brush aside her friend's endeavours without hurting her feelings? "Abigail, while I appreciate your efforts, I am not ready to consider such a thing as marriage."

Abigail patted her hand. "Of course you don't need to make a decision right now." Short-lived relief burst through Sera. "Over dessert you can indicate whom you prefer, and we can finalise the candidate in private later."

"Ah, the murderess is among us," one man said, to a titter of laughter.

Before Sera could fling an angry retort, Abigail glared at the individual. "I will have no unfounded accusations under my roof, Sir Reginald. You will mind your tongue or take your leave."

With a broad face and equally broad torso, Sir Reginald resembled a block of wood. From his comment, he obviously possessed the intellect of a tree stump, too. 'I will mind my tongue if Lady Winyard minds her fingers. Those more knowledgeable than I say a woman mage poses a risk to us all."

'Ignorance, which you have in abundance, is a far greater danger," a familiar voice replied, but his was not the one who made warmth rush through Sera.

Laughter erupted, aimed at Sir Roust, who flushed and stared at the drink in his hand.

Arwyn Fitzfey stood in the doorway, resplendent in silver and pale green. His blond hair shimmered like spun gold, and even Sera admitted his legs were well displayed in his silk stockings. A collective sigh heaved through many of those present as the half-Fae approached. He took Sera's hand and bowed over it. 'Lady Winyard."

"Yet again you leap to my defence, Lord Fitzfey." Sera smiled at the king's bastard, then glanced over his shoulder to drop a dead fly from the chandelier into Sir Reginald's glass as he took a sip. She choked back a laugh as he swallowed and gagged.

'I could not imagine a more noble cause. Your quest to serve England is symbolic of the struggle of all women and working-class men who wish to be acknowledged in our society." His attention remained fixed on her, even as two women tugged at his sleeve.

Sera had no intention of being a symbol. Nor did she wish to be a martyr. She simply wanted control of her life. 'I intend to conduct myself with honesty and hope my hard work will speak for itself."

Abigail clapped her hands, possibly before the conversation veered too far into politics. "Let us go through to dinner. Lord Loburn, will you accompany Lady Winyard?" Lord Fitzfey offered Abigail his arm.

The marquess, as the highest-ranking man save Fitzfey, presented his arm to Sera while the others jostled for position behind them. "I believe, Lady Winyard, that you will be a breath of fresh air through the Mage Council. Too long have those men been shut up in their tower with musty old ideas and practices."

To think Abigail called him dull when he shared her view of the council. Sera found an insightful dinner partner in the marquess that sparked a lively discourse. Much of the conversation at the table skimmed over Sera. She had no experience of the balls or soirées they dissected, nor did she know the individuals served up for criticism.

As another course was cleared away and more plates presented, some of the talk touched on the uprisings in France and America. These then led to a discussion as to whether there should be a loosening of rights in England.

"All Englishmen, men and women, should be given the vote and an equal say in the governance of our land," Arwyn said.

"Steady on, Fitzfey," Lord Mercer said from farther along the table. "Some might support suffrage for men, but women cannot be allowed to vote. Their minds are better occupied with housekeeping and child-rearing. Besides, they would need to be guided by their husbands or fathers, which would only result in a duplicate vote and a waste of time and effort."

Some men murmured their agreement.

"Most women have more sense than these useless bucks," Lord Loburn muttered under his breath.

Sera agreed with him. Kitty would run intellectual circles around any man at the table except, perhaps, her dinner partner. "Who says women cannot take an active role in politics and understand the surrounding matters? We have only to look at our queen to find refutation of that notion. I assure you, gentlemen, women are quite capable of learning about any number of topics, not solely those of housekeeping and child-rearing."

"Quite so, Lady Winyard. I believe you have quite a touch with horticulture?" As hostess, Abigail directed the conversation back to a more ladylike topic.

Gardening wasn't quite the same as taking an active role in society, but there was a certain freedom in imagining gardens and forests she could one day nurture into life, which would endure for centuries. "My magic has an affinity for nature, and I do confess to enjoying time spent in a garden."

"My orchid could do with a magic touch. It seems rather dull and has failed to flourish. Blasted thing is so temperamental. I am either too solicitous or not solicitous enough," Lord Mercer muttered into his wine.

Sera wondered if raising orchids was some new hobby among the fashionable set. Certainly, the blooms could be seen as a sign of wealth, with their rare beauty and sensitivity to temperature.

"Perhaps I could help, Lord Mercer? I was rather successful in coaxing Lord Branvale's orchid into bloom." The gentlemen stared at one another. One snorted into his glass, another had a coughing fit, and Lord Mercer went a shade of pink not dissimilar to the flower under discussion.

While Sera had lived a restricted life under Branvale, it was not a sheltered one. She had a wide range of servants as her family and conversed with the tradesmen and merchants who flowed in and out of their door. From the men's reaction, she realised she had made a fundamental blunder.

"Ah," she said, setting down her wine. "You are not referring to the plant at all. It is now upon one of you gentlemen to educate me, so I do not make such a mistake in the future."

They all stared at each other, nonplussed, but none answered. Then Lord Loburn cleared his throat. "As you might have discerned, an *orchid* is not a plant, but a particular type of woman."

"It is a way of referring to a mistress?" If so, it was a clever code word to allow them to discuss such a topic at dinner without censure from the ladies present. Although from the scowl on Abigail's face, the topic would not be allowed to continue.

Lord Loburn frowned. "*Mistress* is too crass a word for this type of woman. She is noble, unspoiled, an ingénue, if you will. Having fallen on difficult times, she is cared for by a wealthy gentleman. Such gentlewomen, unused to the hardships of the world, require a specific environment in which to thrive."

"You mean like a ward, then?" It was not uncommon for a wealthy man to take over the care and education of a noble woman bereft of her family.

Lord Loburn flashed an embarrassed smile. 'A ward could became an orchid when she reached a certain age, and if she so desired. For there is a difference in the type of relationship."

Given the flustered look of Lord Loburn and the way in which the other men found the contents of their plates fascinating, Sera suspected the difference between a ward and an orchid was...intimate relations. Which sounded exactly like a mistress to her. But men perceived some nuanced difference, and certainly not all wards were preyed upon by their guardians.

"Thank you, Lord Loburn, that has cleared up the topic for me." He really was helpful and reminded her somewhat of a young Mr Napier. Intelligence burned in his eyes and he seemed willing to help without resorting to being condescending about it.

The information swirled in Sera's head as she applied it to a previous conversation. Contessa Ricci and Lord Branvale hadn't argued about a *plant* over dinner. They had argued about the treatment of a *young woman*. But which of them kept the delicate *orchid*? And had one of them stooped to murder to keep their secret?

Given what she knew of Branvale, Sera simply couldn't imagine him cosseting a young woman. Certainly neither she nor his children had received such tender care. That left Contessa Ricci—a vampyre who would require someone to sustain her. What if that noble woman kept a few such *orchids* to meet her needs? Given Branvale's views on Unnaturals, what if he had discovered her *greenhouse* and demanded an end to it? What if he had threatened to notify the authorities?

Scenarios spilled over in Sera's mind, and every one of them cleared her of any suspicion of murder.

She needed to talk to Lieutenant Powers and Mr Miles. Tomorrow, of course. She couldn't exactly storm out of Abigail's house and go in search of them.

Dinner ended and everyone adjourned to the drawing room for the anticipated highlight of the evening—Abigail would sing. She could have toured the world enchanting audiences, but her parents preferred to keep her talent shut away from the public. They thought it made her more valuable, like an expensive jewel hidden in a vault and only shown to a select few.

Chairs were arranged facing the pianoforte. Sera took a seat in the front row. Abigail stood with one hand resting lightly on the instrument while the woman who would play took her seat. Shuffles and coughs fell into silence as everyone waited. A few opening chords on the pianoforte drifted across the audience, and then Abigail began to sing.

Sera recognised neither the song nor the words as they washed over her. But they wrapped around her and tugged on her senses. She closed her eyes, each note and syllable almost like a physical caress. Her friend sang of love that flowed through each person. The first stirrings of attraction so like spring.

218

Of their own volition, Sera's hands moved, and she constructed a meadow. As love erupted between the couple, she crafted bright green leaves on the surrounding trees. Lush grass waved with the tune. Then the relationship deepened into the passion of summer and the field burst into riotous wildflowers of intense orange, deep blue, and stunning pink. The song continued to soar, as love matured into the seed heads and textures of autumn. As the performance reached its crescendo, one of the lovers drew their last breath. Sorrow blanketed the land in winter snow and the world stilled.

As the songstress held the last note, the field shimmered and vanished like mist under the sun. The guests leapt to their feet, applauding Abigail, then they turned to clap for Sera. Buoyed by their praise, Sera curtseyed and gave a glad smile to her friend.

What a success! The night would be the talk of London for days.

Conversation swelled as the guests discussed what they had witnessed and how Sera's magic had brought the song to life. People clustered around her, marvelling at how she wrought flowers and trees from thin air and made them dance and sway to the music. Sera answered questions as best she could until her throat protested and the clock chimed two in the morning. With a yawn, she declared it time to seek her bed and replenish her magic.

Abigail linked arms with her once more as they walked to the front door. But in the tiled entrance, once the footman had rushed to signal the carriage driver, her friend rounded on her. Her eyes glistened with unshed tears. "How *could* you, Sera?"

"How could I what?" What terrible *faux pas* had she committed? Over dinner, she had made sure to watch which item of cutlery her friend picked up first, and she'd eaten nothing with her fingers.

Oh. Had it been the talk of *orchids*?

"You stole my moment with your *flowers*." Abigail placed one hand on her forehead and turned to face the wall. "And not the wretched orchids, either."

Sera's stomach plummeted. Never had she wanted to hurt Abigail's feelings. "I—I'm sorry. Your song so moved me, I couldn't help but create the imagery you inspired. Your guests were enchanted and, I think, it enhanced the spectacle for them."

"You were certainly a spectacle." A harsh tone skated over the last word. Abigail turned back, her face composed but her features stiff.

Sera managed to swallow a defensive reply. "Please forgive me, Abigail. I am not much used to company and was carried away in the moment." The words grated over her tongue, but she managed to say them.

Her friend nodded, satisfied with the apology. "Very well, we shall say no more of it. I know you are not used to being in refined company and you were probably keen for some attention." Then she patted Sera's arm. "This shows how much you need someone at your side, who, being older and more worldly, can direct your efforts and tell you when you may, or may not, use your magic."

Sera stared at her friend, stunned. The impact of

what she'd said hit as hard as any blow by a boxer. *To be told when she might use her magic?* That sounded like the worst sort of prison sentence.

No. She most certainly would not be governed by anybody.

Not even a friend who was supposed to love her.

EIGHTEEN

After a solid night's sleep, Sera didn't rouse until midmorning. Having wandered down the stairs in her robe to seek a cup of hot chocolate, she discovered her plans to find Mr Miles and Lieutenant Powers disrupted by the yellow light creeping from under the lid of the mage correspondence box. Within rested another assignment issued by the council.

Westbourne Green. Mr Parker. Ten o'clock this morning.

She knew little of the area to the west of London, apart from the fact that it was pastoral. Something to do with sheep, perhaps? Her attention wandered to the small clock on the mantel, and she hurriedly pushed back the chair. The clock's hands stood only a few minutes from ten. She would barely have time to dress before the carriage collected her.

"Vicky!" she called as she dashed up the stairs, tugging off her robe on the way.

With the maid's help, and a little magic, she was dressed in her clean riding habit of plain green wool as the clock struck. While society expected ladies never to be outside without a parasol, Sera had work to do, and a delicate umbrella would be an impediment. A hat would suffice, assuming the wind didn't tug the ribbons loose. Fortunately, she possessed a practical and unadorned straw hat, which she tied firmly under her chin.

Elliot flung open the door as the carriage rolled to a halt outside. Yet again, the Mage Council treated her like the unwanted bastard at the dinner table. The carriage they sent was old, and with chipped and peeling paint. A dent on one side of the wood suggested the driver had had an altercation with another carriage...or possibly a charging bull.

She plastered a smile on her face and took the offered hand to help her inside. The smile stayed in place even as she surveyed the moth-eaten curtains and thin cushions on the seats.

"This will only make me stronger," she muttered under her breath as she sat.

With nothing to do on the journey, she closed her eyes and travelled inside her body. With each day, her magic coursed more loudly through her veins. Voices in ancient tongues whispered of the things she could do. She wanted to gather the power to her and blast it out. But Londoners wouldn't appreciate her exploding anything in the city. Not to mention that expending a great deal of energy could make her exhausted for days, or in extreme cases, render her unconscious.

Through the fringes of the city they travelled and out past Hyde Park. The view outside her window was pretty, with its rolling fields, abundance of wild flowers, and grazing sheep. The carriage halted at the edge of a meadow. Three men were clustered to one side, one leaning on a shepherd's crook.

They openly stared as she descended from the carriage, and she wondered if, during her contemplations, she had sprouted another head.

"Mr Parker?" she enquired of them. The driver the Mage Council sent had stopped at this particular meadow. Surely he knew where to deposit her. Was this some sort of prank?

The man with the crook glanced at his companions, shrugged, and approached her with a wary look in his eye. "Aye. That's me."

"I am Lady Seraphina Winyard, sent by the Mage Council." Distrust and disinterest were her two constant companions. No one believed her capable of the tasks set her. She was too young, too female, too untested.

"Is he coming, then?" Mr Parker peered around her, as though waiting for someone else to step from the shabby carriage.

"Who?" Sera drew a deep breath and keep her tone measured, while inside she balled her fists in frustration.

"The mage we asked for," he said slowly and with a tone similar to the one used to talk to a simple child.

"I am the mage the council has sent to assist you."

She laced her fingers together in front of her stomach, and a ripple of power sparked over her knuckles.

"Women can't be mages. That's a man's job," one of the other men said, and moved to stand at his companion's shoulder.

"Contrary to what people are told, men and women have equal ability when it comes to magic. What women mages have lacked is the opportunity," she said as clearly and politely as she could.

Three men now frowned at her. This wasn't going the way she planned. Mr Mulvaney in the East End had readily accepted her help. Of course, he had been trying to turn back a rising tide of sewage, not enjoying a sunlit meadow.

She tried a different tactic. "Don't let my exterior bother you. I wield as much magic as my older masculine counterparts. Try not to think of me as a woman, but as a mage."

Doubt remained etched on their faces. This would need a practical demonstration. What to conjure? She took inspiration from her surroundings.

Sera created the creature in her mind, then let the magic flow around the image before she began to mould it with her hands. Silvery strands formed in the air and gathered together. Within a few seconds, a shimmering crystal horse stomped in the meadow, his body transparent, but jewel-like. When he shook his mane, music tinkled across the field.

The men gasped. "She can do magic!" one exclaimed, and he nudged his companions in case they couldn't see the magnificent horse.

Not satisfied with her creation, Sera continued to work. She added wings. The crystal horse neighed and flapped them. Then he reared up and leapt into the air. With a few powerful downstrokes of his wings, the horse flew upward. He circled the field before spiralling higher into the sky to transform above them as a rainbow that shot back down to earth.

Sera stared at the trio. Waiting.

The dumbstruck look remained on Mr Parker's face, but he remembered his manners enough to slide the cap from his hair and bow his head to her. "Well, I'll be. Pardon me, milady, but we've been asking the Mage Council for help for months now. Never thought they would send help at all, even if...well..."

She smiled, knowing exactly how he probably felt. With each task set her, she was finding her reception to be the same. The common folk had asked for assistance, only to be ignored. Now the council sent them the upstart girl. Except Sera intended to pervert their plan. The Mage Council thought to humiliate her by placing her among the working class. Instead, she helped the people who needed it the most and found an immense sense of satisfaction in what she did.

Now that she had eased some of their doubts, they could get down to work. "How can I assist? And what a glorious place you have here. How I long to be surrounded by such beautiful fields."

A smile of pride flashed over Mr Parker's face. "The fields would be much better if not for the chafer grub. It's eating all the grass roots and then the other animals

226

are digging holes to find them. It's making the grass sickly."

"You are battling the chafer grub?" When she used to dig in the garden on Branvale's property, at times she would uncover the fat, creamy larvae with their black tips.

The shorter of the three men pulled his cap off before speaking. "Yes, milady. We have a plague of the things. They affect the pasture quality, which in turn upsets our sheep and cattle."

She was to defeat bugs? Well, everyone had their own unique battles. "Let us have a look at the problem and then we can decide on a course of action. Could you turn over a bit of sod, please?"

The men exchanged frowns and shrugs. One was leaning on a spade. He walked over and paused. Then he cleared his throat. "Um. Here?"

Sera nodded. "That will do. Thank you."

He thrust the spade into the soil, trod on the blade, and then lifted out a sizeable chunk of earth. Sera knelt on the ground to a horrified gasp from Mr Parker. Apparently mages weren't supposed to kneel in a meadow. Ignoring the men, she picked over the clump of soil. Several of the repulsive grubs wriggled away from the exposure to the light. Birds called out above, spotting the tasty meal.

Mr Parker crouched beside her. "You see, there are too many of them. The land needs a few, to be sure. But these ones are munching their way through all our grass and making bald patches."

Now that she cast around, she spotted the damage

from both the grub and the creatures digging up the land to dine upon them. "What would be a balanced number of grubs to earth for this pasture?"

He scratched his chin and stared off into the distance. Apparently arithmetic required some concentration. After a long minute, he spoke again, "In a patch the size of this here on the spade, we'd rather only see one or two. There must be ten munching on the roots."

"So, we need a ninety percent reduction." A pang shot through her for what she was about to do. The death of any creature, even a pest, made her pause. While she respected Mother Nature, sometimes the balance became upset, and she needed a little help to redress things. "I shall do this field first, and we will see if it works."

She clasped her hands together and bowed her head, meditating on what she had to achieve. Once she had the process and result firmly fixed in her mind, her magic coalesced inside her, and supplied the words for the spell. Sera whispered under her breath as she rolled her hands, crafting the spell into a ball. Then she flung out her arms. A wave shot across the meadow, rippling the grass. Birds in the trees took flight and rose as one with squawks and calls. Sheep baaed in alarm and ran to a far corner to huddle under the trees.

Then silence fell. Even the birds held their tongues.

Sera closed her eyes and asked forgiveness of the earth for her actions. A ripple spread across the paddock and tiny cream bodies popped to the surface.

Far above, birds called out spying the feast spread out for them.

'It's done," she said to the men.

They glanced among themselves. They were an untrusting lot.

'Why don't you turn over another sod and we can have a look," she suggested.

The man with the spade dug another hole and upended the sod. The four of them gathered around. Mr Parker knelt and teased apart the soil. He had the clump nearly spread out before he pulled one lone wriggling chafer grub free of the dirt. A handful more deceased ones shook free of the earth. "Well, I'll be."

Huzzah! It had worked. Sera contained her excitement and acted as though working such spells were an everyday occurrence for her. She turned her attention inside for a moment. While the magic expended had drained her a little, her body still held more in reserve. Since the council had sent her out to the countryside, she may as well make good use of her journey. "Are there other fields affected?"

"Yes, milady. All of them hereabouts. The grub don't respect no boundary lines and they go where they want." Mr Parker waved to the fields on the other side of the road and beyond.

They kept her busy all morning, moving from one field to the next. In each, she reduced the number of chafer grubs and left only one out of every ten. Hundreds of birds flocked to the pastures and feasted upon the remains of the unlucky grubs. The suspicion in the men's eyes disappeared as they turned over clumps of soil in each field and saw for themselves the reduced numbers. Whispers turned to chatter, and frowns to smiles.

At midday, one of the men rode off on his horse and returned with a basket. They shook out a blanket for her and sat in the sun to share a plain, but welcome, luncheon. Sera closed her eyes and a sense of peace washed through her. Westbourne Green appealed to her, with its open spaces and lush meadows. Away from the bustle and smell of London, but close enough to travel into town.

An idea entered her mind. 'Is there any land for sale around here?"

Mr Parker nodded. "There certainly is, and might I say, you'd be right welcome as a neighbour, Lady Winyard."

She would ask Mr Napier to make enquiries. Buying a plot of land would give her something entirely her own, and earning the necessary amount would give her a goal to keep in mind. Already she could imagine the sort of magical forest she could create to surround her home and let her live free from prying eyes.

By afternoon, Sera's hems were soiled, and her hands coated in earth. 'Is there anything else that can be done to help repair the health of the pasture?"

Mr Parker rubbed his jaw. "Seaweed is mighty useful. But it's a long trip to the ocean to get it."

Sera ground her fingers over her palms to remove the worst of the accumulated dirt. "What do you do with seaweed?"

"We soak it in barrels of water until it turns the

colour of strong tea. Then we spread the water over the fields. It fertilises it, you see, puts the goodness of the ocean into the soil. Then the seaweed is tilled into the soil as well," he explained.

She couldn't resist a challenge, and plucking seaweed from the ocean would have them talking about her abilities. 'I might be able to scoop some up. Where would you like it delivered?"

Mr Parker stared at her with a slack jaw. Then he shook his head with a soft chuckle. Did he think her incapable or mad? 'Over there by them trees would be useful, if you could manage it, milady. There's a water supply nearby, and we can place the barrels against that hedge for the soaking."

'I shall see what I can do." She closed her eyes and reached out with her mind. High above, she touched the birds and sought their assistance as payment for the grub feast. From one avian friend to another, she jumped, heading toward the shoreline. After a minute, she reached the coast. The seagull circled over the sea. There. A large patch of seaweed. The next bit would be more difficult.

Sera wrapped the floating mass in a spell. Then, as her mind flew back to her body, she jerked on the leash and pulled the seaweed with her, rather as an angler pulled a line once they had a bite.

The men cried out as a *thump* shook the ground under their feet. Opening her eyes, Sera grinned. A pile of seaweed sat in the exact spot Mr Parker had pointed out. A few stray pieces took their time to materialise in the air above the field and drop on to the pile.

"Thank you, milady! We'll not forget your kindness." The men slapped each other on the backs.

A wave of satisfied exhaustion washed over her. No, they'd not forget. The Mage Council underestimated her. There were far more working-class people to help than there were nobles or mages. Right under their noses, she would quietly amass loyal followers. These fellows would swell the ranks of an army she began with the families of the toy-bearing children. Each good action she took recruited more soldiers who would, if called upon, support her.

Those who thought her a pawn had forgotten one important rule of chess. If the pawn were to make it across the board...it became a queen.

Thoughts of winning games tumbled from her mind when she returned to her modest home. Another carriage waited in the road, this one a glossy black with the shimmering purple and gold emblem of the Mage Council on its door.

Sera hopped down from the ratty old carriage and approached the glistening, pristine one. She peered in the window but saw only her own reflection. A trickle of magic from her tired hand and the glass turned transparent—Lord Ormsby waited within and appeared to be either reading or dozing off.

The driver jumped down to open the door, and his movement jostled Lord Ormsby. The Speaker of the Mage Council shook himself and a book slid from his lap to the seat.

"Get in. I have been waiting for some time." He gestured to the opposite seat.

Sera couldn't find a shred of sympathy for him. He must have known she was out, since he allocated their tasks. She glanced up at her home, where Elliot watched from the top step. Then she climbed inside the vehicle and the door slammed shut. All noise outside disappeared, and the windows turned opaque once more.

She settled her skirts around her, dirty hems and all, as though they were embroidered silk. "I have been in Westbourne Green, as instructed. I believe the farmers are satisfied with my work."

His eyes widened as he glanced at her attire. "You did it?"

At least the sturdy wool hid the grass stains from kneeling in the fields all day. "Yes. I reduced the grub population in their fields and found them a load of seaweed to fertilise their soil. I also successfully dislodged the obstruction causing sewage to flow in the streets of the East End the other day."

His jaw dropped, and he stared at her. Then he snapped his teeth together with a grunt. "I am here because all of London is talking of your unauthorised use of magic last night."

Ice trickled down her spine. His words were eerily similar to the sentiment voiced by Abigail. Granddaughter of the former Speaker. "I attended a party and conjured an entertainment after dinner. I wasn't aware any act of magic had to be authorised by the council. Do all mages follow such a rule?"

Lord Ormsby picked up a walking stick and clasped one hand over the silver bauble on top. "You are young and prone to hysterics. Many are concerned about your lack of control. It is one thing to have you deal with insects and waste, quite another to cast near nobles. If things got out of hand, you could have injured someone, as you nearly did poor Branvale. It is not to happen again."

What a load of nonsense. Sera drew a long breath through her nose. It wouldn't do to test her powers against the older mage while confined in the carriage. Most likely they were jealous she'd stolen a few lines in the newspaper and taken attention from them. "I am as in control of my abilities as any mage, and will use my power with all the freedom granted us by Parliament and the Mage Act."

His brows drew closer together, and he pursed his lips, considering his next words. His face contorted in what she assumed was supposed to be a smile, and he adopted a less severe tone. "We are only concerned for your safety. A young woman should not be unguided in this world, and you are our responsibility. An amendment is before the House to place you under the council's governance until a suitable marriage is contracted."

Sera's temper raced through her veins and set fire to her blood. She stood in the cramped space and put one hand on the door handle, needing to escape before she blasted off the roof with a fireball. "Thank you for your concern, but until that amendment passes—*if* it passes—we have nothing more to discuss. Good day, Lord Ormsby."

Sparks prickled over her skin as she stalked up the path. The council would put neither leash nor muzzle on her, and she would bite off any hand that tried.

NINETEEN

Sera stormed up the path and through the open door. In the parlour she paced before the fire, shaking her fists as she swore under her breath about the Mage Council and interfering men who wanted to control her life. Elliot stood in the doorway, leaning one shoulder against the frame.

She raged as she replayed the terse conversation. "The gall of him! To say I need to be controlled. That I am hysterical. That I—"

"Have set fire to the settee," Elliot interrupted as he pointed behind her.

"What?" She spun in the direction of his finger. One of the sparks bouncing off her form had leapt to the settee and smouldered on the fabric.

With a swipe of her hand, she doused it. Then despair extinguished the rage, and she dropped to the warm seat. Mr Miles had once told her not to give the Mage Council any fodder for their delusions. She'd nearly given them all the evidence they needed to push their ridiculous amendment through Parliament! Imagine if in a fit of rage she set fire to her own home and burned down the neighbourhood. The only safe place to put her would be in the Repository of Forgotten Things. The magical prison where dangerous things were left to be erased from time.

"What if I am what they believe me to be?" she whispered in a small voice. She stared at her hands. One small spark could have caused disaster, and she'd never noticed it. What if she made a mistake on a larger scale? Her stomach flopped and heaved. Imagine if in removing the grubs from the field, her spell had gone awry and instead culled precious sheep or even the men standing beside her.

The lunch she'd eaten some hours before now churned and considered a reappearance. Sera clasped one hand over her mouth and leaned forward, drawing breaths through her nose to ease the burning sensation.

"Don't listen to them." Elliot sat beside her. "We believe in you, and you would have put out any fire before it spread. Are you telling me none of those high-and-mighty mages have ever made a mistake?" He nudged her with his shoulder.

She let out a sigh and leaned back to stare at the ceiling. Of course they made mistakes, but they were held to a different standard. "They are watching my every move, waiting to pounce when I fail. Assuming, that is, they can't blame me for Branvale's death." That reminded her of her need to find Mr Miles and Lieutenant Powers. She had to share what she knew of *orchids* and the poison.

But where to find Mr Miles? Sera had no idea where he resided or spent his days. "Elliot, where would I find Mr Miles?"

His lips quirked, and he jumped to his feet. "Not down the back of the sofa, then? Have you tried looking under your bed?"

She'd let him have one more joke about it, then she would give him a frog's legs. Although he seemed to read her mood and swallowed the next quip.

"He left a card. I expect that might give us the required clue." He winked and produced the card from his jacket pocket.

"How long have you been carrying that around, waiting for me to ask?" She took the item and ran a finger along the top.

Elliot plucked her straw hat from the floor, where she had tossed it during her fit of temper. "He gave it to me the first time he called here, as any gentleman would."

The calling card was plainly yet boldly stamped.

Mr Hugh Miles
Surgeon

Then an address in Soho, not too far away. Would he be in his rooms, or out somewhere with the lieutenant continuing their investigation? As much as her curiosity wanted to see what sort of home the surgeon kept, she needed to talk to both men.

"Where would I find Lieutenant Powers?" If she tracked down one gentleman, she might find both.

'I shall ask my little birdies. Should have an answer for you in an hour or so." He tapped the side of his nose and headed out the door.

Birdies? Somehow she imagined Elliot with rat-like minions, scuttling about in the dark and ferreting out information. Birds would be handy allies to spot the gentlemen on the street below. But skimming with a sparrow's mind required her time and attention. She would let Elliot try first, giving her time to send a message to Kitty. Sera had ensorcelled two pieces of paper, so they might correspond with one another. She still wanted to craft a mage silver ring for her friend, but the exact spell required access to the locked part of the mage library.

She retrieved the sheet of paper from the desk drawer and found a message waiting. Kitty had read the reports in the newspaper of the *field of love and sadness* Sera had crafted to complement Abigail's song, and wanted to know how it had been received by the hostess.

The visual display had ruffled the singer's feathers. Sera would think on some gift for her, to smooth over the bump in their friendship. She'd forgotten how closely Abigail followed society's many unspoken rules. Sera rubbed a finger over Kitty's words to remove them from the page. Then she dipped her pen into the bottle of ink and wrote her reply.

THE GUESTS WERE COMPLIMENTARY, *but I should have asked Abigail first. Visited today by Ormsby. He warned that I am not to conduct UNAUTHORISED displays of magic again and that the amendment to the Mage Act progresses. Please beg your father to do what he can to stop it!*

HAVING CONVEYED the pertinent bits of information, she slid the sheet back into the drawer. Handling the ensorcelled paper reminded her of the one she'd found under Branvale's bed. In her next quiet moment, she would check whether the spell had uncovered anything yet.

Elliot appeared as she finished her correspondence. "The surgeon returned to his rooms earlier this afternoon. You should be able to catch him there. Alone. If that's what you want." He raised one eyebrow.

Alone. That one word bounced around in her head. Abigail would swoon if she knew Sera intended to visit a man unchaperoned. But she needed to discuss the poison, so that outweighed any concerns of propriety. "I shall call on him. His rooms are not too far away and I think I may walk."

"Of course, milady. Also, this came for you." He held out an envelope bearing the royal seal on the flap.

The court used old-fashioned methods of delivering messages, even though the royal couple had their own mage correspondence box and the spells to use it. Almost as though they didn't trust the invisible method, in case it went awry and broadcast their missives to the population at large.

Sera slit open the envelope to find a summons to

appear before the monarch the next day. "My presence is required before the queen tomorrow. Perhaps they, too, want to chastise me for creating a field of wild flowers, while Tomlin is celebrated for turning the Thames purple and making fish dance upon its surface."

"Or they might want you to do something similar for the whole court. Stop being such a misery guts," Elliot said.

She stuck out her tongue at him. At times, he reminded her of an older brother, giving either support or a kick when she needed it. As much as she hated to admit it, he was right. Time to stop wallowing in her misery and do something productive. "I shall call on Mr Miles first, then tomorrow I shall find the lieutenant."

Elliot saluted her and turned, his shoulders shaking with silent laughter.

Impertinent footman with his utter disregard for her new position. Sera rose and followed Elliot to the entrance, where he held her hat and a cloak. Humour sparkled in his eyes and his lightness rubbed against her and eased her dark mood. Let other households keep their stuffy footmen and overstarched butlers. With all the levity Elliot brought to their little home, she could never replace him.

"I'll be back before dark." Sera adjusted the cloak around her shoulders and fastened the clasp, then pinned on the hat.

Children played in the street outside and called out to her as she passed. Sera returned their greeting and then whispered a spell to make iridescent bubbles appear around the group. Delighted laughter bounced off the buildings as the youngsters chased the floating spheres.

Sera enjoyed the late afternoon walk and the constant activity of London after so many years of being restricted by Lord Branvale. She hardly noticed the change in the neighbourhood's tone until she turned into the lane where Mr Miles lived. Partway along the road, she stopped outside one particular building to stare up at its battered facade. Her new home seemed a smart terrace by comparison. The area had seen far better days, and the buildings displayed their neglect. Children with grubby faces sat on steps and lacked any of the toys that the children in her neighbourhood clutched.

"I'm looking for Mr Miles," she said to the group clustered on the step.

One boy pointed upward. "Very top, milady, in the attic."

"Thank you." Sera rolled her fingers together and produced a bright red ball that she held out to him.

The lad's jaw dropped. "For me?"

"As a thank you. It is rather bouncy, so don't throw it too hard at anything solid." She winked.

The lad took the fist-sized ball and bounced it on the bottom step. The ball soared higher than his head and his friends gasped. By the time Sera reached the door, the group was having a lively game in the street, the red ball zinging among them.

Several flights of rickety stairs later, she reached the

last landing. A narrow door hid a dark set of stairs leading up to the attic. "Why doesn't a surgeon keep a room on the ground floor?" she wondered aloud as she took the last few stairs. Another door blocked her way, and she rapped upon it and waited.

The door was flung open. Bright light illuminated Mr Miles from behind, and she squinted at the sudden change from shadow to sun.

"Lady Winyard? Whatever are you doing here?" He held out a hand to assist her up the last step, as though he helped her aboard a pirate ship. He wore no jacket or waistcoat, but an apron such as a butcher might wear, covering his clothing. His shirtsleeves were rolled up past his elbows and exposed the thick muscles in his forearms.

"I needed to speak to you about the poison." Having reached the attic, she paused to catch her breath and soak in the surroundings.

Skylights in the roof at one end of the garret flooded the space with light and the surgeon appeared to have set up his work area where the light was best. At the other end, the room was cast in perpetual shadow, but she made out a bed and a nearby chest of drawers.

Shelves held cages with mice scurrying about their lives. Another shelf was crammed with books. The wall at the very end of the room had a circular window some eight feet in diameter. Next to it sat a rectangular planter that sprouted a familiar type of greenery. Sera walked closer and touched a small purple flower. "Are you growing potatoes?"

He rubbed a thick leaf between his thumb and forefinger. "They take little time or effort and are appreciated by my neighbours when they are ready. It seemed a better use for the dirt I found in the corners up here."

Sera glanced down. The worn floorboards appeared to have been swept. Next, she turned to the long, narrow table in the middle of the space he used as a workbench. An assortment of vials and saucers was scattered over the top, along with an open journal to pen notes about his studies.

"Why do you keep a room in an attic?" she asked, the purpose of her visit delayed as she indulged her curiosity.

"It gives me privacy from all but the most determined visitors." His eyes crinkled with the width of his smile. "And I enjoy the light from the windows and the view over the rooftops. But, alas, it is not practical for much of my work, which requires protection from sunlight and a chillier temperature to prevent decay."

He took her hand and led her to the round window. London stretched before them and smoke curled from chimneys jutting from slanted roofs. The late afternoon light cast it all in a soft glow. From his attic, the surgeon had a bird's-eye view of the city. All sorts of birds flew past, but from where she stood, Sera didn't need to touch a mind to soar over the rooftops.

"The Mage Council sent word of their findings to Lieutenant Powers today and they will confer with the queen tomorrow." His soft, rumbly voice came from beside her and something in his quiet manner and soft tone made emotion churn inside.

That would explain her summons to the royal presence. "Excellent. I came to tell you of my findings. I discovered that the poison used was the death cap mushroom."

"That is what the Mage Council found." He gestured to a worn sofa in the middle of the floor that seemed to divide bedroom from the living area. The once vibrant green brocade had faded from the sun to a watery hue. In spots the threads were frayed and pulled, as though a cat had used it as a scratching post.

"Through further analysis, I teased out the spell cast over the poison. It not only accelerates its action, but amplifies the effects." Sera rushed through her findings.

Mr Miles drew a breath and his smile fell away. He rose and stalked to the window.

"You still think I did it, even when I present evidence to the contrary." Sera whispered the words to Mr Miles' broad back.

The young surgeon stood at the window, one hand curled in the frame above his head, his attention on something out in the shadowed street. A sigh made his shoulders heave. When he spoke, he addressed the view out the window and did not turn around. "The Mage Council found differently. They have advised that a spell halted the effects of the poison, allowing the murderer time to distance themselves from their crime. Lord Ormsby will tell the king tomorrow that Lord Branvale ingested the poison at least two days before his death."

No!

Despair clenched her insides and her breath came in

shallow gasps. Once such news became public, all of London would call her a murderer. That would give the Mage Council the support they needed to push through the amendment to the Mage Act and control her every action. Guilty or not would be irrelevant. Never again would she walk free. Panic rushed up her throat as the implications slammed into her.

"They would place me under Lord Branvale's roof when he was poisoned, which corroborates their claim that I did this. But they are wrong. He consumed the poison mere hours before his death. You must believe me, Hugh, please. I am innocent." Once, Sera had believed she did not care about anyone's opinion. Now, faced with losing this man's good opinion, she realised how much she cared what he thought of her.

He turned with the faintest trace of a smile on his lips. "Ask me that again, if you don't mind."

He would tease her, at a moment like this, when her life hung in the balance? It took a few deep breaths to control the shudder in her limbs before she could repeat the words. "You must believe me."

He paced closer and crouched down before her, then took her hand, clasping it between his. "The other bit, where you said my name. I would hear it again."

"Hugh. Please," she whispered her entreaty. His Christian name had flown unbidden to her lips in her moment of need.

He raised her hand and kissed her knuckles. "I believe you. But we will require proof to convince the king and queen when the Mage Council delivers their findings."

Her shoulders sagged, the situation hopeless. "It is my word against theirs, and they already cast me as inexperienced. I can imagine what they will say if I claim the opposite." She recalled the wisp of the spell contained in the vial. There was her proof, but no one save another mage would understand how it was constructed or be able to interpret it. Who could she trust? Lord Pendlebury was the only one. What if he sided with Lord Ormsby?

"I had already tested the substance I found in Lord Branvale's stomach. Yesterday I sacrificed one of my mice. The poor creature sickened and died within three hours. Even allowing for the difference in size and weight between a mouse and Lord Branvale, I saw no evidence of any lingering magic to delay the effect. If such were true, the mouse should still appear healthy today."

Sera stared at her hand. An odd tingle had rippled over her skin when he'd kissed her knuckles. It took some effort to concentrate on the meaning of his words. He had tested the poison and proved her findings. The Mage Council lied. Relief surged through her at the glimmer of hope he offered.

"You believe me." How much easier it was to face the oncoming battle when she knew at least one man stood by her side. Particularly a man as solid as...Hugh.

He let go of her hand and sat beside her. Then he gestured to his workbench. "I was in the process of examining the mouse and comparing the damage to that suffered by Lord Branvale. Do you wish to observe?"

Sera shook her head. "No. I cannot watch you autopsy one of nature's creatures. Nor would I wish to give the Mage Council any wriggle room to say I altered your findings."

"I have yet to confer with Lieutenant Powers, but it seems most likely that Lord Branvale was poisoned while dining with Contessa Ricci." His arm stretched out behind her on the settee.

Sera rose to her feet before she succumbed to an urge to lean into his side and forget about the world for a few stolen minutes. "There was more I wished to share. I have learned that an *orchid* is not a plant at all, but what some men call a kept woman of delicate disposition and noble birth."

Hugh's eyebrows shot up as he stood. "Truly? I have not heard such a phrase before. I shall inform the lieutenant. A woman seems a more likely subject of an argument than a flower."

"I thought the contessa's Unnatural state might have been the source of the disagreement between them, but if what you say is true—they may have fought over a woman." As ideas swirled through her mind, the despair shrank. There were still avenues for the investigator to pursue, and she held tight to her belief that the truth would prevail.

She would yet slip the leash the Mage Council sought to place around her neck.

247

TWENTY

Hugh escorted Sera to the narrow attic door. "Contessa Ricci must sustain herself somehow. Lieutenant Powers has been questioning the local authorities to ascertain if there have been any corpses found drained of their blood and bearing two puncture marks. I confess to knowing nothing of their habits. It would make a fascinating study if she would allow me to observe her."

"You assume her thirst kills her victims. If she wishes to escape unwanted attention, far better to keep them alive and perhaps cosseted...like an *orchid*." What books did the Mage Council hold about Unnatural creatures such as vampyres? She had failed to plant a blade of grass, but remained determined to pass their silly test and gain access to the knowledge locked away behind an ensorcelled door.

"There is a limit to how much blood a person can lose. I wonder how much a vampyre must imbibe at any one time." The frown returned to his brow, and he rubbed his chin.

Sera could see his mind whirring with calculations. While she couldn't answer the question about fluids and quantities, she could ferret out one of the contessa's secrets. 'I shall turn my mind to the question of her dining habits while I leave you to finish your examination. I look forward to being present when you tell the council they are wrong."

'I wouldn't dream of presenting my findings without you," he murmured. He held out his hand to help her down the first steep step.

Sera was grateful for the darkness of the narrow stairs to the main landing. Hugh couldn't see the blush that heated her skin at his words. Once out on the street, she hastened back to her home. A plan formulated in her mind as dusk fell around her.

Approaching her terrace home, she rang the invisible bell to summon Elliot. He flung open the front door as she reached for the latch.

'I need your help," Sera blurted out.

'Of course you do. What is it this time?" He slid her cloak from her shoulders, shook it out, and hung it and her hat on a hook.

'I need to determine whether Contessa Ricci is keeping a woman somewhere." Or could it be a young man? During Abigail's dinner, she hadn't thought to ask Lord Loburn if an *orchid* was always one gender. Flowers possessed both, and she shouldn't close her mind to other possibilities.

He arched one dark brow. "Another night-time expedition?"

Sera crossed to the parlour and dropped to the settee. With a flick of her hand, she created a cheerful blue and green flame effect in the fireplace. "The lady in question is an Unnatural known to favour the cover of darkness, so yes, we will venture out after nightfall." She had kept her men's clothing, since they were so much more practical for nocturnal activities.

"I'll have someone watch the address, in case she heads out before we get there." Elliot plumped up a cushion and then dropped it down behind her.

"Thank you." It had been a long and exhausting day, and it would still be many hours before she could seek her bed. Putting her feet up with a cup of tea would ease her tiredness before dinner.

After a meal and friendly conversation below stairs to revive her spirits, Sera headed upstairs to change into trousers and a waistcoat. Then she laced up her newly cleaned boots and grabbed a navy wool coat. Before donning her cap, she scrubbed her hands over her face to alter her features to those of the younger sibling of Elliot.

She met the footman, dressed in a similar manner, in the entranceway. Full dark settled over the city as they set off down the stairs and along the road. Nocturnal London emerged from the shadows and took over the streets and alleyways.

"Do you plan to watch her house all night? What if she stays in?" Elliot asked as he hailed them a carriage to take them closer to their destination.

"Good grief, no." Sera had no intention of being chilled to the bone and stiff from endless hours of a pointless vigil. "Once we get there, I expect you to charm someone in the household and determine whether she intends to venture out tonight."

"Can't you work your magic and find out?" He tapped the side of his head in the gloomy interior of the hired conveyance.

"No. There is a limit to our power. We cannot enter the thoughts of mortal men." How much easier so many things would be if she could reach into a man's head and pluck out the thought or memory—or truth —she needed.

"So you don't know what I'm thinking?" He stroked his chin, and even in the dark, a gleam sparked in his eyes.

She laughed. "I don't need magic to know what you are thinking, Elliot Bryn. It is written all over your face. And no, I will not be part of your plan to lure some barmaid who thinks I am your brother into a dark corner."

"It doesn't have to be a *dark* corner," he muttered and turned back to regard the view out the grimy window.

As luck would have it, they didn't need Elliot to charm a scullery maid. The lady in question was stepping into her carriage as theirs stopped at the top of her street.

"Follow that carriage at a discreet distance," Sera instructed their driver.

"How am I going to know which one it is when the streets get crowded?" he asked.

Sera considered her options and conjured a spell in her mind. Then she focused on the other vehicle as she whispered the incantation under her breath. On the last word, she snapped her fingers. One lantern at the rear of the carriage spluttered, then it relit itself with a greenish tinge.

"That should help. Follow the green lantern." She settled back next to Elliot, curious as to where the contessa went in the evening. Covent Garden, perhaps, to take in the entertainment? Or might there be some underground society of Unnatural creatures that met when God-fearing Londoners were tucked up in their homes?

After winding through the streets for what seemed like an eternity, eventually their carriage slowed and then stopped. "She's getting out," the driver said.

Sera and Elliot hopped out, and Sera pulled a coin from her pocket and pressed it into the driver's palm. "Thank you."

Elliot whistled through his teeth. "Do I get one, too?"

"Only if you behave until we return home." The footman made a valid point, though. Sera expected much of him for a servant's pay. Not that he did much during the day—it wasn't as though she had family or numerous visitors for him to attend.

Sera looked around as Elliot joined her. People came and went along the busy road, but there didn't appear to be taverns or theatres in the vicinity. Up ahead, the contessa wore a red velvet cloak and, with the hood thrown back, her pale skin appeared luminescent under the full moon.

"Come on, before we lose her," Sera whispered, smacking her companion in the stomach.

"Cool your heels, lad. It's not a race," Elliot said as a couple walked past them.

"What is this area?" Sera asked.

Elliot took long but slow strides, and after a few paces, she adjusted her stride to match.

"Houses of ill repute," he muttered out the side of his mouth.

Oh. That would explain the men hurrying back and forth, heads ducked and hats pulled low as though they didn't want to be recognised. Others lingered on the footpath, smoking cigarillos and either silently enjoying the night, or holding rowdy conversations with other men. Music and laughter drifted from open windows and wafted along the cobbles.

They followed the contessa past a brightly lit house, and another where three women stood by the front door and called out invitations and descriptions of what could be found inside. Sera's ears heated as she received quite a different education from the one conducted in the Napier family classroom.

Elliot pulled Sera to a halt as their quarry climbed a set of stairs. The door to the house swung open to admit her as she gained the top step. A single light burned in a street-level room. From behind the drawn curtains came only a hint of shadows.

"Now what? We can't just barge in and introduce

ourselves. Do you want me to go round to the kitchen door?" Elliot crouched and retied his boot lace to give them time to survey the house.

Sera glanced up and down the street. "I need to be closer. Do you smoke?"

"What? Why?" He stood up and straightened his cap.

"I'm going to find a way to see what is happening inside, and I need you to make it look like we are having a conversation." She led the way along the road to the low wall of the neighbouring property. At about waist height, it gave her something to lean upon. They would appear to be two men deciding which premises to enter for their night's entertainment.

"I was giving it up. Many of the girls don't like it," he muttered as he patted down his pockets and pulled out a battered tin box with a trio of hand-rolled items inside.

Sera clicked her fingers and produced a pale flame with which to light his cigarette.

"Now what?" he asked as he drew on the end.

"If anyone walks by, do what you do best—talk. I won't be able to answer until I return." Sera let her mind wander and consider the problem before her. Magic provided the answer.

He tilted his head back to blow smoke away from them. "Where are you going?"

"Inside." Sera leaned on the wall and set free a tendril of magic toward the house. Through the brick it wormed, burrowing into the room beyond. The next bit was trickier. She needed a set of ears and eyes. The invisible strand of magic brushed along the walls of the parlour until it found a suitable vessel. Under a sideboard, a mouse had emerged to test the air, searching for a meal.

Sera wrapped the creature in her spell, and once her mind joined with that of the mouse, she crept closer to a foot of the sideboard. The room soared to gigantic proportions before her, the ceiling so far above her furry head that the mouse's brain interpreted it as a type of unchanging sky. The sole lamp on a side table cast a soft glow in one spot, leaving the rest of the room in shadow.

A woman sat on a settee before the fire and did not move as the contessa entered.

"You are chilled, Vilma," Contessa Ricci said instead of a greeting.

"I cannot warm my bones tonight," the woman called Vilma replied.

The vampyre sat and took the younger woman's hands in hers. "Have you dined this evening? You should have bone broth and warm bread to restore your vigour."

"You worry too much. I am simply tired." Vilma smiled and touched the contessa's face, brushing aside a loose strand of hair.

The contessa captured the woman's hand and kissed the palm. "Let me warm you, if you are willing?"

"Yes," Vilma murmured.

The contessa drew the other woman into her arms. Vilma sighed and angled her face away, exposing her neck. The contessa nuzzled the pale skin. A sudden inhalation of breath filled the room, followed by a moaned exhale. Further soft moans from Vilma accompanied a wet sucking noise. Sera had heard similar sighs before at Branvale's house, when one of the maids used to receive nocturnal visits from a gentleman caller in a dark corner of the servants' yard.

"What did you see?" an overloud voice seemed to shout in her ear.

Sera shook her head, disoriented as her mind disconnected from the mouse and flew back to her body. For a moment, everything appeared too tiny, and she wondered what had happened to her fur.

"You gasped. What was it?" Worry pulled at Elliot's brows and he took Sera by the upper arms to steady her.

"The contessa is with a young woman she called Vilma. She is cold, even though the weather is mild, and she sits before a fire." She would ask Hugh if he could diagnose any condition from such vague symptoms. "The contessa was solicitous of her condition. Then said she would warm Vilma."

Elliot shook her, his eyes now bright with curiosity. "Don't stop just as the story is getting good. How exactly is the contessa warming her up?"

"She put her arms around Vilma, who arched her head to expose her throat." She demonstrated. "The contessa appeared to be kissing her neck, and the woman moaned. The mouse detected the sound of sucking, which I assume is the vampyre feeding." Sera stared at the house. Should they tell someone? Was it even a crime for a vampyre to feed upon someone if it appeared to be voluntary? She had questions for Lieutenant Powers. Perhaps he would know.

"Did this Vilma moan in pain from having her blood drained? I wonder why she didn't fight." He let her go and ran a hand over the back of his neck as he stared at the lit window with its drawn curtains.

"I don't know. From the little I heard, there was no animosity between them. On the contrary, it was solicitude. Nor did the woman appear to resist or fight against the feeding. The sound she made would indicate that she...enjoys what is happening between them."

"Really?" A speculative gleam sparked in Elliot's dark eyes. "There are fellows who would pay handsomely to watch that."

Sera slapped the footman in the chest and then tugged on his jacket lapels to lead him away. "Do try to keep your mind on the matter at hand. How much do you think Branvale knew of what goes on between the contessa and Vilma? Enough to cause an argument about it?"

Elliot cast one backward glance and then fell into step beside Sera. "He didn't exactly chat to his staff. If he mentioned it to anyone, it would have been Jake. Perhaps he let something slip while undressing in the evening after a little too much to drink?"

"Then I need to talk to Jake." Another reason surfaced in her mind: the suppressant syrup that Branvale brewed for his valet.

But that could wait. What she needed more urgently was a few hours' sleep before her appearance at court in the morning. Thank goodness nothing stirred at the palace before ten.

Once home, Sera fell into bed and slept soundly, only waking when Vicky drew back the curtains and presented her with a breakfast tray. After eating and a quick wash, the maid helped her dress in the simple gown with its sweet pea embroidery. It might not be a suitable dress for attending the monarch, but she didn't have the extensive wardrobe of other women of the court.

Let them see her as lacking the artifice of other courtiers. If they thought her feeble of magic and mind, it would ultimately work to her advantage.

The sun hid behind clouds and cast London in a dull light as Sera alighted at the palace and was ushered through the corridors. This time, the attending courtier took her along a different route, before pausing at a set of dark walnut double doors. He coughed to the footmen stationed on either side. One reached out and grasped the handle, opening the door for them.

Ridiculous that her guide couldn't open a door himself. It was just as well Nature limited who possessed magic, or all of the court would glide around on floating chaises and never lift a finger for themselves. There and then, she vowed never to rely on her magic to undertake tasks she could do herself.

Sera entered a plush drawing room easily the size of an entire level of her little home. Carpets in deep colours were scattered across the floor. The walls were panelled with dark wood to the height of the chair rail, then a rich green wallpaper above that made her think of twilight in a forest. Chandeliers lit with magical steady flames cast a soft golden glow on those below. Settees and chaises were placed around the room, all in complementary brocades of green, gold, and copper. Chairs and side tables filled the spaces between and were used by the many courtiers and nobles present.

The queen sat on a settee before a fire so large it could have roasted an entire cow. The flames sparked purple and silver and threw out a soft warmth. What a shame the mage responsible hadn't added a faint lavender fragrance to mask the odour of those courtiers who didn't believe in bathing more than once a month.

The queen's spouse was absent, which probably explained why everyone else was allowed to sit. The king was notorious for making the courtiers stand for hours on end. A cluster of ladies sat on delicate chairs behind the queen. Lady Abigail flashed a quick smile that reassured Sera that their small *contretemps* was forgiven, before her friend resumed her serene and slightly bored look.

Beside them, and under a landscape painting of cows grazing in a field, stood Lieutenant Powers and Hugh. After the previous day, she no longer thought of him as *Mr Miles*. He smiled openly at her and lent her a strand of confidence, something she needed when she gazed at Lords Ormsby and Tomlin, seated opposite the queen. The Speaker of the Mage Council pursed his lips. Tomlin's expression remained inscrutable behind half-lidded eyes.

Luckily, she had been forewarned as to what the Mage Council intended to say about the poison. Sera steeled herself for what was to come, curtsied, and waited to be acknowledged.

"Lady Winyard, excellent. The king is indisposed and will not be joining us. Now that you are here, we can proceed," Queen Charlotte said.

"Proceed, Your Majesty?" She stood and regarded the monarch with wide-eyed innocence.

Intelligence burned in the queen's eyes and she peered at her newest mage. "Lord Ormsby and Lieutenant Powers are to tell us how their investigations progress into the death of Lord Branvale. We thought it pertinent for you to be present."

"Thank you for including me, Your Majesty." She clasped her hands over her stomacher, but kept her grip light so as not to betray her nerves. Had the queen arranged a private audience so that after Sera was denounced as a murderer, she could be seized by the other mages?

If so, she would not go quietly. She closed her eyes and touched the magic inside her. It surged through her veins in answer. *Let them try*, it whispered.

TWENTY-ONE

The queen gestured to a footman, who placed a plain ladder-back chair close to her and in front of where Hugh stood. She gestured for Sera to sit. The surgeon had promised to provide proof to support Sera's findings, and she could do nothing now except place her fate in his hands.

Lord Ormsby cleared his throat and stood, taking up a position by the fireplace. When he had everyone's attention, he began. "The Mage Council's finest mind, Lord Tomlin, has worked tirelessly to discern the nature of the poison used to kill our brother."

Sera bit back a snort. Tomlin hadn't worked *that* tirelessly, since he'd taken a day off to entertain the court and distress the poor fish going about their lives in the Thames.

"Through the application of his efforts, Lord Tomlin has discerned a natural element as the base of the poison." Lord Ormsby's voice boomed from his barrel-shaped torso, and Sera suspected he was incapable of a quieter voice. The courtiers gasped at the news, as though the younger mage had achieved some amazing feat.

Again, Sera had also determined that. In fact, given that Mr Miles had hypothesised from the effects he'd observed that either arsenic or *Amanita phalloides* were the main suspects, it took no magic at all to say a *natural element* had been used.

'Further, as we suspected, the poison was ensorcelled. A twisted mind used magic against Lord Branvale." Here, Lord Ormsby paused and stared directly at Sera. She met his gaze while whispers erupted among those present.

'I shall allow Lord Tomlin to present his findings in more detail and explain his process." The Speaker of the council gestured to Lord Tomlin, who joined him by the fireplace. When the younger man remained silent, Ormsby nudged him with a sharp elbow.

Lord Tomlin glanced at Sera and his Adam's apple bobbed as he swallowed. Were the lies he was about to spew blocking his throat?

Avoiding eye contact, he spoke to an empty chair. 'By careful application of my magic, I teased apart the individual components of the poison. The element used resisted my efforts, but by applying pressure I was able to crack through the barrier behind which it hid."

Sera rolled her eyes. How typical of a man to apply brute force to a problem, even a magical one. She preferred the delicate touch that had resulted in the element's revealing itself.

"The base of the poison is the death cap mushroom," Lord Tomlin said. Several courtiers broke into applause.

"Was his last meal sautéed mushrooms?" someone asked.

"We were provided with the menu, and it did not include any fungi-based dishes," Lieutenant Powers spoke up from behind Sera.

"Nor did I find anything in his stomach contents that resembled mushrooms," Hugh added.

Queen Charlotte turned to the surgeon with a frown. "You looked at what his stomach contained?"

The surgeon stepped forward and stood beside Sera. If she reached out, she could touch his hand and draw on his strength. But not with Abigail watching. Or the queen.

"Yes, Your Majesty, as part of my autopsy. I conducted a detailed examination of his stomach to ascertain approximate time of death. Food moves through the digestive system in a predictable manner, and there was not a great deal of time between Lord Branvale's last meal and his demise."

"How extraordinary," the queen murmured. Then she waved her hand at Lord Tomlin. "Continue."

Tomlin shuffled from foot to foot and appeared to have trouble spitting out what he needed to say. "The next part of my task was most difficult and complex. A mage must find the spell hiding within the sample. It took me some days and much concentration to discern the magic contained within the fluid. I found that, um, the spell used was...well, it was rather complex and involved two separate and yet different castings."

'My young associate found that first, a delaying spell was cast over the poison that made it sit dormant for two days after Lord Branvale ingested it. When the number of days had passed, the other spell activated, and the poison took his life." Lord Ormsby finished up for Lord Tomlin.

Such a finding by Lord Tomlin placed the blame firmly on Sera, who would still have been under Branvale's roof if these men were to be believed. Her analysis had found one spell only—not two. The only magic present in the sample was an accelerant.

She refused to hold her tongue and jumped to her feet. 'No, you are wrong. There was no delaying spell. In fact, the opposite is true. An amplifier was used in the poison to speed up its effect. I found that Lord Branvale consumed it mere hours before it took his life."

The queen looked from Tomlin to Sera and arched one eyebrow. 'What say you, Lord Tomlin? How is it possible that two of our mages could reach such different conclusions?"

Lord Tomlin clasped and unclasped his hands. Then he cleared his throat twice. 'As I said, there were two different spells used. Lady Winyard has correctly identified one. Someone did use magic to enhance how the poison reacted within the body. Effects that should have been felt over some days or weeks were compressed into mere hours. After, of course, the poison emerged from the liberation effect of the other spell present." He added the last in a hurry, after another elbow prompt from his superior.

Lord Ormsby waved a dismissive hand in her direction. "Lady Winyard found the more obvious spell. What she failed to find was the time delay enchantment that let the poison slumber for two days. Or perhaps she has some other motive for claiming the spell acted immediately upon Lord Branvale's ingesting it?"

Sera's stomach plunged through the floor as her fears were confirmed. The council sought to lay the blame at her feet. Ormsby's words portrayed her as a murderer, lying to protect herself. Had she missed a second spell? She cast her mind back to the wisp she had teased from the sample and captured in a vial. No, there had been only one casting trapped in the bottle. She grasped hold of her confidence in her analysis. Tomlin had made a mistake. Or he was lying. She glanced around the room as ladies twittered and courtiers bent their heads together. Dark looks were cast her way, heavy with silent accusation. It took all her resolve to remain calm.

"Are you both certain of your findings?" the queen asked.

"I am, Your Majesty. There was no delay in the action of the poison." Sera kept her voice strong and clear.

Fabric rustled as everyone turned to stare at Lord Tomlin. Under the scrutiny of those assembled, his shoulders slumped.

"Of course he is sure." Lord Ormsby answered for him.

Hugh picked up a leather valise at his feet and walked to a low table, where he deposited it with a soft thump. "If I might make a suggestion, Your Majesty. While I do not possess any magic, a practical demonstration will resolve the conflicting results in a way that all here can observe and understand."

"Oh? This sounds most interesting. Do elaborate, Mr Miles." The queen leaned forward to watch as the surgeon removed a small cage containing three mice with grey speckled fur.

"This is no need for this, Majesty." Lord Ormsby gestured to Sera and his face turned a deeper shade of red. "Obviously, this woman is lying to save her own skin. She should be confined for the safety of everyone in London until this matter is resolved."

The queen waved a dismissive hand at the Speaker of the Mage Council as Hugh proceeded.

Next, the surgeon withdrew a squat bottle made of green glass so dark it was nearly black. He held it to the light and a dark substance oozed up one side. "This is the sample I recovered from Lord Branvale's stomach. I shall feed a tiny amount to one of these mice. If Lady Winyard is correct, any effect will happen quickly. If Lords Tomlin and Ormsby are correct, well...things will be rather dull while we wait for two days."

Sera sent a silent thanks to the surgeon for once again coming to her rescue. The poor mouse would give its life to prove her correct, and reveal the underhanded tactics of the council. She wondered if that was what had made Tomlin hold his silence. Had Ormsby forced him to say he'd found a delaying spell? Was there still a scrap of integrity in Tomlin's heart?

"This is preposterous! Never before has the word of

a mage been questioned. The results of such a performance cannot be trusted. A mouse is much smaller than Lord Branvale, so of course it will kill a tiny creature faster." Lord Ormsby continued to bluster while Tomlin remained oddly silent at his side, fixated on his shoes.

Lieutenant Powers detached himself from his spot under the painting and stepped forward. "To those without magic, this will prove which analysis is correct. When someone is accused of murder, it behoves us all to embrace any opportunity to reveal the truth."

"I can assure you, Lord Ormsby, that I have calculated the difference in mass between Lord Branvale and the unfortunate mouse. I shall administer a dose to the mouse that is proportionately the same as what the contents of his stomach show Lord Branvale consumed." Mr Miles continued to remove instruments from his bag. A bowl the size of a fist was followed by a leather roll with smaller instruments, then another cage.

"Continue, Mr Miles. I agree with the lieutenant that a practical demonstration must go ahead to add weight to the findings about the nature of the magic used. How odd it is that our mages have reached such different conclusions. One can only conclude that one of them must be mistaken, but who?" The queen's keen gaze swept from Sera to Tomlin.

Tomlin coughed and looked away. "Discerning any trace of a spell from such a small sample is a most difficult task, Your Majesty..." His voice faded away under Lord Ormsby's glare.

With each passing moment, and as Lord Tomlin's discomfort increased, Sera became convinced the other mage knew only too well that there was no hibernation element. Which meant Ormsby had coerced him into saying there was. She would enjoy seeing how this played out and watching Ormsby swallow his accusations.

"If you would select the victim, Your Majesty." Hugh held the cage out to the queen.

"Must I?" Unlike her ladies, who clustered together in fear at the three small furry creatures, the queen peered through the bars at the curious animals.

Hugh turned the cage to reveal one creature hiding in a corner. "I thought that for his service to the Crown, the other two mice might be retired to a warm hedgerow to live out the rest of their days."

"That seems fair. One is sacrificed, but two are rewarded," Queen Charlotte said.

Sera hoped the same didn't apply to mages.

The queen waved her finger back and forth before pointing to one with its nose pushed through the bars. "I choose this one, with the dark grey swirls on its fur. As to its companions, do find them a hedgerow with no cats nearby."

"Of course," Hugh murmured as he placed the cage upon the table and undid the hook. Reaching in, he took hold of the unfortunate creature and closed the lid again. "Would you mind, Lieutenant Powers?" The surgeon held out the mouse to the army officer.

"Happy to assist in uncovering the truth." He took the mouse in his cupped hands.

Sera couldn't watch. The tiny animal's sacrifice upset her stomach. Across the room, Abigail was alone among the ladies in following the events. Her friend's expression was unreadable apart from a slight frown marring her smooth forehead.

Instead of watching the poison be weighed and administered, Sera chose to study a portrait of the king for some minutes. Then Hugh announced the deed done. He called out the exact time from his pocket watch, and as Sera turned, he made notations in a battered journal. One mouse sat alone in the small cage. His companions were placed back in the valise, to be liberated in a comfortable spot in a garden.

"Yes. Well, the passage of time can affect a spell. It is entirely possible the hibernation element might have degraded or even worn off entirely by now," Ormsby muttered as everyone in the room stared at the mouse.

"And yet Lord Tomlin found it, implying it is still very much present. By his analysis," Lieutenant Powers said.

Each time she listened to the lieutenant, Sera liked him more. Particularly when his statements made Lord Ormsby squirm.

The grandfather clock in the corner marked off the seconds and then chimed the quarter hour. The queen called for a card table and refreshments. Then she summoned three of her ladies to partner in a game of Commerce. Lord Ormsby seemed to grow more confident with every minute that passed, as did Lord Tomlin, whose posture grew straighter. Sera rose and prowled the room, animating the paintings to divert herself. A charming scene of women picnicking under a spreading tree came to life as Sera touched it with magic. Women chatted and passed items across the blanket. Birds alighted in the tree above and in the distance, sheep grazed.

Courtiers with nothing else to do gathered to watch the painting. Emboldened, she moved to the next one, a rather stern portrait of a man from the Tudor era with a starched ruff around his neck and an assortment of dogs at his feet. At a wave of her hand, the man breathed through his long nose. The dogs became bored and wrestled with one another. One knocked into a plinth and sent the urn upon it crashing to the ground. The growing crowd around Sera burst into laughter.

"What is going on?" Queen Charlotte called.

"Lady Winyard has brought the paintings to life, Your Majesty," a courtier answered.

Lord Ormsby frowned and puffed out his cheeks. Sera stared at him, silently challenging him to denounce her for her *unauthorised* use of magic.

"Well done, Lady Winyard, for seizing the initiative while we wait. Why aren't you two entertaining us, Ormsby?" the queen barked at the Speaker of the Mage Council.

Lord Tomlin made a lapdog perform tricks. The little spaniel walked across the floor on its hind legs, to the delight of the ladies. Sera cringed at his using the poor creature against its will. Lord Ormsby conjured a dire piece of music, where each chord dropped heavy in the room. The man either possessed no musical ear at all, or chose to express the struggles of the small mouse with the slow, funerary composition.

As Sera pondered how to animate a still life of a bowl of fruit, Hugh announced the passage of two hours.

"The mouse is shaking." He held the small cage before his face and visually examined the tiny prisoner.

The surgeon gave those assembled regular updates on the deterioration of the mouse's condition. Sera could only glance in its direction, while it suffered to prove her innocence. It hid in a corner among a handful of hay, Hugh intent on any change. More time passed, and Hugh opened the cage to examine his patient more closely.

After several long minutes, he closed the lid and held the cage between his palms. "The mouse is deceased, Your Majesty. The poison took two hours to show its effect, and death followed within the hour, giving a total elapsed time of slightly under three hours."

Sera bowed her head at the creature's passing and offered a silent prayer of thanks for its sacrifice.

Lord Ormsby waved his hands in the air. "This proves nothing—"

"On the contrary, this piece of evidence proves much." Lieutenant Powers approached the queen. "This demonstration by Mr Miles enables me to narrow down when Lord Branvale ingested the poison. We now know that due to the accelerant cast, it was at most three hours before his passing."

"This also validates what Lady Winyard told us,

that the poison acted rapidly and without delay." Queen Charlotte narrowed her gaze at the two male mages.

Lord Ormsby snorted. "Lord Tomlin found that first."

Lord Tomlin squirmed, cleared his throat, and knitted his fingers together. "In light of this, I will have to reconsider my findings. I might have made a miscalculation or, more likely, another element contaminated my sample with a hibernation enchantment. That aside, Lady Winyard and I are in agreement that the effect of the poison was amplified, achieving in a few hours what would have taken nature some days or weeks."

Sera stared at her fellow mage. Never had she expected him to admit to an error, although his actions saved him from being called a liar before the whole court. If he could make an attempt at being noble, so could she. "I am grateful that this shows I could not have been responsible, Your Majesty."

"Carry on, Lieutenant, and find the poisoner." With a wave of her hand, the queen dismissed them all. She rose from her seat and swept from the room, followed by her ladies.

Lord Ormsby took Lord Tomlin by the arm, their heads bent together as they left. One man listened, the other had much to say.

Sera waited for Hugh to pack away his mice and supplies and then joined him and the lieutenant on a slow walk through the palace.

"Thank you, Hugh, for once again coming to my rescue," she said.

His face brightened into an expansive smile. "My pleasure."

She held tight to a small measure of relief that she had now become much harder to convict as being responsible for Lord Branvale's death. Of course, some might still say she had crafted the poison and sent another to tip it into her guardian's food or drink.

"I wanted to share some information with you, Lieutenant Powers, that sheds a different light on Contessa Ricci's argument with Lord Branvale." Sera crafted a spell to stop anyone listening in on their conversation and then opened it over their heads like a parasol.

"Oh? Do tell, Lady Winyard." The lieutenant's eyes lit up.

"I have learned that an *orchid* is a particular type of young noble who has fallen on difficult times, kept by a more wealthy patron, and that the contessa maintains a young woman called Vilma." What tragedy had touched Vilma's life that she gave her blood to a vampyre in return for a roof over her head? And was such an arrangement any better or worse than the bargain struck by a man's mistress?

Powers smoothed one end of his curling moustache. "I, too, have discovered that little fact about these particular house plants. But this is new information about the young lady concerned—is she being held against her will?"

Sera replayed what the mouse had seen that

273

evening. Such versatile and useful little creatures who lent their ears and eyes for her purposes. Or even their hearts, as one just had. "I do not believe so."

"Let us call on the contessa and see what she has to say for herself." Lieutenant Powers crooked his elbow for Sera in invitation, and with a reluctant glance at Hugh, she took the lieutenant's arm.

TWENTY-TWO

They climbed into a carriage, the two men taking the rear-facing seat opposite Sera.

The lieutenant pulled a small book from his pocket and consulted his notes. "We can now assume that Lord Branvale had approximately three hours from the time he consumed the poison to the time it took his life. Our only question now is, *where* was he poisoned? The contessa told us that Lord Branvale dined early, at around eight, and then left her company after their disagreement at approximately eleven. Yet Jake Hogan said he was awakened at one by the mage's complaint of an upset stomach. Either we are missing something that occurred during the two hours between eleven and one, or someone is not telling the truth."

Hugh pushed himself into the corner of the carriage. He had the appearance of a bear trapped in a too-small cage. "If the valet was correct about the onset of symptoms around one in the morning, his lordship

275

had to have ingested the substance around eleven at the latest. How cold-hearted, to sit across the table from someone and watch them sup on poison."

"Given she is undead, can she be anything but cold-hearted?" Powers snapped the little book shut. "We will call on the contessa first. Then I shall return to the mews to see if the driver remembers what time he fetched Lord Branvale. If he did indeed leave the contessa early, it is not impossible that he went somewhere else afterward for a nightcap. Lady Winyard, do you know if he attended a gentleman's club?"

Sera considered what little she knew of Lord Branvale's personal life. "I don't believe so, but I suppose he could have been invited by a noble. Is it possible Jake was mistaken about what time Lord Branvale returned home?" Worries brewed inside her. Jake was either mistaken, or the contessa had lied to divert the investigation.

After the initial burst of conversation, they rode in silence to Mayfair. Hugh hopped down and held out a hand for Sera. They trailed behind as Powers strode up the path and rapped on the glossy front door. The butler showed them through to the grey and silver parlour and announced he would fetch the mistress.

The men stood as the contessa entered the room. Today she wore a gown of deep grey with silver embroidered vines and bright red roses. Her hair was loosely gathered at her nape in a shocking state of sleepy undress. Sera thought her a storybook figure, but was the contessa the wronged princess or the scheming witch?

"Ah, you have returned. Am I to be vindicated or accused?" She swept aside her skirts and invited Sera to sit beside her on the settee.

Lieutenant Powers leapt straight to the heart of their visit. "I have a few points I wish to clarify, Contessa Ricci. You say you argued with Lord Branvale the night he dined here. Was that about Vilma, or your condition?"

The contessa exhaled a huff and rose. She paced before the window overlooking the street. Sera watched the other woman's stiff back and wondered what thoughts raced through her mind. Did she expect to be denounced and dragged out into the streets? Sera pondered what to say that might reassure the contessa, as they had no intention of exposing her as a vampyre. But if she had indeed poisoned Lord Branvale, well... there would be an awkward situation if they attempted to hang her.

"I am sure the lieutenant will leave you undisturbed, as long as you abide by the laws of England." Sera glanced to the Lieutenant Powers for reassurance, and he nodded. "I am aware of Lord Branvale's opinions about Unnaturals, but I do not adopt the prejudices of others without question. In my experience, it is better to form one's own opinions of others based on how they act, not what one is told." In Sera's limited experience, those who were noble by birth often had the greatest difficulty in understanding noble actions. Hugh, for instance, possessed a kind heart and noble nature, despite his lowly rank.

"Lord Branvale saw *my condition* as something that

could be reversed if he found the appropriate spell."
Contessa Ricci shook her fist and then turned it into a
dismissive gesture accompanied by a *hrumpf* from the
back of her throat.

That didn't make sense to Sera. If Branvale sought
to remedy the contessa's undead heart, he should have
been crafting some sort of resurrection spell. She leaned
back on the settee to study the other woman. "But
Lord Branvale brewed a preservative spell for you. That
would not have altered your condition."

With a swirl of silk, the contessa turned and
prowled to the settee. Her lips pulled into a grimace as
she rested one hand lightly on the fabric. "He was fasci-
nated by me, but I was never subjected to his experi-
ments. He respected my position and wealth. No, Lord
Branvale sought out Unnaturals hiding on the streets
on whom to test his brews and spells."

"I did not know." Sera's mind raced, thinking of the
poor creatures hunted, so that her former guardian
could test castings to reverse their misfortune. Had he
helped them, or subjected them to more misery?

"I have heard whispers of such practices. There are
those who call themselves *scientists*, who experiment on
Unnaturals to see how they differ from us." Hugh
clenched his hands into massive fists.

"Yet he knew of your condition and could have
exposed you. That must be a perilous state in which to
live," Lieutenant Powers said in a low tone.

"He would never dare say anything about the
state of *my* heart, not when he harboured so many
interesting secrets of his own." The contessa fluttered

her hands in the air, and Sera imagined her surrounded by butterflies, each with a secret painted on its wings.

The lieutenant huffed in soft laughter. 'Mutual blackmail?'

'A crude description. I prefer to say we kept each other's confidences. He never revealed my secret and so I will not disclose his.' The contessa resumed her seat next to Sera.

'What about the potion he sold you?' Sera still couldn't follow why she needed the deep red liquid.

Contessa Ricci waved a hand in front of her face to shield her eyes. 'The monthly potion I purchased was for the jugs of blood a butcher delivers here. The brew keeps it from spoiling.'

'You can drink an animal's blood?' Hugh leaned forward, his expression keen and open.

'Yes. It sustains me.' The contessa picked up a cushion from beside her and smoothed a scarlet tassel. She seemed to need something to occupy her hands, or they took over the conversation.

'If your needs are met by an animal's blood, why do you maintain Vilma?' the lieutenant asked.

Her hand stilled with the tassel across her palm like a streak of blood. 'A man might drink several tankards of cheap ale, but savour a small measure of a fine brandy.'

'Ah.' The lieutenant leaned back in his chair and stroked his goatee to an even finer point.

Sera recalled the scene she had witnessed while touching the mouse's mind. There had been something about the intimacy between the two women that speared an ache through her. "You care for her."

A hand caressed the fabric of the cushion. "I care for both Vilma and her mother. I gave them a home when Vilma's father died, and his entailed estate went to a cousin who turned them out without so much as a penny."

The lieutenant closed his notebook and slid the tiny pencil down the gap in the spine before returning the item to his pocket. "There are those who would say that, lacking either a pulse or a soul, you are incapable of caring for another."

Contessa Ricci turned a bold, dark stare on the army man. "How many men possess both, and yet are incapable of the slightest empathy toward their fellow man? I would argue that neither a pulse nor a soul dictates who has a place in my heart."

Powers barked a short laugh. "I can appreciate Lord Branvale's fascination for you, Contessa. But our conversation does not advance us any closer to who served the mage a poisoned draught, and he did dine last at your table. Did Lord Branvale savour an unusual brandy that night before he left here?" He spread his hands in an apologetic gesture.

"No. He finished his supper around nine, and we adjourned to my library, where we played chess and talked until eleven. He eschewed any drink, as he wanted his mind clear to concentrate on our game. You must look elsewhere for your murderer, Lieutenant. I had no reason to kill a man who kept me so entertained by torturing himself with his secrets." She stood and the two men jumped to their feet.

Sera didn't want to leave. She wanted to press the contessa further about what secrets her former guardian harboured. How had she existed under his roof for so many years and not glimpsed a hint of what he hid?

Like the ensorcelled paper under his bed. With the events of the last few days, she had not checked to see if any text had revealed itself. Perhaps she had best start there.

"Thank you for your time, Contessa Ricci," Sera murmured as she paged through thirteen years in her head, searching for clues.

The contessa took Sera's hand and clasped it to her heart. "Do call again, Lady Winyard. While I enjoy reading reports of you in the newspaper, I would much prefer to hear your tales in person."

"I would be delighted." There was much Sera could learn from the contessa...once they were both cleared of any wrongdoing in Lord Branvale's death.

Sera climbed up into the carriage and settled into her seat. She gazed out the window but didn't see the grand houses. Rather, her mind conjured the busy kitchen below stairs in Branvale's home.

"Assuming the contessa told us the truth, the timing does not work," Hugh said. "If Lord Branvale consumed nothing after nine, he would have been exhibiting symptoms by eleven and dead before Jake Hogan says he was awakened at one," Hugh said.

'Or Jake lied," she whispered to no one in particular.

'Unless Lord Branvale went somewhere else after leaving here and imbibed the poison there, then yes, the valet did not tell us the truth about when the mage woke him." Lieutenant Powers rapped on the roof and the carriage lurched as the horses pulled them to their next destination.

'Did he have any reason to dislike Lord Branvale?" Hugh asked in a gentle tone.

A sigh heaved through Sera and she refocused her attention on his broad, kindly face. 'I thought I knew the people I shared that house with, but after talking to the contessa, I am questioning everything." Complaining about Branvale was a common topic of discussion over their meals, but from what she recollected, none of it had the hard edge that would lead to plotting murder.

Then a line in the old mage's journal floated before her mind. 'He brewed a potion for Jake. A suppressant."

The surgeon leaned forward, his fingers close to brushing her skirts. 'Both his sister and mother suffer a congestion of the lungs. The suppressant might have been to stop the cough."

Sera shook her head. That didn't sit right. 'Branvale never mixed anything for his staff when we were sick. I did what I could, or we went to the local apothecary."

The lieutenant had the inquisitive gleam in his eyes. 'It was unusual, then, that he supplied a remedy for his valet's family? Could it have been more than ordinary cough syrup?"

"That is what I wonder," Sera murmured.

The carriage jolted to a stop, and Powers grasped the door handle. "I'll not be long. I want to be certain of the time the driver from the mews collected Lord Branvale from the contessa's home."

"Do you know what was in the syrup?" Hugh shuffled along the seat, so he sat directly opposite Sera. His long thighs pointed to the middle of the carriage or their knees would have touched.

"No. Unless he wrote down the formula somewhere, I would need to examine it to tease apart the components, as I did with the poison." What would a suppressant do, if not stop a violent cough?

Lord Branvale sought out Unnaturals hiding on the streets to test his brews and spells. Had he tested some potion on Jake's family? But Sera had served beside him for years. Jake was no Unnatural. Thoughts became rabbits multiplying in her mind, scattering to disappear down burrows where she couldn't pursue them. A blast of fresh air pulled them all back into one main worry —Jake.

"The driver is adamant he retrieved Lord Branvale at eleven, and deposited him directly at his door with no detours," Powers said, resuming his seat.

They exchanged glances, but remained silent. Jake had lied, then, about when Branvale had returned home, to erase two hours. Time enough to poison his master. But why?

They journeyed in silence from the affluence of

Mayfair to the narrower and darker streets of the East End. The faces changed outside the windows, from the freshly scrubbed and hopeful to those worn down by their lot in life. Sera imagined how she could make life easier for the poorest in London. While entertainments might distract them for a time, a full belly and a warm bed at night seemed more important.

'Stop here!' Powers rapped on the roof.

The carriage lurched, and the lieutenant jumped out first. Sera emerged last, and Hugh took her hand and tucked it into the crook of his elbow. He drew her closer to his side as they walked across the filthy cobbles.

Sera smiled. The surgeon's unnecessary protective streak amused her. She could strip the skin from the bones of an attacker with the flick of her wrist, should she need to. Nor would water ever splash at her gown, so there was no need for a man to take the road side as they walked. But his consideration of her was endearing.

Powers took the lead, trotting up the tenement's stairs as they wound their way upward. Shouts from behind closed doors shuddered through Sera, and a sharp but damp odour drifted past her nostrils. Her feet stopped at one point when the feeble cry of an infant reached her ears.

"This is why I do what I can to help them," Hugh murmured from beside her.

'I am a mage, and yet this makes me feel powerless." How could she alleviate the suffering of so many on her own?

"Choose a place to start, and do one thing. Small changes build bigger ones." He squeezed her hand, understanding her internal struggle.

One small thing could make a difference. Like planting a blade of grass in a barren landscape.

"Why don't you knock?" The lieutenant leaned against the wall beside one particular door.

Hugh rapped, and they waited. The door opened a sliver and an eyeball appeared. Then it rolled sideways and alighted on Sera.

"Sera!" Jake exclaimed as he opened the door. "My tea's gone cold."

She smiled at the familiar joke and stepped around Hugh's bulk to hug the valet. "Jake. I'm so glad to see you. I've been worried."

Jake pulled her into the room where his sister lay asleep on the sofa, her feet up and a book open in her limp hands.

"How are your sister and mother? Did the syrup help?" Hugh asked in a low tone, as though he did not want to wake her.

"The syrup made no difference and neither of them is improving." Jake hardened his jaw as Lieutenant Powers entered and closed the door behind him.

Sera put her hand on Jake's arm. "What was in the brew that Branvale gave you?"

His Adam's apple bobbed up and down. Then he ran a hand through his hair before throwing them up in the air. "I don't know, Sera. They got so much worse once they started sipping it. I have the empty bottle still, if that might help?"

"Let's see what we can discover." She glanced at the lieutenant and gathered a strand of magic to her. She whispered words along its length and then sent it to curl around the army man's head.

Let me try to help them, before you take over, the spell murmured in his ear.

He nodded and leaned on the wall to inspect his spotless fingernails. Meanwhile, Hugh approached the prone woman drawing irregular breaths.

Jake opened a drawer and retrieved a cordial bottle with thick yellow glass, and handed it over. Sera removed the stopper and peered within. An acrid smell hit her nostrils, but she couldn't quite identify it. Angling the bottle, she spied a few drops in the very bottom.

"Could I trouble you for a saucer, please?" she asked.

With the saucer in one hand, she sent a spiral of magic into the bottle and coaxed the remaining drops of syrup along the side of the glass and then drew them down to the saucer. As she had with the poison, Sera smeared the little she had over the ceramic and then stood by the window.

"Do you remember what Lord Branvale used to say about Unnaturals?" she asked as she coaxed apart the thick syrup.

Jake's hands tightened into fists. "It was no secret that he didn't think them human, but he also thought some of them were handy. People think them worse than criminals, but how many live right under our noses and hope no one ever stumbles onto their secret?"

Rather like the contessa, although wealth and a title offered insulation from public opinion. "Which is a ridiculous and unfounded prejudice. I am sure Unnaturals are people like you and I, going about their lives and trying to do their best for their families."

Jake nodded and appeared to choke up. Tears misted his eyes and he bit on his knuckles.

Hugh joined them. "I admit that I am rather flummoxed. Your sister's lungs are full of congestion. The syrup should have cleared the mucus and eased her breathing."

Sera held her palm over the saucer and let the ingredients and the attached spell filter through her mind. A tickle rippled over her palm and pricked at her skin, almost as though the potion taunted her for thinking it nothing more than a suppressant. "There is something else at play here."

She squinted at the smear and sent another drift of magic over the scant remains. What was hiding within it? A vision of a woman with white eyes, her head thrown back as she screamed, burst into Sera's mind. When the syrup flowed down her throat, it stifled her cries. That made no sense, unless the brew treated a different condition.

An Unnatural condition.

"Why do your sister and mother scream?"

TWENTY-THREE

Sera tapped the saucer. "This is to suppress a scream, not a cough."

"Scream?" Hugh glanced to the unmoving woman.

Jake stared at his sister and shook his head. His mouth formed a soundless *no*.

"Jake, I need to know why Branvale created a spell to stop your sister and mother from screaming." Sera set the saucer on the table.

The former valet continued to stare at his sister. From the bedroom, his mother emerged clutching a brown shawl around her shoulders. Ignoring the strangers in her home, Mrs Hogan gently lifted the girl's shoulders and sat beside her daughter.

After drawing a deep breath, Jake managed to whisper, "No one can ever know."

Sera placed a hand on Jake's arm, turning him to face her. "How many years did I keep it secret that you spat on Branvale's boots and, more than once, into his dinner? You know I would never tattle on family. You have to trust us. Please."

His chest heaved as he struggled to push out the words. He spoke in short bursts, as though each syllable caused him pain. 'My Ma. She's...an Unnatural. So's Edith. She takes after Ma. I mostly take after Da. He was normal, you see. But I have Ma's eyes." He pointed to their unusually pale grey.

Mrs Hogan watched them with her eerie stare and pulled a blanket over her daughter and herself.

'What sort of Unnatural, Jake?" Sera thumbed through types of creatures in her mind and could think of only one who emitted a soul-piercing scream.

Jake swallowed, then he scrubbed his hands over his face. 'Banshee."

Hugh let out a sigh. 'Lord Branvale gave you a potion to stop their screaming. No wonder they are congested. You are suppressing the very essence of who they are."

'How did Branvale know?" Lieutenant Powers pushed off the wall and approached on silent feet, like a cat stalking closer to an unsuspecting mouse.

'It was last year. Da had been ill for some time. Ma sent Edith to fetch me when he took a turn for the worse. Branvale was there when Edith collapsed and let out her shriek. He told me to make her be quiet. I blurted out that I couldn't, because our Da's soul was passing. That got his interest. Said he would use his magic to make her normal." Tears welled up in the valet's eyes and one escaped to roll down his cheek. Jake wiped it away with the back of his hand.

Mrs Hogan hugged her daughter and rocked her gently, as though she were still a youngster. Or like a mother unable to do anything to save her child except offer the comfort of her embrace.

"You spoke true when you said Lord Branvale woke you at one in the morning to complain of stomach pains—because you had given him something when he returned home at eleven that caused his condition." The lieutenant spoke in a soft tone, as though reassuring a spooked horse.

A sigh heaved through Jake, and he hung his head. "I didn't think you'd figure it out. I thought you'd blame whoever he had dinner with. When he got home that night, I poured him one final nightcap as I undressed him. I had to, Sera. He said if I didn't let him cure them, then others would take them away to experiment on. But God help me, he was killing them. It had to end."

"Where did you get the potion you mixed in his drink?" Lieutenant Powers asked.

"Bought it in a dark alley from some fellow I'd never seen before." He dragged his hands through his hair and glanced at Sera from under half-lidded eyes.

Her heart broke for the valet. All those years he'd sought to protect his family, and she had never known. She might have been able to do something. "Why didn't you come to me? We could have figured something out."

A sad smile touched Jake's lips. "You don't know, do you? How deeply you're caught in his web."

Sera thought it about time some of these secret

spiders were chased out into the daylight. But before she could say a word, an ear-splitting scream pierced her brain and her vision turned white. She cried out as she dropped to her knees, her hands clasped over her ears. The cry set every nerve on fire.

She tried to grasp her magic, but the lancing sound dashed it from her reach. The second time she tried, she managed to touch the tingle in her veins and throw up a shield. The keening diminished enough to let Sera craft a stronger spell. On the sofa, Edith and Mrs Hogan had their heads thrown back and their mouths stretched wide as they emitted the otherworldly cry. Keening for a soul about to depart. But whose? Life was a fragile thing among the poor in the tenements.

"He's gone!" Lieutenant Powers shouted, and bolted out the open door.

Hugh helped Sera to her feet as she threw a hasty type of umbrella spell over the grieving sister and mother to dampen the sound. The two banshees clung to one another as they screamed. Leaning on the surgeon, Sera staggered out to the hallway. A flash of a bright red jacket came from a narrow door at the end of the corridor.

"He's gone to the roof." Hugh grabbed her hand. Doors opened and residents flowed out, blocking their way.

"What's that godawful noise?" they shouted, and stared down the hall.

Sera's spell reduced the keening to a low sobbing that faded by the time they pushed through the crowd and reached the rickety stairs to the roof. The wood vibrated with their footsteps. The lieutenant's shout of "Stop!" drifted over them. Light spilled down the narrow stairwell as the two men in front of them burst out into the open.

Hugh pulled Sera up the last step and onto the flat roof. Wires strung on posts held aloft washing and flapped like ghosts urging them to turn back.

"Where is he?" Sera pushed a sheet out of her face. She couldn't ruin the hard work of the women by tossing aside their laundry on the dirty rooftop.

Shadows flitted past and Sera ran after them. Hugh used his larger bulk to wrangle washing before becoming enmeshed in a tangle of petticoats and underthings. With a twist of magic, Sera sent the items off to dance with one another and the path before them cleared. A shaft of sunlight pushed through the clouds to illuminate the two men in a mad dash for the edge of the building, Lieutenant Powers almost within tackling distance of the fleeing valet.

"Jake!" Sera screamed.

He never turned.

He never slackened his pace.

One moment he was pounding across the roof, the next he simply...disappeared.

Sera's shocked mind took a second to register what happened. Then she lashed out with her magic, hastily crafting a net to catch the falling man. She flung her creation through the air and over the side of the building. Desperate to snag hold of a foot, a hand...anything.

Faster, she pushed the spell. If she were quick enough, she could catch him before he hit the cobbles below. Her mind plummeted with the magical net when a muscled arm looped around her waist and abruptly broke her flow. Sera's mind snapped back, and a smack jarred through her body.

'No!' she cried out, clawing at the arm that held her even as she still tried to halt Jake's fall.

'He's gone, and I'll not lose you this day, too.' Hugh hauled her backward.

Only then did Sera realise she had been about to fling herself off the rooftop after Jake. Cries went up below and a crowd huddled around the prone form of the valet, his arms and legs at impossible angles to his body. Then a mist smudged the scene as tears blurred her vision.

'No. I could have caught him.' Sera grabbed hold of Hugh's lapels and shook them. 'Another second and I would have had him.' She could try again. There must be a way to turn back time enough to make her attempt successful.

Hugh wrapped her in a firm embrace. 'Sometimes even magic cannot stop the inevitable.'

'Damn.' Powers stood on the edge of the roof and stared down. 'I must go down. Join me when you can.'

Sera pushed Hugh back a few inches. '*You* must go to Jake. You can fix such injuries, can you not?'

'Do you think you could stay with his family while I assist?' Even with a man injured or dying below, his eyes crinkled with worry for her.

'Go. I will sit with them and do what I can until you return.' She shoved him in the direction of the lieutenant and the two men took off at a trot to vanish down the stairs.

Her stomach churned as she crossed the rooftop at a slower pace. A banshee screamed to mark the passing of a soul, not when someone was merely injured. Had Edith and Mrs Hogan screamed to distract them and allow Jake to escape? Or had the imminent death of their brother and son finally enabled the women to break free of Branvale's potion and let loose their mind-piercing cries?

On the floor below, the ghoulish residents had dispersed, no doubt drawn by the spectacle outside. Sera walked down an eerily deserted corridor back to the rooms occupied by the Hogan family. Within, she found mother and daughter with their arms wound around each other, their heads bent together.

Sera's spell held around them, but their ear-splitting screams had diminished to the sobs of the bereaved.

With nothing she could do, Sera paced the confines of their rooms, one hand touching the wallpaper as she walked. Under her breath, she whispered an incantation. She added layers of insulation to shield any loud noises. With each pass, she ensured air and light could penetrate the barrier. Around and around she walked, perfecting the enchantment. Tiny holes in the spell allowed lighter noises to escape. Laughter and chatter would seep through like a light breeze. Shouts and screams, though, would be ensnared in an impenetrable web. Her eyes grew heavy with the effort.

Satisfied with her work, Sera then dismantled the hastily erected umbrella spell she had cast over the women. She helped them up off the floor to sit on the sofa. Edith sobbed against her mother's chest. Mrs Hogan regarded Sera with near white eyes, rimmed with bright red by her grief.

Unable to face what happened out on the street, she instead busied herself in the kitchen. First, a shovelful of coal to revive the fire. Then she filled a kettle and set it to boil. By the time Hugh appeared, Sera had brewed a pot of tea, given a cup to Jake's mother and sister, and was drying dishes. She grasped a towel between her hands and hope surged up in her chest.

"We could do nothing for him," he rasped. "He has been moved to a nearby location."

Sera swallowed her tears and poured tea into a mug, which she pressed into Hugh's hands. "Thank you for trying. I don't understand why he...jumped."

Hugh took a slurp of hot tea and then gestured to the huddled women. "To protect them."

An odd way to protect them, by sacrificing himself. But after his confession, Jake faced execution for the murder of a mage and either way, his family was lost to him. Sera turned the valet's actions over in her mind. There had to be more to what he'd done. Like examining a potion, if she angled it the right way in the light, she would discover the missing clue.

"Look, milady, the colour has returned to their cheeks." An ember of excitement flared into life behind Hugh's sad eyes.

Sure enough, as the banshees keened for their lost relative, the pink flush of health returned to their faces.

Although somewhat blotchy from the depths of their grief.

'I am pleased some little good has emerged from this tragedy. I hope they are both restored to health. If only they were seen as no different to any other Londoner going about their lives." Who would protect them now? Only another Unnatural would understand the knife edge they walked, until such time as Parliament recognised their right to exist.

Sera poured herself a mug of tea and sat at the table. The brew went untouched as she warmed her hands on the mug, her thoughts swirling. The surgeon likewise sat in silence, one watchful eye on his banshee patients. Life returned to the building around them, and the sounds of normal arguments, laughter, and pounding footsteps returned.

A sharp rap preceded the opening of the door, and Lieutenant Powers stepped inside. He nodded to the women on the sofa, then joined Sera and Hugh at the table. 'I have sent off my preliminary reports and advised the queen that Lord Branvale's death is resolved." He omitted any mention of murder, murderers, or poison from his brief summary. For which Sera offered silent thanks. Edith and Mrs Hogan had been through enough.

"What will happen to his family now?" she asked.

The lieutenant's lips tightened in a grimace. "There is little I can do, I am afraid. Once it is known Unnaturals reside here, there are those who might seek to capture them for their own purposes. The law offers them no protection. If only there was someone who could, someone who would be sympathetic to their condition."

Exactly Sera's line of thought. "Yes, if only there was someone who might shelter them."

Powers rapped his knuckles on the table. "I must go and will not detain you. I'm sure you also have much to do, Lady Winyard." He stood and held Sera's gaze. A silent understanding formed between them.

"Indeed." After the lieutenant left, she approached the bereaved family and laid a hand on Mrs Hogan's arm. "Pack only what you can carry. I will return and do what Jake asked of me. I shall take you somewhere safe."

Mrs Hogan nodded and placed a hand over Sera's. "Thank you."

"I will do what I can." *Do one thing. Small changes build bigger changes.* Helping these women would be one step toward achieving a much bigger change—an equal right to exist for all Unnaturals.

Twilight brushed over the city by the time Sera walked up her front stairs. She had paid a visit to the contessa and negotiated a safe place for Edith and Mrs Hogan. The two women would take up residence in the house occupied by Vilma and, once recovered, would be found work within the household to suit their abilities. In return, Contessa Ricci would receive her monthly preservative potion at no charge. Sera also promised to dine with the vampyre monthly when she delivered it, as her guardian once had. The latter part was no hardship; on the contrary, she looked forward to her first such dinner with the Italian noble.

Elliot held the door open and narrowed his gaze at her. "You look done in."

"Jake did it," she murmured as she walked inside.

The footman's eyebrows shot up as he shut the door. "Bloody hell. I knew he didn't like Branvale, but never suspected it went as far as murder."

Sera stripped off her cloak and handed it over. "None of us did. He did it to protect his family. Branvale found out they are Unnaturals and was forcing Jake to feed them a potion he brewed to try to *cure* them. He was treating Jake's family as an experiment."

A low whistle came from Elliot as he hung the cloak on its hook.

"I thought I knew him. How could I have lived with Jake for so many years and not known his struggles?" She placed her hands in the small of her back and arched to relieve a dull ache.

Elliot stared at her for a moment, then huffed. "You know as much as people let you see. We all hide things. Why don't you go up to bed before you collapse and litter my tidy hall? I'll send Vicky up to help and have Rosie bring you a tray."

"Thank you." Her feet grew heavier with each step, but Sera had one thing yet to do before she climbed into bed. Stopping at the linen closet, she dug out the hidden sheet of paper. Her spell had revealed a brief message, written in an unfamiliar hand. The words from Lord Branvale's anonymous correspondent.

Keep her with you, however you can

To ensure her safety, the council must believe her feeble,
with little power, and of no consequence
There cannot be another Nereus

All Sera thought she knew of the previous thirteen years exploded into thousands of tiny, glittering pieces. The bracelet Branvale had snapped on her wrist had dampened her power. *To ensure her safety.* How odd to consider that he had, in his cold way, kept her alive. Thoughts and beliefs realigned themselves. What if he'd never thought her inferior or defective, but had followed these instructions and had sought the extension of his guardianship to keep her from whatever her unseen opponents intended?

Who, or what, was Nereus? So many questions without answers.

"Tomorrow," she muttered.

No more would she be a pawn, moved by unseen players. She would learn their secrets, disrupt their game, and then beat them at it.

Twenty-Four

The next morning, Sera sat at the desk before the parlour window and looked up to see the looming figure of Hugh Miles mounting the stairs. She composed herself as Elliot showed him through—the footman grinning behind the surgeon's back.

Hugh took her hand and bowed over it. "I wanted to see how you were holding up this morning."

Sera stared at his large hands and wondered what sort of stitch such thick fingers could make. "I berate myself for failing to help Jake earlier. Part of me feels guilty that his actions clear me of suspicion. However, unless we find who sold it to him, I am sure some will claim *I* made the poison that Jake poured into Lord Branvale's glass that night."

He let go of her hand. "You have an unexpected ally in that regard."

"Oh?" Curious, she rose and moved to the settee, gesturing for Hugh to take the armchair.

He sank into the chair and propped his elbows on the arms. 'Lord Tomlin, on hearing the news last night, said that any gifted apothecary could have crafted such a poisonous potion."

Sera leaned back and let those words ripple through her. A most unexpected ally, after he'd tried to claim the poison had had a hibernation effect imposed on it. Perhaps a twinge of guilt made him speak up now, before Lord Ormsby silenced him again? Not knowing the other mage very well, she decided to cast a charitable light on his actions. "That was an unusual step for him to take. Almost gallant."

Hugh's eyebrows drew together. 'Hardly gallant, after he first tried to place the poison in your hand. I have other news, too. Apparently, when the council sent soldiers to the Hogan family rooms this morning to seize the Unnaturals, they found no trace of his mother or sister."

Sera widened her eyes and resisted the urge to bat her eyelashes. 'Really? Vanished? Well, let us hope that after these horrid events, and wherever they may have gone, they find a small sanctuary of quiet and safety."

He started to say something, changed his mind, and placed his fingers over his mouth. But humour sparkled in his gaze. 'I, too, hope they are safe and protected. I think Jake would have appreciated that."

'With one problem resolved, I now need to find a way to tackle the next obstacle in my path." Sera stared at the ceiling as she considered how to gain access to the locked library.

'Might it help to talk through this problem aloud?" Hugh asked.

There was no harm in discussing the issue with the surgeon. It might clarify her thoughts to have his opinion. 'The mage tower at Finsbury Fields contains a locked library that holds knowledge the council has gathered over the centuries. To gain access, I must plant a single blade of grass in the tower's wasteland of a courtyard. It sounds simple, but it is a test of strength and precision. The earth there is drenched in magic and quite barren. I have tried repeatedly and failed. Now all I hear in my head are their voices telling me I am a feeble woman and that only a man can plant a seed."

Hugh made a sound in the back of his throat and tented his fingers. 'A man might plant a seed, but only a woman can nurture it. Without her, it would wither and die. I am relieved to hear, however, that the council is not so enfeebled that they fail to recognise you are a woman."

Sera swallowed a laugh. But his words made an idea spark in her mind.

He leaned forward. 'You have a unique type of magic, unfamiliar to them. Use your abilities to nurture life. Is this not what you have fought against—being forced to follow their methods?"

She stared at him. The solution was so blindingly obvious. For years she had tried to warp her magic to fit the male mould imposed by Branvale and the council. What she needed to do was break free of their chains and embrace who and what she was. A woman. One who reached for the warm touch of Mother Nature when she cast.

"You are brilliant, Hugh. If it wasn't considered impertinent, I would kiss you." Ideas blossomed as to how she could pass the Mage Council's test and leave them in no doubt of her ability.

"I wouldn't tell anyone. Your secret impertinence would be safe with me." The surgeon met her gaze. Then he blushed and stared at the ceiling.

Good humour bubbled through Sera. She approached his chair, leaned down to take his face in her hands, and kissed him on the lips. His body stilled, as though he was too scared to move, but he most definitely kissed her back.

Then she broke it off. "I have to go. Will you come back for our celebration tonight?"

He pushed out of the chair. "I wouldn't miss it for anything, milady."

"Elliot!" she called, her idea setting fire to her feet. Snatching up the cloak from its hook, she swirled it to her shoulders. Hugh nodded and took his leave, whistling a cheery tune as he walked away.

"That doesn't count for our bet, by the way," Elliot muttered when he appeared.

"What doesn't count?" Sera fastened the clasp and settled the drape of fabric around her body.

He rolled his eyes toward the open door and the broad receding back. "You kissed him. He still has to work up the courage to kiss you, and his time is running out."

"Well, he may feel a little more motivated now."

Sera grinned at the footman and practically danced out the front door.

She hailed a carriage to take her out to Finsbury Fields. Unable to sit still, Sera perched on the edge of her seat and tapped a foot the entire way. At the nondescript tower, she had to slow her footsteps and rein in her eagerness. She stared at the dry and cracked ground, and a moment of self-doubt grated up against her resolution.

The old weathered door swung open to reveal Lord Pendlebury in his purple robes. "What do you seek?" he intoned.

"I seek admittance to the library," Sera replied. Honestly, their rituals were pointless, but if they wanted a display, she would give them one.

"First, you must prove your worth to access our collected knowledge. Grow a blade of grass in this earth." He swept out an arm to encompass the packed earth surrounding the mage tower. Parts were so dry, there were cracks in the ground deep enough for mice to hide in.

"Must it be only a single blade of grass?" she murmured.

Lord Pendlebury's brow furrowed. "Mages throughout history have found *that* a near impossible task. But I wouldn't say no to a shade tree out here, if you feel up to growing a mighty oak."

He spoke in jest, but Sera took his words to heart. She glanced around the area between the tower and the enclosing wall. In one spot was a small patch of grass, no more than a foot square. These were the blades of grass planted by a succession of male mages. Sera wouldn't even call it a *lush* patch of grass. It struggled in the barren landscape with too little water and too much sun, as though London's notorious rain never touched the ground here.

She knelt and placed her palms on the dirt. With head bowed, she closed her eyes and reached out with her magic. Down through the cracks she tunnelled, and bit back a cry at the pathetic state of the soil. Parched, drained, with no one to nurture it into health. Mother Nature had abandoned this stretch of land. Or, more likely, the mages had excluded her.

With Branvale's shackle removed from her wrist, magic surged through her veins. Sera let her power seep into the ground like a gentle rain. It trickled through the cracks and splits. All the while she sought the goddess who supported all life on earth, entreating her to answer her daughter's call and help revitalise the soil.

A tendril of answering power reached up to meet Sera's and entwined with it.

"Thank you," she whispered. Together, the two types of magic cultivated the dirt under the solid crust. Moisture and nutrients were added. Only when she imagined that she turned over a rich compost, did Sera visualise the seed she required. She coaxed it into life in the renewed soil, adding a breath of warmth as extra encouragement. A root poked out and burrowed. Then a shoot pushed through the surface and wriggled. As it grew taller, a leaf emerged from one side. Inch by inch, the seedling grew.

A gasp came from behind her. The browned grass

turned to a deep, healthy green as the sapling continued to grow. Branches sprouted off the main trunk and still it stretched toward the sky. When the tree reached six feet in height, it stopped growing and shook its limbs. Bright green leaves burst into life along the bracts.

Sera rose and brushed off her skirts. Then she smiled at Lord Pendlebury. "An oak, as requested. A few more years and we shall be able to take tea in its shade."

He stared with a slack jaw. "How, Lady Winyard, did you achieve such a feat when we have all struggled with a blade of grass?"

She had drained herself to the point of exhaustion, and her bones were turning into liquid. If she didn't sit down soon, she would embarrass herself by falling over. All things she would never reveal to another mage. Nor would she mention that her unique magic allowed her to seek the help of Mother Nature, the most powerful force known to humanity.

Instead, she tilted her head and managed an open, innocent expression. "I do not know, Lord Pendlebury. I suspect my spell went awry. I was merely trying to grow a bigger and healthier stem of grass."

He appeared to be on the brink of saying something, then his mouth slammed shut. A wide smile lit his eyes. "You are a marvel among us. Let me escort you to the library, since you have most ably demonstrated your ability. None of our fellow mages will be able to miss the tree on their way in and out now."

Exactly. Every time they came to the tower, there would be the proof of her ability, spreading its shade and protection over their efforts. Let them chew on what that meant.

After some hours in the locked library—some of them with her head on her arms—and clutching the more immediate spells she sought, Sera returned to her home for a well-deserved rest before the street celebration. When sunset cast the buildings in a deep golden glow, Sera stood in the street and surveyed their hard work.

People had dragged out their tables and chairs and set them up in two rows. Cloths in white, red, and green covered the tables. Strands of tiny magical lights wound back and forth between the buildings and lit up a rectangle below. Women began carrying out heavy trays laden with plates. More emerged from Sera's kitchen—she had dipped into her first advance to ensure everyone would go home with full stomachs tonight. Her funds even stretched to three kegs of ale. Elliot had found three musicians, who sat on crates and played fast and jaunty tunes.

Children flowed from open doors, laughing and chasing one another, and the adults followed. Hugh appeared, towering a head above the others, and greeted her warmly. Sera tugged him to a table to one side and poured him an ale as everyone found a seat for the feast. By the time full dark enveloped them, the group existed in their own wonderland of delicious food and raucous conversation.

"You need to say something." Elliot nudged her when everyone had a plate full of food and something to drink.

Sera stood and cleared her throat.

"Higher." Elliot gestured upward with a thumb.

Hugh stood, took her hand, and helped Sera up on a chair. "Thank you, everyone, for coming tonight and for welcoming me into your neighbourhood. I wanted to show my appreciation, but I'll not bore you with a long-winded speech. To new friends! Let us eat, drink, and be merry."

People cheered and raised their mugs to her. Grinning, she assumed her seat and conversation broke out as the meal recommenced. Afterward, Sera took a quick sip of ale and then walked to the empty space beside the tables. Cracking her knuckles, she drew on her magic to begin the evening's entertainment. First she created an expanse of ocean, the waves lapping against the cobbles. Upon the water appeared a pirate ship. The boys roared and raced to stand closer, jostling each other to point out pirates scrubbing the deck, others climbing the rigging, and one in the crow's nest peering off to the horizon.

One by one, in the ocean mermaids materialised, their hair braided with shells. Each mermaid rode a sea unicorn, like a seahorse but with a twisted horn in the centre of its forehead. That delighted the little girls, who clapped and promptly set about ensuring each girl had her own mermaid to cheer on.

A battle ensued, the mermaids defending their fishy friends and sunken treasure from the pirates, who cast their nets overboard and fired off their cannon. The mermaids won by sneaking under the boat to allow their unicorn seahorses to poke holes in the hull. The boys booed as the ship sank and the pirates struggled in the ocean. Being kind-hearted, the mermaids summoned turtles, each large enough to carry a pirate back to land.

Her tableau over, Sera dropped into a chair while people clapped, and Hugh passed her a mug of ale. Elliot waved to the musicians, who struck up a lively reel. Men and women danced in the streets. Someone asked Sera, but she apologised, pleading that she was worn out from her efforts for the moment.

"You have made a remarkable impression on the neighbourhood, Lady Winyard." Hugh's serious brown eyes focused on her.

"Sera," she murmured over her ale. Perhaps the exertion, the company, or the ale warmed her skin.

"Pardon?" A tiny line wrinkled his brow.

"My friends call me Sera."

"You would number me as one of your friends?" Now a glint of humour winked in his gaze.

She set down the mug and adopted a serious expression. "I do not have a particularly large number of them outside of my devoted staff. If you require an exact number, sir, you would be my third."

He picked up her hand and kissed her knuckles. "I would be honoured to be friend number three."

Friend. The word drifted through her insides and warmed her. A quiet voice asked, *More than friends?* She smiled. *Perhaps.*

There was something intriguing about the young surgeon. He had been the only one strong enough to take her hand and absorb her excess magic as she lifted

Branvale off his feet. But she was young and had no intention of rushing into any such decision. First, there was much to enjoy about her newfound freedom.

'Do you feel up to a dance now?" he asked, having retained hold of her hand.

'I think so." The country dances were more to her liking than the court dances. She danced with many of her new neighbours, including one where she held hands with a number of the little girls.

Only as the children dropped from exhaustion did the night come to a close. Parents swooped in to pick up a sleepy bundle and carry them off to their homes and bed. Older children dragged their feet and asked for *just a little longer* in tired voices. Sera waved good-night to Hugh and then retired to her doorway to watch each neighbour safely to their door.

Elliot joined her in the cooling hours of early morning. "What's our next adventure?" he asked.

'Oh, you're going to like it. We're going to unearth Branvale's secrets."

How, she didn't yet know. But Lord Branvale had been tangled in a web that ensnared her, and Sera intended to find out where every sticky thread led.

With a little help from her new friends.

Seraphina's battle for independence continues in
A Dangerous Ruse...

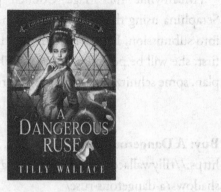

Tournament of Shadows
Book 2: A Dangerous Ruse

Her opponents have her cornered, unless Sera makes an
unexpected move...

Seraphina continues to pick at the secrets entangling her, when during a ball she spots a piece of enchanted jewellery eerily similar to the one she once wore. But before she can find out about the origins of the magical bracelet, its owner is murdered.

At least this time no one is blaming Sera.

To find the missing bracelet before it falls into the wrong hands, she must uncover the murderer. Her friends gather to investigate—could it be someone in the visiting Austrian delegation or are older grudges at play? They need to stop the person responsible before another life is lost or worse, many lives are irrevocably ruined.

Meanwhile the Mage Council plots to corner Seraphina using the oldest tool they have—forcing her into submission. If they lay their hands on the bracelet first, she will be powerless to resist. What she needs is a plan, some schnitzel, and a dangerous ruse...

Buy: A Dangerous Ruse

https://tillywallace.com/books/tournament-of-shadows/a-dangerous-ruse/

History. Magic. Family.

I do hope you enjoyed Seraphina's adventure. If you
would like to dive deeper into the world, or learn more
about the odd assortment of characters that populate
it, you can join the community by signing up at:
https://www.tillywallace.com/newsletter

TILLY WALLACE

Vintage Magic

Tilly drinks entirely too much coffee and is obsessed with hats. When not scouring vintage stores for her next chapeau purchase, she writes whimsical historical fantasy novels, set in a bygone time where magic is real. With a quirky and loveable cast, her books combine vintage magic and gentle humour.

Through loyal friendships, her characters discover that in an uncertain world, the strongest family is the one you create.

To be the first to hear about new releases and special offers sign up at:
https://www.tillywallace.com/newsletter

Tilly would love to hear from you:
https://www.tillywallace.com
tilly@tillywallace.com

f facebook.com/tillywallaceauthor
BB bookbub.com/authors/tilly-wallace

9 780473 620370